HEATHER PECK has had a  was both farmer and agricultu and alpacas, reared calves, bro in international negotiations, s from Chernobyl to bird flu, managed controls over pesticides and GM crops, saw legislation through parliament and got paid to eat KitKats while on secondment to Rowntree.

In the second half Peck chaired an NHS Trust, worked on animal welfare, sailed a boat on the Norfolk Broads, volunteered in Citizens Advice and the Witness Service and vaccinated humans against Covid. Two golden threads have run through everything, her fascination with words and her Gran's wise advice: 'You can do anything if you try hard enough.'

She writes about the countryside and the animals she loves, the industry (farming) she holds in deepest respect, and issues she is passionate about.

Peck's main protagonist has grown with each story and his life has changed in ways she couldn't have predicted at the start. She'd like to meet him. www.heatherpeckauthor.com

# FIRES
## OF HATE

### Heather
### Peck

SilverWood

Published in 2022 by SilverWood Books

SilverWood Books Ltd
14 Small Street, Bristol, BS1 1DE, United Kingdom
www.silverwoodbooks.co.uk

ISBN 978-1-80042-195-0 (paperback)
ISBN 978-1-80042-196-7 (ebook)

British Library Cataloguing in Publication Data
A CIP catalogue record for this book is available from
the British Library

Page design and typesetting by SilverWood Books

*To Gary*


*who has put love and laughter back into my life*

# Acknowledgements

My very sincere thanks to Geoff Dodgson for finding time in his busy life for a meticulous reading and extraordinarily helpful detailed comments on an early draft; to Alison Tayler for her encouragement and to all at SilverWood Books for your help and support.

# List of Characters

**Police**

The big boss: Chief Superintendent Margaret Tayler

**Main investigative team:**

DCI Greg Geldard

DI Jim Henning

DS Chris Mathews

Constables Bill Street, Jill Hayes, Steve Hall and Phil Knight

Ned, senior crime scene investigator

Also, DI Sarah Laurence

George and Mollie/Mildred, forensic anthropologists

**Legal team**

Ms Farrar and Peter Leavenham, defence solicitors

Mr David Gadd, defence barrister

Frank Parker, Crown Prosecution Service

Sir Frederick Seymour QC, prosecuting barrister

**NASA (National Agricultural Science Agency) staff**

Prof Craig Bennington, deputy CEO and Professor of Ethology

Prof Lily Lai (analytical chemistry)

Jan Littleboys, chemist team leader

Jack Haigh, chemist

Pat Nichols, chemist

Ken Ashby, Bennington's PA

Hazel Partner, IT services

**Friends from other books making a reappearance**
Ben Asheton, first responder

Paula Asheton, his wife

Mrs Pritchard, exceptionally precise secretary

Bobby, Greg's cat

Lukas Jankauskas, ex-poultry farm worker

Esther Jankauskas, interpreter, his wife

**Crooks from *Glass Arrows***
James Metcalfe and Dragan Bakalov

**Emergency Response**
Bob Crawford, CEO, Norfolk and Norwich Hospital

Commander Fisher, Silver Command, fire brigade

Plus miscellaneous animal rights activists, research staff etc

# Glossary

| | |
|---|---|
| A&E | Accident and Emergency |
| ANPR | Automatic Number Plate Recognition |
| EDP | Eastern Daily Press |
| HR | Human Resources |
| IED | Improvised Explosive Device |
| NASA | National Agricultural Science Agency |
| N&N | Norfolk and Norwich Hospital |
| PTSD | Post Traumatic Stress Disorder |
| SIO | Senior Investigating Officer |
| Sitrep | Situation Report |

# 1

## North Yorkshire, March 2001

The face at the upstairs window was frozen into stillness. No more tears, not now. Jack had used all the tears the day before, when his father had found him and his pet heifer hidden in the dell beside the beck. Even the sheltering branches and makeshift lodge of netting and leaves had not hidden them from the man who had spent his own childhood building dens on this same farm. Jack had begged and pleaded with his father all the way back to the main steading.

'Blossom has no symptoms,' he kept wailing. None of their cattle had any symptoms. Killing them all just wasn't fair. And Blossom was special. He'd reared her by hand. He won the young handlers' competition with her. She lived separately from the main herd. Why couldn't they wait and see if she had the virus? Surely just one didn't matter? He could keep her away from everyone. No one need know. And, after, at least she would have some of his father's decades of breeding, decades of hard work. Not all their bloodlines would be lost.

Jack had deployed every argument at his disposal, and every word had fallen on deaf ears. His father had dragged him, and Blossom, all the way back to the killing pen and handed her over to the Ministry vet, still without looking at Jack. The vet had looked at him though, and gently suggested he go indoors. Jack hadn't wanted to leave. He could see Blossom was frightened. He didn't want to leave her to face the captive-bolt pistol and the fear alone. But his father made him go.

At the door of the house, he turned to take one last look and was shocked to see his father had tears coursing down his face. At that, he went in silently and stared through the window for the rest of the day.

In the middle distance was the long bank of burning bodies and the glow that lit up the sky. Somewhere amongst that tangle of legs and heads was his Blossom. Dead like all the rest. Not because she was sick and needed to be put down for her own sake, but because of some daft rule dreamed up by bureaucrats who'd never got up at dawn to bucket feed a calf before school. Never spent their weekends feeding, washing and grooming until she shone. Never taken pride in training an animal bigger than they were to walk obediently on a halter. Never won their trust to the point that she would face strange noises, strange sights and strange experiences just because he was with her. But now the trust, the learning, the polish were all gone, along with every cow and calf on his father's farm. The cattle sheds stood empty. The milking parlour was unused and Flash, the collie, hung around the yard bewildered by the lack of a job to do.

That was when the hate was born. The hate of officialdom. The hate of rules that imposed cruelty under the guise of practicality. And the hate of everyone who treated animals as though they were inanimate, insentient.

By March 2002, things were different, of course. The compensation cheque in his bank account, Jack's father managed to source some new stock that had bloodlines derived from his own lost herd. It was some comfort that he could handle cows again that had traits he recognised from old Gillyflower, Blossom's mother, and even some from the older line, named after Queens by his father. There was a great-granddaughter of Lizzie, and another of Old Anne. He added some Jerseys to improve the butterfat content of his milk, and Jack's mother tried her hand at ice cream. Even Flash, slightly overweight from too much time off and forgetful of the details of her role, got back into the swing of things. The only one who could not forget was Jack. He refused his father's offer of a calf to rear and train. He couldn't forget Blossom, nor the way he had betrayed her trust. He wouldn't, couldn't take that risk again.

By August 2007, Jack was faced with the choice of staying on at school in the autumn or following his father into farming. He knew what his father wanted, but the memories of 2001 were hard to shake off. A chat with a sympathetic master at the school suggested a middle way. He was fairly good at science. He could stay on, take science A levels and perhaps study some aspect of farming later on. It pushed into the distance the moment when he would have to tell his father there was no way he would ever be a dairy farmer.

Then the news broke. Foot and mouth in Surrey, and this time it was *all* the government's fault. By the time the source of the outbreak was confirmed in September, Jack's decision was made, set in stone, and a fire lit in his mind that would never go out. Official incompetence had killed twice in less than six years; once through a poor decision and the second time by actual, direct government-created contamination. He would never again put his heart into anything the government could kill. And when he got the chance, he would act to protect the government's innocent victims.

# 2

## Near the River Bure at Acle, June 2018

Reflections from the river rippled on the roof of the conservatory as DCI Greg Geldard gulped down his morning mug of hot black coffee. Perched on his left shoulder was Bobby, his one-year-old tortoiseshell cat. She was rubbing her head up and down his newly shaved cheek in what he took to be approval, but knew was really an appeal for a drink of milk and some cat treats before he left for the day's work. Glancing at his watch and noting that time was pressing, he rushed round the small cottage, placing quantities of cat food in five different locations so that Bobby had to do some hunting in order to get fed. It helped keep her busy while he was gone, and he knew that this was likely to be a long day. Then, with one last rub of her head, he placed her on her favourite windowsill and dashed out to his car.

It was now just over three months since he had charged one James Metcalfe, and his Romanian sidekick Dragan Bakalov, with a complex mess of crimes from murder to smuggling. At last, the case was being heard in Norwich Crown Court. He and some colleagues were due to give evidence. He'd spent the day before, and indeed most of the evening, going over the files and his private notes. This had been his first big case in Norfolk and successful convictions really mattered to him and the whole team. He and Jim Henning, his DI on the case, had spent hours asking each other questions, trying to pre-empt the likely lines of inquiry from the defence barristers. The Crown Prosecution barrister had done the same with them both but, as Jim said, it wasn't his questions they needed to fear. If anyone tripped them up, it would be Ms Farrar from the defence team.

The traffic was slowing as it approached the roundabout onto the A47 and Greg looked at his watch again as he pulled up. If the driver of the car alongside the red BMW 3 series coupe had looked sideways, he would have seen a bull-necked, fresh-faced man in his thirties with mid-brown hair and a determined expression, tapping his steering wheel either in frustration or to music. The bulging briefcase tossed carelessly on the back seat would have revealed him to be a professional of some kind. He would probably not have guessed, first off, policeman.

By the time Greg drew into the car park near the Norwich law courts, his safety net of extra time had been seriously eroded by traffic delays. He swung out of the car and grabbed his briefcase in one move, slammed the door and headed for the exit, only then recognising the man in the liveried vehicle alongside.

'Hi, Ben. So you're on today too?'

Ben, slim, hair greying and sporting 'first responder' uniform looked up from his car keys. Attacked in the line of duty by the Romanian enforcer Dragan Bakalov, he'd been lucky to get away with no worse than a flesh wound.

'That's right, provided they get to me,' he replied. 'I've been told that, as one of the victims, I'm likely to be called early, but you know what it's like.'

'Don't I just. I probably won't see much of you inside until we've both given our evidence. They tend to keep us police separate, as you probably remember. The Witness Service will be looking after you. Are you going in the public gallery after they've finished with you?'

'If I have time. But I'm on duty this afternoon, hence the first responder signs all over my car. I'll probably leave when they adjourn for lunch.'

'If I've given my evidence by then, do you have time to meet up?'

'Again, depends on timing, but probably not. How about we meet for a drink later? The King's Arms is sort of halfway between you and me.'

'You're on. See you later.'


Chris Mathews, Greg's forceful detective sergeant, was already waiting in the room set aside for police. Today she had let loose her vivid colour sense by topping a sober black trouser suit with an orange and pink scarf. The trainers peeping out from the hem of the trousers were orange too. As so often, Greg mentally reached for the sunglasses.

'Morning, Chris. Jim here?'

'Yes. He's just gone for some coffees from the snack bar. He's bringing you one too.'

'Good man. All ready for the questions?'

'I think so. I just wish this had got to court while it was all fresh in my mind, but I suppose a few months isn't so bad.'

'Could've been worse. And at least they didn't get bail, so they've been safely tucked away. Have CPS been in yet? Do we know what today's timetable is?'

'Not yet,' answered Chris. 'Still waiting to see. I hope you've brought something to do while we hang around.'

Greg pulled his laptop out of his briefcase. 'Always paperwork to catch up on,' he said, and made himself comfortable at the table in the corner. By the time Jim returned with the coffees, the CPS barrister had arrived, brisk, flustered and hot. All as normal.

'The good news is,' he said, 'we're still scheduled to start at ten or shortly after. Both the accused have arrived and are in the cells. Their defence is making a bit of a fuss, but it's something and nothing. I think we'll go ahead more or less on time. The line of questioning from me is as we discussed earlier. Nothing new there. The usher will fetch you when we're ready. Oh, and lose the scarf,' he said to Chris. 'Don't want to antagonise the judge.' And he bustled out again.

There was a pregnant silence. Greg and Jim looked at the floor. Chris sighed and pulled off the offending, fluorescent item.

'Worth a try,' she said. 'At least he didn't notice the shoes.' She regarded her neat, gaudy foot with some complacency.

By the end of the afternoon, Chris, Jim and Greg had given their evidence. Ben had also been questioned and cross questioned. On that basis, it was hard to see how Bakalov could avoid being sent down. When the victim of a stabbing survives to tell the tale, and is backed up by brawny members of the lifeboat crew who intervened to make that survival possible, the perpetrator is surely caught red handed. The fate of James

Metcalfe, however, still hung in the balance. Charged with a range of offences from acting as an unlicenced gangmaster, through wildlife smuggling to three murders, the evidence was a complex mix of forensic science, data extracted from a car computer database and witness statements. After a thorough grilling on the circumstantial nature of the evidence amassed against him, Greg found himself unable to call it.

Greg arrived back at his cottage just as his mobile rang. Opening the back door with his briefcase in one hand, the phone tucked between shoulder and ear, he attempted to fend off Bobby's urgent greeting while also making coherent sense to his boss.

'How'd it go,' asked Margaret Tayler, Chief Superintendent. 'CPS is playing his cards close to his not inconsiderable chest, but did seem cautiously optimistic. What was your take?'

Suppressing a smile at the reference to the barrister's generous proportions, Greg replied, 'I think we're home and dry on Bakalov, definitely on the attempted murder of Ben Asheton and probably on the charges relating to the murder of the worker dumped in the river and the arson of the gamekeeper's cottage. As for Metcalfe, the jury haven't heard all the evidence yet. Jim, Chris and I have had our turn, but they've yet to hear from forensics. I'm pretty certain the smuggling charges will stick, and if they do then we have a good chance on the rest.'

'Good. When do you think you'll finish up there?'

'Tomorrow, hopefully. Defence haven't finished taking evidence yet, and I'd expect the case to go on for another two days at least, but they should be done with us by Thursday.'

'Again, good. The work's stacking up, Greg. The county lines case needs some attention. I feel it's losing impetus. And I've had an odd phone call from the government lab on the Science Park. They've asked for advice on security.'

'Isn't that a job for uniform?'

'Normally, yes, but it seems they've had a specific threat. They're being a bit cagey, but they've requested CID involvement and in view of the almighty cock up that was the last attack on the GM trials, I think you or Jim had better take a look. I'll send an email with what I know.'

'OK, thanks. I'll deal with it as soon as we're free of the court.'

Greg turned his attention to Bobby, currently making a game attempt to slaughter his post.

'Come on, Bobs,' he said. 'Let me at least see whether I want to read it before you shred it.'

Leaving the cat with the adverts for pizza takeaways and the local free press, he picked up the stiff, official-looking envelope with the printed label and opened it with a knife from the magnetic holder on the kitchen wall. Then froze. It was not entirely unexpected, but a bit of a shock all the same. A formal communication from his estranged wife Isabelle's solicitor, inviting him to divorce her on grounds of adultery.

He sat down at the battered oak kitchen table and placed the letter carefully on the surface, bottom edge neatly aligned with the table edge. He placed his hands on either side and sighed. Bobby arrived on the table top, marched over the letter and rubbed her head on his neck.

'Quite right, Bobby,' he said. 'Deal with it later. We've got more important stuff to do first.' And he took the cat into the sitting room for a quick game of chase the feather. When he left to go to the King's Arms, the letter still lay where he had left it.

Jim and Ben had already made themselves comfortable in the bar when he got there. Having bagged one of the tables in the bay windows, they'd spotted the arrival of what Jim termed the 'flash red car' and a pint was waiting on the table.

'Thanks,' said Greg. 'Anyone eating? I could do with something to help soak this up.'

'Pity not to,' said Jim and snagged a copy of the bar menu from a passing waitress.

'Is Chris joining us?' asked Greg.

'She said not,' replied Jim. 'Said she was off tomorrow and had some stuff to catch up on first.'

'I nearly died on the spot when he told her to take off the scarf,' said Greg.

'Me too, but she told me after it's a sort of running joke between them. Every time she's in court she tries it on with one luminous item of clothing to see if she can get it past him.'

'Well I wish you'd warned me. And while we're on the subject, you should have warned me about the cat's name.'

'Cat's name?' asked Ben, trying and failing to look innocent.

'Come off it. You all knew about the row between Sarah and Chris about naming the kitten and none of you tipped me the wink. If I'd known, I'd have picked something neutral.'

'Whereas you picked Chris's suggestion and Sarah has been out of sorts ever since.'

'Rubbish. She's much too sensible to take offence over such a minor matter.'

Ben and Jim exchanged glances. 'You think? Well, possibly, but there's nothing like two strong characters in one office to generate heat,' remarked Jim.

'So long as they generate light as well, I'm OK with that. So what's everyone having?'

After their meals of pie and chips, with a side helping of court hearing review, all three were ready to call it a day. Just in time, Greg remembered to ask Jim about the laboratory and its mysterious security issue.

'I could pick it up on Friday afternoon,' said Jim doubtfully, 'but that's assuming I don't get held up in Norwich on the county lines case.'

'No problem, I'll call in myself,' said Greg. 'I haven't been over there yet, so it's a chance to find my way about.'

Back home, curtains drawn and settled cosily in front of the view of the river from the conservatory windows, glass to hand and Bobby back on his lap, Greg treated himself to a sip of his favourite single malt. It was no good. The official letter was picking at the edges of his mind and he couldn't settle. With a sigh, and the cat over his shoulder like a stole, he returned to the kitchen and picked it up. It was an officially worded and straightforward request that he divorce Isabelle on the grounds of her adultery. He tapped the stiff envelope on his teeth as he thought, then put it down on the table at his elbow and decisively drank off the last of his whisky. On the face of it, a not unreasonable request, but he had a strong feeling there was something more to it.

'Bed, Bobby,' he said. 'And tomorrow I think I need a word with the soon to be ex.'

# 3

## Queen Mary University, London, 2010

The crowd in the students' union bar was thinning when Jack was suddenly joined by the glamorous but intense girl he had seen the day before at the Compassion in World Farming meeting in the chaplaincy.

'Hi, we didn't have a chance to speak yesterday. I'm Meg. You're Jack, I think.'

Jack was flattered she had found out and remembered. 'That's right.'

'I asked who you were after the meeting,' she said. 'I was impressed by what you said about welfare at slaughter. Are you going on the demo on Friday?'

'The one near Ramsgate?'

'Yes. Are you going on the bus?'

'Yes.'

'Sit with me on the bus? I'd like to discuss what you said about slaughter.'

She waved in response to his delighted nod, and dashed off.

The bus was booked to leave the Mile End Road at four in the morning. Even getting to college at that time of day was a challenge, and Jack reflected that it showed the dedication of the CIWF club members that they were prepared to get up so early. Looking round, he amended that to 'stay up so late', as it was apparent quite a few on the coach had not been to bed at all that night. Meg was there, comparatively bright eyed and bushy tailed. He joined her on a seat near the back of the bus. Most of those around them settled down for a nap during the two-hour journey to Ramsgate.

Dressed for a rough day in jeans, warm jacket, and with a beret pulled over her long, mid-brown hair, Meg still looked stunning. 'All clear on what we do at Ramsgate,' she asked. 'It's the first time you've been on one of these isn't it?'

'Yes. And yes. In fact,' and he grinned, 'I'd pretty much decided to follow the crowd. It's mainly a case of blocking the lorries peacefully isn't it?'

'Yes. If we can.' She looked around, but most of their immediate neighbours appeared to be asleep and the old coach rattled and growled enough to cover most of what was said.

'As I said, if we can, but sometimes the lorry drivers aren't too careful about what they do, and some of us may need to be a little more, shall I say, forceful. I wanted to know if you'd be up for that. If you'd help out?'

'Doing what,' asked Jack, torn between caution and excitement.

'Possibly chaining ourselves to a lorry. Possibly the odd smashed windscreen. Nothing too desperate. But if we're serious about stopping this filthy trade, some of us think we need to make our point more forcibly. Defra just isn't listening at present.'

'Defra never listens,' he grunted. 'And OK, I'm up for that, provided no one gets hurt.'

'Well, of course, that's what we hope,' she agreed. 'But we can't guarantee it. And these folk are making money out of animal suffering. Perhaps a bit of pain for a big gain isn't a bad exchange. But if you're nervous...' She left the sentence dangling.

'I said I'm up for it,' he said. 'Now, you said you wanted to talk about welfare at slaughter.'

'On the way back,' she said. 'We should get some kip now.' Closing her eyes, she rested her head on his shoulder.

On the coach on the return journey, nursing some bruises and what was probably going to be a black eye, Jack found his memory of events very confused. He had a clear picture of getting off the coach and listening to yet another briefing from a CIWF official. He'd stressed the importance of peaceful demonstration to the point of tedium and, as a result, lost the attention of many of his hyped-up audience. Jack's coach-load met up with some others, and the demo was nearly 200 strong when they got to the port and deployed along the access road. After that, he mainly remembered noise, activity and confusion. A bit like going to war, he thought later.

Meg kept a hold on his sleeve for much of the time, so he followed her, willy-nilly. They started off orderly enough, lining the road with banners and a lot of shouting. When some livestock lorries approached, they formed human barriers in the roadway. It was only when security guards, and later police, started to clear them out of the way that it got a bit rough. By nine o'clock the police had them kettled in a corner by the port entrance, the trucks had gone through, and most protestors were assessing the damage. Jack wasn't the only one with some bruises. Neither the police nor the security team had been too gentle. The black eye he reckoned he got when he was trying to protect Meg from a flying fist. He hoped she'd noticed. Meg herself seemed energised by the violence, and dismissive of the complaints from the CIWF officer who'd deplored some of the rougher tactics. An element of the crowd, mainly middle-aged ladies, shared the official's concerns and there was a clear split of opinion between those who espoused the non-violent route, and the livelier student contingent. The official's parting words were to the effect that if they couldn't abide by the rules, they wouldn't be welcome under the CIWF banner. That didn't seem to depress anyone's spirits.

After a stop on the way home to stock up with beer and snacks, Meg returned to the subject of slaughter.

'I was impressed by what you said the other day,' she said. 'About how if farmers knew what went on after they took their stock to market, they'd be more careful about where and how they sold them.'

'It's true,' he said vehemently, over his fish and chips. 'My father was always careful after the first time he saw how a slaughterhouse treated the stock. They've improved somewhat since the old days, but he saw sheep awaiting slaughter penned alongside baskets of severed heads, with blood running under their feet.'

'You see much worse than that,' said Meg. 'If you think it's improved, you're fooling yourself.'

'How do you know?'

She looked around again and dropped her voice. 'Because I've seen it. That's what I wanted to talk to you about. I belong to a small group.'

'In CIWF?'

'No. Separate. But with very similar aims. You've seen today that CIWF just doesn't go far enough. Not in our view anyway. So we set up our own action group. We've been putting CCTV in slaughterhouses. Undercover obviously. Then sharing the footage. It's horrendous, honestly. If you're interested I'll show you, but I warn you, you'll be shocked. If you're up for it, I thought you might like to join our group.'

Jack turned in his seat, his chips, for the moment, forgotten. 'What do you want me to do?'

'Help us break in to slaughterhouses and fix up cameras, then retrieve the footage. We need to get in quietly, so they don't go looking for cameras. Or we infiltrate the staff, and get in that way. I thought you might be able to help. We might even ask you to go undercover, but I warn you, that would be tough.'

'I'll look at the footage you have,' he said with a remnant of caution, 'but yes, I'll help if I can.'

As Jack had cause to reflect later, it was ironic that, having chosen a university in the Mile End Road, about as far from rural England and agriculture as he could possibly find, it was there he was enlisted to fight abusive slaughter methods.

His first outing was nearly his last. The phone call came late one evening.

'Be outside Mile End tube, 2200 tomorrow. You'll be

picked up by a van. You'll know the driver. Dark clothes. Reply as advised.' The call ended.

Jack replied 'yes' by text, and reflected that if push came to shove, he could refuse to get in the van.

Outside the tube station as instructed, wearing dark jeans and a black puffa jacket over a dark hoodie, he was impressed when a white van pulled up exactly on schedule. As it happened, he only vaguely recognised the driver, but Meg leaned out from the passenger seat.

'Get in the back,' she instructed as the rear doors opened. There were two other folk already in the van, neither of whom he recognised. They nodded, but said nothing. Jack sat on the bench seat opposite and also remained silent. The atmosphere was not conducive to conversation.

Judging by the road noise and the way the van swayed, it reversed direction then soon joined a main road. Within forty minutes, they were pulling up and Meg opened the rear doors.

'OK. The target is just up the road. The van will stay here to keep out of range of the perimeter cameras. Our CCTV was inserted a week ago. We're here to recover the cameras. The driver stays with the van, in case we need to leave in a hurry. You and you,' she pointed at Jack and one of the others, 'you'll go into the slaughterhouse and get the cameras. Mick knows where they are,' she said to Jack.

'You,' – she pointed at the remaining shadow standing by the van – 'we'll create a diversion near the main gate, to distract the security guard.'

She looked back at Jack and Mick.

'Give us ten minutes, then go for it. You'll hear us.'

Mick handed Jack a pair of black gloves and a balaclava.

'You'll need these,' he said quietly, and picked up an enormous pair of bolt cutters.

'How did you get in last time,' asked Jack as they skirted the perimeter fence. 'Won't they notice if they keep getting holes in the fence?'

'Last time I went over the gate,' Mick said shortly. 'But since we released the other footage, all the slaughterhouses in this group have tightened up their security. We have a friend inside who tipped us off. Now shush. We're nearly there.'

Mick had picked a spot where trees grew relatively close to the fence. As he went straight to the spot, Jack assumed he had scouted it out beforehand. A quick look round, some fast snips with the bolt cutters, and Jack helped bend the wire back to create a snag-free entrance. Once inside the perimeter, they skirted the building to approach it from the side away from the main entrance.

'Waste materials are collected from this end,' muttered Mick. 'It smells a bit.' He wasn't wrong. It stank. Even Jack, used to farmyards, was taken aback. The roadway ran up to big double doors, with a pedestrian door alongside. Mick listened, then used the bolt cutters again, this time on the padlock securing the main doors. They pulled one open a foot or so with a squeal of door catching on lintel, then slid inside.

'You keep a look out here,' instructed Mick. 'We need to secure our escape route, so that's you. Any problems, shout. And then run.'

Jack must have looked surprised.

'If you get a problem, it's too late to be secret,' said Mick drily. 'By then, it's speed or nothing. I shouldn't be long. The cameras are in the stunning area and the slaughter hall.' He disappeared into the dark, and Jack tucked himself behind the door, watching both out into the yard and, as best he could, into the dark spaces of the abattoir.

It seemed hours before he heard Mick returning. It had started to drizzle, turning the light glowing near the front gate into a fuzzy blob. At that moment, he spotted a moving shape in the yard outside. He put out a warning hand to Mick and they both waited behind the big door, hoping the security guard did not come close enough to spot the severed padlock. It was a forlorn hope. The guard may not have been super-active but he had his instructions and checking every door and gate was among them. He shook the doors, exclaimed as the padlock fell on the floor and bent to pick it up. Mick gave the door a savage push, knocking the guard to the ground, and shouted to Jack, 'Run!'

They both shot through the gap and past the sprawling guard like greyhounds from the traps. Mick had the advantage, starting first, but Jack's long legs soon caught up. Behind them they heard the guard shouting at his walkie talkie and knew they would soon have added problems. Jack reached the fence first and dived through the hole. Mick followed, was held up slightly by his coat catching on the wire but pulled himself free. Judging by the noise, reinforcements were approaching round the perimeter.

'Separate,' gasped Mick, and dashed off to the left, towards the van. Jack went right.

He soon lost himself in the wood, but kept running until he emerged into an open area with the fences of a housing estate in front of him. As he went over the back fence like a gazelle, and through the untidy garden beyond, he heard shouts in the distance and knew that outrunning his pursuers was not going to be an option. He pushed the garden gate open and slid silently through. The household bins were out for collection all down the street. Into one he pushed his balaclava, and into another his gloves. That bin had a pile of newspapers in the top. He took the top one, folded it neatly under his arm and walked boldly down the pavement, whistling as he went. He walked straight into a couple of the security guards as he turned the corner.

'Whoa,' he exclaimed. 'You nearly bowled me over there. Where's the fire?'

The guards didn't even pause, seeing a respectable young man apparently on his way home.

'Seen anyone running?' one of them asked.

'No,' he said. Then, 'Oh wait, I did see someone turn the corner as I came into the road, but I thought it was a jogger.'

'Where?'

'Back there,' he turned and pointed.

'Thanks.' And the two guards trotted off, following Jack's outstretched arm.

Jack wondered how long he'd got before they came back. He was careful not to hurry as he walked away, just in case they turned to watch him. Once round the corner, he legged it to the main road and leapt on the first bus that came along. It turned out to be going to the station, so the journey home was easy after that. His phone buzzed when he was on the train. It was Meg.

'Where are you?'

'Train to Liverpool Street,' he said.

'Any problems?'

'No. What about Mick?'

'He's with us in the van. With the footage. Well done, Jack. See you tomorrow.'

# 4

## Norwich Science Park, 2018

As advised, Greg approached the Science Park from the A47 rather than tackling the traffic- and student-clogged route through the city. He had to pull up twice by big information boards bearing maps that stated 'You are here', and struggled to identify the most efficient route between where they claimed he was and where he wanted to be. At last he stopped by the security gate to the National Agricultural Science Agency, also known as NASA, and was pointed to visitor parking and reception.

Just a short wait later and he was directed to a small meeting room equipped, encouragingly, with a coffee machine and a plate of wrapped biscuits. A tall lean man with tousled grey hair and a grey goatee bustled in just as he was sitting down at the table. Greg got to his feet again and took the hand proffered him.

'DCI Greg Geldard,' he said.

'Professor Craig Bennington, deputy CEO,' said the other man. 'Thank you for coming so quickly.'

'No problem. I'm new enough in Norfolk to welcome the opportunity to familiarise myself with different parts of my patch. I've been briefed, but I must admit I'm not exactly sure why I'm here. I gather you've had a threat of some kind?'

'Yes. Look, I'm conscious I may be making a fuss about nothing, but after the problems last year over the GM crop trials, I thought we were better safe than sorry.'

'That was before my time I'm afraid, but I gather there was a problem with the security set-up for the trial.'

'Yes. I'm not blaming the police, don't get me wrong. We took advice from your colleagues, but when we hired the security company our then CEO went for the cheap option and it didn't work out. The men supposedly guarding the trial plots didn't see the point of standing guard over a load of plants and skived off to the pub once darkness fell. The activists got to the trial plots and destroyed the lot in one night. So you'll understand why we're feeling a bit sensitive.'

'And this time, Professor?' prompted Greg.

'This time it's not GM crops, it's animal rights activists. And do please call me Craig.' He unfolded the file in front of him on the table and pulled out a letter in a plastic sandwich bag. 'You can see my staff watch *CSI*,' he said wryly.

Greg pulled the letter towards him.

'But where are my manners?' exclaimed the professor. 'Can I get you a coffee while you have a look at that?'

'Thank you,' said Greg. 'Black, no sugar.'

While the machine behind him hummed and gurgled and the plate of biscuits was put on the table, Greg read: 'Stop the torture of apes and monkeys or suffer the consequences. Take this warning seriously. We have the means to take action.' It was printed on a sheet of plain photocopy paper, by the look of it by a bog standard laser printer.

'Thank you,' he said. 'I'll take it and get it checked for fingerprints et cetera but I wouldn't hold your breath. As you say, everyone watches *CSI*.' He turned the ziplock bag over and noted a plain white envelope was tucked in behind, the professor's name printed on it in similar fashion.

'Good. You kept the envelope. Why do you think it was addressed to you rather than the CEO?'

'I'd guess, because I'm a professor of ethology.' As Greg looked blank he translated, 'Animal behaviour. Our organisation chart is in the public domain, not least in our annual reports, so it wouldn't be hard to work out who was the most senior member of staff likely to be involved with animals.'

'Who handled the letter and the envelope?'

'God knows how many before it arrived in my office, but since then only my PA, Ken Ashby, and me. After us, no one. Ken put it in the plastic bag.'

Greg helped himself to an orange-flavoured shortbread. 'And the reference to apes and monkeys?'

'Well, that's the odd bit. The only primates we experiment on here are human. And they're all volunteers as you'd expect. We don't have any non-human primates, nor any reason to have. We do have an animal unit – I'll take you round if you like – but apart from a small number of farm livestock most of our specimens have at least six legs.'

For a second, Greg wondered wildly about genetic modification, but Craig went on, 'As in, most are insects. We have the National Bee Unit here, so we have several thousand bees. And because of our work on pest control, we have hundreds of cockroaches, mites and so on. But as far as experimental animals are concerned, we don't even have rats or mice. In fact we did wonder if the Bee Unit is what prompted the reference to apes. The plans for the laboratory are also in the public domain, and there is a reference to an apiary. I suppose to the uneducated that might mean apes. But it does seem a bit far-fetched.'

'Never underestimate the relative lack of intelligence of the average criminal,' remarked Greg. 'In all modesty it's one of the reasons we catch them. I knew a chap in North Yorkshire who fled the house he'd just burgled on a winter's night and realised he was leaving clear tracks in the snow behind him. His solution was to take his shoes off!'

Craig laughed. 'In that case, that may be where they're coming from. But let me show you round, then you can see what we have here, and also what precautions we've taken.'

Craig led Greg across the echoing, double-height atrium of the entrance hall to a door at the back. Greg noted he had to use his security pass on a key pad to open the door.

'All doors are secured, except the main entrance,' explained the professor. 'A security pass is coded so that it will only open the doors you need to go through, depending on your role. I have clearance for almost everywhere but, for example, someone working in the analytical labs wouldn't have access to the animal unit. Moreover, every time a pass is used to open a door, the ID and time are logged on a central computer. Passes are limited as to time and day too. So if someone doesn't normally work weekends, the pass only activates Monday to Friday.'

'What about the main entrance?'

'That works on a proximity detector, so in working hours it opens when someone with sufficient body mass – ie a person –

approaches the door. During those hours, the reception desk is manned and a security guard is on call. In any event, that only gives you access to the reception area and the canteen. All doors leading off are secure. It works fine,' he remarked, as he led the way down a gravelled path to a high fence beyond, 'except when a group of geese off the lake decide to have a look around. Four or five geese have enough body mass to trigger the door opening. We have had some in reception a couple of times, much to the receptionist's consternation.

'This is the only pedestrian entrance to the animal unit,' he said as he reached the gate in the fence. 'The top half of the fence is electrified and the whole fence is alarmed, so if anyone tries to cut a hole in it, it sets off an alarm.'

'What about vehicle access?'

'There's a vehicle gate further round the perimeter,' Craig replied. 'That too is alarmed and electrified. And it's secured outside normal working hours. In general it's only used for deliveries.'

'Deliveries of what?'

'Lab materials, feed stuffs, PPE, sometimes stocks of insects and so on. Very occasionally farm animals, but mostly we maintain a stable population of those, so they neither come nor go. They're housed in appropriate buildings or graze the fields behind.'

'Who makes the deliveries?'

'All specialist materials come from a couple of companies who supply lab materials etc. We use companies that supply other animal units, so for obvious reasons their security measures are really tight. Other stuff, ordinary office stuff like paper, ink cartridges and so on, they're delivered to the main lab and brought over here by our staff as and when required.'

Once through the electrified fence, Greg looked around with some interest. There was a mixture of buildings, all single storey, but while some looked like typical laboratories, others were plainly farm-style livestock buildings.

'My research interest is in how we can adjust the way we keep farm animals in order to maximise their welfare and well-being,' remarked Craig. 'Even small tweaks in environment can have a big impact on their ability to exercise normal behaviours.'

'Is that important?' asked Greg, looking at the small flock of sheep grazing a paddock and the pigs in a field with arks, seemingly not minding the drizzle.

'Very,' came the reply. 'For all sorts of reasons. Happy animals grow faster and breed more efficiently. But not only that. An animal keeper is legally obliged to provide their animals with the Five Freedoms, and one of those is the freedom to express normal behaviour. I'm guessing you didn't know that?'

'No, I didn't,' said Greg.

'Embodied in the Animal Welfare Act,' said Craig, opening the first door. 'I sometimes think that if pet owners knew what legal obligations their guinea pig comes with, they might think twice. And how much better pets lives would be if they did. Anyway, some of these animals are also used in feeding trials, but nothing that imposes a welfare burden. The Bee Unit is through here.'

Greg hung back a little, trying not to make it obvious but reassured to see that, indoors at least, there were no bees flying around. Through the window he could see some hives a safe distance away.

'We tend to keep the bees and the sheep apart,' added

Craig. 'They don't seem to mix happily. I'm not sure whether it's because the sheep knock the hives over by scratching on them, or because the bees get their feet caught in the fleeces.'

Making notes of the security measures he could see, the CCTV cameras and secured access points, Greg reflected that the visit was proving quite educational in a number of ways.

A general look round the rest of the laboratory later, and the two men returned to the small conference room where they had started.

'More coffee?' asked Craig.

'No thank you,' replied Greg. 'I should be getting back. I'll take the letter with me and get one of our folk to pop in to take some fingerprints for elimination purposes, if that's OK? I'll also do a report, but I have to say I think your security is pretty thorough. I may have a couple of suggestions to make, but nothing very much. We'll raise your threat level and I'll ask local patrols to call by as regularly as they can manage. But as I'm sure you know, we're a bit thin on the ground and won't be able to do much more unless you get more explicit threats. Please do contact me if you get any more approaches.'

'One thing,' he added as he was leaving. 'The most obvious weak spot is in your own staff. If it's OK with you, I'd like to send my sergeant along to talk to your HR team about the precautions they take and how they screen new recruits. Your security essentially depends on only certain people having access to the buildings at prescribed times. But if those people are moles, you have little defence.'

Part way home and just as he was navigating the slow section of the A47, Greg got a call on his mobile. Checking his dashboard, it was a Norwich number he didn't recognise, he answered on the hands free.

'Lewis and Collins, solicitors,' said the disembodied voice. Recognising the company name from the recent letter, Greg had a sinking feeling he knew what this was about.

'My name is Jane Rogers and I'm your wife's solicitor,' said the voice. 'You should have received a letter from me. I appreciate it may have come as a shock, but I'm ringing to see if you are willing to comply with your wife's request. And to ask if you have a solicitor acting on your behalf.'

Greg thought for a moment, scowling in his rear view mirror at the van tailgating him, presumably under the impression that the fifty miles per hour speed limit didn't apply to him.

'Yes, I got the letter,' he said. Then, realising the scowl was translating into tone of voice, he tried to smile, and went on, 'I didn't know there was any rush.'

'I think your wife feels that, as you've now been separated for over a year with little or no contact, it's time for you both to move on.'

Greg thought some more, then replied, 'Please tell her that I'll consider her request, but I want to meet her first. I should be able to manage an early evening meeting between now and the weekend. She can choose when and where.'

'I'm not sure your wife will be keen on that,' said Ms Rogers, sounding a little flustered.

'Look, I'm not planning on making a scene,' interrupted Greg. 'She's welcome to choose a wine bar, a restaurant, even the cathedral if she wishes. I just want a quiet chat before I draw a line under the last few years. I don't think that's unreasonable.'

'I'll pass the message on,' said Ms Rogers, just as the white van behind Greg surged past at an illegal and risky eighty miles an hour in the fifty limit.

'Well, sod that,' said Greg. Then, realising the phone was still live he said hastily, 'Sorry, that wasn't intended for you. I'm on duty and I need to take action,' as he hit the button for the blue lights and closed up behind the van.

Later that evening, as he brought Jim Henning up to date on his visit to the Science Park, he admitted, 'It was petty, I know, but there was a certain satisfaction in scaring the bejesus out of that idiot in the white van. I rather enjoyed making like a traffic cop, prowling round checking tyres, bodywork, pointing out he had neither tax nor insurance, then finding some very dodgy-looking kit in the back and threatening to charge him with going equipped for theft.'

'The paperwork's going to drown you,' remarked Jim.

'No, I got lucky there too. While I was still checking things over and thinking exactly that, a patrol car pulled up behind us, so I handed over to them. They were happy enough and I got to go home.'

'So, what are you going to do about Isabelle.'

'Wait to hear when we can meet up. Then I'll sign the divorce papers, obviously. There's no mileage in dragging things out, but I want to hear from her own lips why there's now such a hurry.'

'Presumably she's planning to remarry?'

'Perhaps so. Nothing to do with me now is it? But it'll be a cold night in hell before *I* take that route again.'

'You say that now,' said Jim, 'but…'

'And I mean it. If I change my mind, I'll take you to dinner at Midsummer House.'

'Wow, you mean the Michelin-starred place in Cambridge?'

'The very one,' promised Greg. 'But I'm safe, I promise you.'

'I *will* hold you to that.'

Just as he went to bed, Bobby prowling the room prior to settling down with him, Greg's phone tinged to an incoming text.

'Tomorrow, the Last Wine Bar, 1800. Isabelle.'

# 5

## Jack and the activists, winter 2016

Jack was nervously navigating the outskirts of Norwich in order to embark on his first day at NASA. His old college mates were hugely entertained by the idea of a fledgling career in rocket science, while knowing full well the initials in this instance stood for the National Agricultural Science Agency.

The battered old Mini, with its idiosyncratic colour scheme of navy and violet, stopped at the security gate. The Norwich Science Park was home to a range of establishments from the Norfolk and Norwich Hospital to the renowned John Innes Centre. NASA was handily situated between the A47 and Heathersett Lane, not far from the John Innes and with most of the other bioscience units within easy reach.

'Name?' asked the liveried guard.

'Jack Haigh,' replied Jack.

'How do you spell it?' asked the guard scanning a list on a clipboard. 'Who are you here to see?'

Sighing at this oft-met request, Jack supplied the spelling and answered, 'HR in the first instance, then Professor Lai. I'm starting work here today.'

The guard ticked off a name on the list. 'Congratulations,' he said. 'For today, park in the visitors' car park, and report to reception. They'll give you a pass for the staff car park that you can use from tomorrow. Welcome aboard.'

Waving a thank you, Jack drove under the raised barrier and parked where indicated.

The receptionist was located at a desk in the middle of an impressive double height atrium. A plaque on the wall to her left announced that the laboratory had been formally opened by a Minister of Agriculture in 1999. She had her list on a computer screen and gave the young man in front of her a warm smile. Tall, blond, fresh-faced and well-muscled from farm work, he was, as she reported to her friend from the HR team, 'Well fit'.

'He's working in the analytical lab,' said the friend, over their salad lunch in the staff canteen. 'With Professor Lai.'

'Oh, I thought he looked like one of the ecologists,' said June from reception, slightly disappointed. 'The chemists usually look more,' she hesitated, 'more office bound.'

'Pale and skinny,' said Kate with a giggle.

'Or pale, plump and bald' replied June.

'As opposed to tall, hairy and tanned?'

'Well I don't know about hairy,' replied June. 'We don't get that far on reception.' And they both giggled again.

The object of their interest was still navigating the formalities of starting work. He had his official pass, and had been lectured on ensuring he used it to log in and out each time he arrived at or left the lab. His car-park pass had been issued, he was clutching a sheet explaining his log-on details for the lab computer network, and he had signed the Official Secrets Act. His mother had been designated the recipient of any emergency phone calls, and his allotted 'buddy' was currently showing him around the site highlights including the gym, the landscaped balancing pond and the workplace nursery. A separate area behind an additional security fence was skirted without comment.

'What's in there?' asked Jack.

'That, oh that's the apiary and wildlife unit,' said his mentor, Kevin, carelessly. 'Access is limited to those who work there.'

Jack looked hard at the small paddocks currently containing a few sheep, and the faceless building with screened windows. Then he followed his guide to the canteen and they settled down for a late lunch.

'The food here's not bad,' remarked Kevin. 'One of the bonuses. So, tell me about you. What did you study?'

'Analytical chemistry at Queen Mary, London, then worked at Imperial,' answered Jack. 'And you?'

'Entomology at UCL. I suppose you're with Lai's crowd?'

'That's right. I believe I'm going to be working on mycotoxins in foodstuffs.'

'Right. Any interest in cricket by any chance? We've a fairly rough team but we do have a lot of fun.'

'Sorry. Not my thing. Chess now, that's my interest. Is there a chess club?'

'Probably,' Kevin was losing interest. 'There's a club for most things.'

\*

Meg had been the link. Demos, slaughterhouse filming, even one raid on an animal research supply hub – despite extended periods of no contact, they had kept in touch all the way from Queen Mary to Imperial. The suggestion to consider a job at NASA had come from Meg. Jack had been chary. He thought his chances only moderate and had liked the look of a similar job in a commercial lab. But Meg had persuaded him, as she always did.

'I don't want to work for the government,' he'd complained. 'I don't like anything about how they go about things. And surely I must be on some list or other of animal rights protestors. They'll never have me.'

'Leave that with me,' said Meg. 'There's ways round these things. We have a reason for wanting you at NASA. Does that make a difference?'

'Who's we?' he'd asked grumpily.

'You know better than to ask that. Just take my word for it. There are plans and you'd be at the heart of them.'

So he'd gone for the job. He'd got it, no problem as she'd predicted, and shortly after had come the text that introduced him to Jan, already known to him at work. He'd been surprised. Yes, she was vegetarian, but so were a lot of people these days. But she'd never broached the subject of animals or animal rights to his knowledge. Never. After a delay of a week or two, which she'd later told him was while she did a few extra checks of her own, she'd introduced herself as his cell lead. The other activist he knew was another chemist, Pat Nichols, working on pesticides in a different part of the lab,. And that was all he knew. Two people. Very little information, and no action.

After six months he was bored and impatient. He missed the camaraderie of the protest events. He missed CIWF and Meg. Most of all, he missed the feeling he was making a difference. All Jan would say was, 'Keep your head down. And wait.'

By the winter, Jack felt he had his feet under the lab bench in more ways than one. Walking across the NASA car park, huddled in his padded coat against the chill of a typical Norfolk wind straight from the Urals, he noticed that the recently returned geese were also sheltering as much as possible, huddled in groups by the perimeter fence. The icy blasts whipped across the balancing pond and flattened the shrubbery. Nothing looked cheerful outside, and it was a relief to scan his pass at the entrance to Analytical Chem and access the warm laboratory beyond. He left his coat in his locker, donned a fresh white lab coat and went to check his results from the day before.

'Hope the sequence ran OK,' remarked his team lead in passing. 'Sainsbury's are chasing for those results before they send that batch of apples for processing.'

'Looks OK,' said Jack, checking the screen in front of him, 'and it seems they're all negative too, so Sainsbury's will be happy. Incidentally, I've had an idea that could speed up these analyses by around twenty per cent.'

'Let's discuss it over coffee,' replied Jan, short haired, fresh faced and in a hurry as usual. 'I'll make sure a few of the others are around as well, and we can give it a good chew over.'

A good chew over was Jan's standard response to ideas and suggestions. It could be frustrating, but mostly it worked. Everyone got to challenge and explore a bright idea before it was implemented. Everyone got to contribute. Jack was amused when she used the same approach in cell discussions.

One evening, he took a walk round the site after work. Even in the dark, the car park and walkways were well lit, the downlighters bright and well placed. He tried his pass on a random door to another lab, and wasn't surprised when it failed to open. He *was* surprised when a car pulled up near him and he was challenged by a security guard only moments later.

'Just taking a breath of air before I drive home,' he explained.

'Then why were you trying to get into that lab?' the guard asked. 'It's not the one you normally work in.'

'No, that's right,' said Jack, thinking quickly. 'I thought I saw a light on and I was going to pop in and turn it off. I hadn't realised my pass wouldn't work.' It was a feeble excuse on the spur of the moment, and Jack could see the guard wasn't impressed.

'Better if you leave that to us, sir,' he said. 'Time to get off home. Now.'

'Right, yes,' said Jack, and returned to his car.

There were repercussions the next day. Jan asked to see him in her office. 'I've been asked to make enquiries about your odd behaviour on site last night,' she said. 'I'll just explain you're a busybody with a penchant for walks in the dark, shall I?'

Jack had grinned sheepishly, but had lost the expression fast when Jan went on, 'But how do I explain your asinine behaviour to the next level? What were you told?'

'Keep my head down and wait for instructions,' muttered Jack.

'And which bit of that wasn't clear?'

He said nothing, feeling sulky and aware he probably looked around five years old.

'If you haven't jeopardised everything, you *may* get some instructions in the next month or so. But one more stupid mistake like that and you're out. Am I clear?'

He muttered something that might have been yes, and she let it go.

'Get out of my sight, and for God's sake keep your head down, as you were told. I have to report this. Twice.'

That had been three months ago and he'd been a good boy since. But he'd mentally given the job another couple of months and he was off. He was approaching the end of his not very long tether.

That evening, Jan called a rare cell meeting. Rare, because on this occasion they met in person rather than via WhatsApp. A nondescript city centre bar, a table in a dim corner and three pints in front of them. The floor was tacky underfoot, the table battered dark wood with tattered beer mats scattered on the surface. Jack thought they looked like the beginning of every spy novel he'd ever read, but no one seemed to be paying them much attention.

'I have some work for you,' said Jan abruptly, breaking across the awkward small talk.

'Pat, I need you to prep some ammonium nitrate explosive. The quantities needed and other details will be WhatsApped to you. All the materials you'll need are being stored in a location that will also be sent to you.

'Jack, I need you to source a cheap car. Buy it privately and pay cash. Give a false name and address obviously. When you have it, deliver it to the same location.'

'We're making a car bomb,' said Jack flatly. It wasn't a question. 'What's the target?'

'NASA, of course,' replied Jan with a studied calm. There was a pregnant silence.

'Why?'

'Wrong question,' replied Jan. 'The decision is taken elsewhere. All you have to decide is will you do it?'

Jack took a deep breath. 'Not if you're targeting people. I've never believed in protecting animals by killing people. I won't do it.'

'Nor me,' said Pat quickly.

'No one will get hurt if we do it right,' said Jan. 'The target is a government facility carrying out work we none of us believe in. The bomb will go off in the car park, well away from the buildings. And there will be warnings.'

'Who drives the car in?' asked Jack, worried it might be him.

'Not your business. A friend.'

Jack drank half his pint at one swallow and wiped his mouth with the back of his hand.

'I can mix the explosive OK, given ammonium nitrate and fuel oil,' said Pat thoughtfully, 'but some powdered aluminium would be good.'

'Everything you need will be at the location you're given. And a concrete mixer, to help with the mixing.'

'OK, he said. 'But you still need some way of setting it off. You can't just use a percussion cap you know.'

'I know. You have a week from the date you are given the location to mix the explosive. Then other people will turn up to load it into the car and add Semtex and a trigger. You must be away by then.'

'Semtex,' Jack exclaimed, only just remembering to keep his voice down. 'You know it can all be traced these days. It has an additive that can be traced.'

'Not this stuff, said Jan with some satisfaction. 'This is old stock. Pre-1990. It'll be fine. Anyway, you just get the car, Jack, and we'll take it from there.'

Jack and Pat left separately, but when Jack got to the station car park he found Pat waiting near his car.

'Are you OK with this? asked Pat, lurking in the shadows by the wall.

'Provided nobody gets hurt,' replied Jack.

'You do realise where the Semtex is coming from, don't you?'

'No idea. Never thought about it. Never expected to think about it to be honest.'

'If it's pre-1990 and untraceable, it's coming from terrorists. Probably the IRA.'

There was a silence as Pat got into his car, then he stuck his head out the window. 'You're not happy about this are you?'

'Not wholly, no. I never expected to get into anything this, this...'

'Criminal?'

'Violent. But I suppose so long as it's only property, government property at that, it's a victimless crime.'

'So you're in?'

'I'm in.'

*

The car was easy. The day after £1,000 arrived in his bank account he checked out the car ads in the *Great Yarmouth Mercury*. It seemed a good idea not to buy too close to his own doorstep. There were a couple of possibilities and he picked one to go and see. It had looked like a private sale, but when he got to the designated street in Yarmouth he found a yard with two or three similar cars parked in it. Better and better. If this was an under-the-counter car sales operation, there was even less likely to be much in the way of paperwork. To add some realism, he looked over all three cars. At least one, he was pretty confident, had been put together after being written off in an accident. That reinforced his impression that the whole operation was illegal.

The short, dark-haired man with bad teeth and strong accent didn't inspire great confidence either. He was vague to impenetrable on the source of the vehicles, and offered no details on previous owners beyond 'careful lady' and 'traveller in ladies' fashions'. Jack decided the car he had come to see, a red Fiesta, was too small for their purpose and looked to be on its last legs. There was also a silver Ford Focus hatchback, price £525. He asked for a reduction for cash, and agreed on £495 after a short haggle. Then he handed over the money, gave a fictitious name and address for the transfer documents and drove it away. He'd hesitated over asking for a receipt for the cash, but judged that the foolishness of leaving without one better fitted the image he was seeking to project. Judging by the noise the clutch made, the car wasn't very long for this world anyway. He left it at the location he'd been WhatsApped; a farmyard with buildings but no farmhouse or livestock. Parking it round the back as instructed, he left the keys under a rear wheel arch and walked into the nearest village, about a mile away. From there, it was a taxi back to Yarmouth to pick up his car from the car park near the magistrates' court (the irony was not lost on him), and back home.

He reported to Jan that evening, again via WhatsApp, and asked what he should do with the remaining £505.

'Whatever,' she replied carelessly. 'Keep it or give it to charity. No matter.'

Jack decided he'd donate it anonymously to CIWF, for old time's sake, and parcelled it up in a brown envelope for posting.

# 6

## The Last Wine Bar

Greg knew Isabelle's chosen venue well. They'd found it in their first few days wandering round the city, and enjoyed both the wine and the bistro-style food, especially – as he remembered – the amazing sourdough bread. Close enough to their rented house to wander over for a drink, it was one of *their* places. Greg couldn't make his mind up whether Isabelle choosing it for this meeting was conciliatory or inflammatory. Not knowing how long he would be there and no longer living near enough to walk, he decided not to take the risk of parking on the street and put the post code for the nearest car park into his sat nav. As so often in Norwich, that proved to be a mistake. He sat blocking the traffic in a busy street, looking at the large and permanent bollards that converted what should have been the entrance to the car park into pedestrian-only access. Muttering evilly, he drove around in circles until he found the vehicular access at the opposite end and at last parked his car. This meant he was now late rather than early, and hot and bothered instead of cool and collected. Grinding his teeth he rushed up the steps to the wine bar and looked round its crowded interior. No Isabelle. He was just relaxing when the chap behind the bar beckoned him over.

'Hi, Greg,' he said. 'Haven't seen you for a while. Your wife said to tell you she's got a table downstairs.'

Greg forced a smile. 'Thanks,' he said, then, 'has she got the drinks in or do I need to order now?'

'She's got a glass of red waiting for you,' replied the barman, turning to another customer as he spoke. 'Enjoy.'

Greg took the steep stairs down to the whitewashed basement, and quickly spotted Isabelle at a quiet table in the corner. At first glance she looked much as he recalled, jewel-coloured top and a silk scarf tossed casually over her shoulders. There were a few other tables in use, and he squeezed sideways between them in order to take his seat. As he lowered himself into his chair, he spotted the reason for Isabelle's sudden desire for a divorce. The polite greeting he'd had in mind went straight out of his head. 'When's it due?' he demanded.

The swelling belly that was forcing her to sit at the table sideways was not the only change in the Isabelle he had known, now he could look more closely. Her hair was longer and, he thought, fairer than nature had intended. It curved softly round her neck and fell forward over her down-turned face. She looked up through her eyelashes, in a Princess Di mannerism that he recognised and remembered so clearly.

'About three months,' she replied. On the table in front of her was a glass of sparkling water, a glass of red wine and a bowl of olives. She pushed the red wine and the olives towards him. 'I hope this is OK. It used to be a favourite.'

'I'm sure it's fine. My tastes haven't changed.' A look of indignation passed over her face and he added swiftly, 'That wasn't a pointed remark. I meant nothing more than I said. Look, Isabelle, if we're going to get through this with a modicum of dignity, can we just assume that we both mean well and start from there.'

'OK by me,' she replied, sipping her water. 'But in that case, why are we meeting at all? We could have left it to our solicitors.'

Greg sipped his wine, put the glass down and turned it slowly.

'We could have,' he said. 'But after all the time we had together, it seemed a very cold way to wind things up. I thought we could at least part civilly, if not as friends.'

Isabelle took her time answering, and Greg ate some olives. 'I suppose,' she said slowly, 'I'm still angry about how we parted. I felt you made everything my fault. You never acknowledged that you had any part in why we broke up.'

Greg felt the heat rising in his face but took a firm grip on his temper. 'Who had cheated?' he wanted to ask. 'Who ran out on the other? Who dumped the other while they were in the middle of the biggest professional challenge of their lives?' In lieu of releasing any of the angry torrent building up behind his teeth, he took another sip of wine. Noticing the white of his knuckles, he hid his hands under the table. 'I'm not sure any of that is relevant now,' he managed. 'Can we just agree that neither of us is perfect but that we both wish the other well.'

Another sip of the water, and Isabelle said, 'Yes, I think we could do that.'

She held out her hand across the table and Greg solemnly

shook it. There was a difficult pause as both took refuge in their glasses again, then Isabelle asked, 'Where are you living now? Have you found somewhere nice?'

'Yes, thank you, a cottage by the River Bure near Acle. It's only small, but it suits me. I even have a cat,' he added.

'A cat! Good God. How did that happen?'

'I always wanted a cat when I had the right place, and my colleagues got her for me when I moved in. She's a tortie named Bobby.'

'Bobby.' Isabelle laughed, sounding natural for the first time. 'Don't tell me. That was your colleagues as well.'

'That's right. How about you, Isabelle? Clearly life is changing for you. Are you happy,' he asked with some difficulty.

She looked at him through her lashes again. 'Yes, I think so. But obviously there are a lot of changes still to come. I want to get things sorted. To be able to look forward again. So, will you sign the papers, Greg?'

'If that's what you truly want.'

'That's what I truly want.'

'Then there's not much more to be said.' He drained his glass and stood up. 'How are you getting home?'

'Paul will take me. He's waiting upstairs.'

'Oh, I see. You didn't want us to meet.'

'I didn't see much point. You aren't going to kick off are you, Greg?' she asked nervously.

'No. I'll sign the papers, Isabelle. And I'm not going to kick off even if I do recognise him. I've better things to do with my evening.'

Greg left swiftly. Once on the ground floor again, he took a swift look round. A middle-aged man with longish hair and a beard seemed to be watching the top of the stairs, but looked away when he caught his eye. Greg hesitated a moment, staring, then pushed the door open and headed for the fresh air. The man's face overlaid his view of the road like a pale hologram, hovering somewhere just above eye level.

'The beard's new,' he thought, 'but I do know that face.' Searching his memory he placed it in the context of an after-performance party. 'Not a singer,' he thought. 'Perhaps a conductor, and older than Isabelle. Older than me.' The face lurked at the back of his mind all the way home. The face, and the memory of Isabelle telling him she didn't want a child yet. She wanted her career.

His phone rang as he was getting out of the car. Juggling keys and cat he entered the house, answering the phone at the same time.

'It's Chris,' said the voice. 'I've just finished at the space agency. I thought I might call in on my way home if you'd like a quick report. And if it's convenient obvs.'

Recognising the popular shorthand for the agricultural science agency, Greg replied, 'Yes, it's convenient, Chris. Do I gather you found something that's bothering you?'

'Yes. Possibly. I'll explain when I get to yours. I'll be about half an hour.'

'You're late finishing. Have you eaten?'

'Not yet.'

'I'll find us something then.'

'Thanks, Boss.'

In the kitchen, Greg found the solicitor's letter still sitting where he'd left it on the kitchen table. 'Might as well get that sorted,' he said aloud, and sat down to append his signature where indicated. Just about to seal the return envelope, he had a second thought, and added a separate letter for Isabelle.

*Thank you for agreeing to see me this evening, Isabelle. I appreciate you may have found it difficult, but I needed to find a way to draw a line under our marriage and move on. Meeting you today helped me do that. It's also made me realise that I've learned something from all this that I think is quite important. And that is, that love once given is the gift that can't be taken back. You don't love me now. But you did once. And I loved you. We both will always have that. Nothing destroys love and no one can take that away.*

*I wish things had been different, but I wish you well, Isabelle, and I'll never regret the time we had.*

*Greg*

He sealed the letter in an envelope, and added it to the paperwork going back to the solicitor before he could change his mind, then picked up a frying pan and some eggs. It would have to be an omelette and salad for supper that night. He reflected that, while it was an odd end to the day, it was better than sitting down in front of a TV and brooding. Work, as ever, would be his saviour.

Chris arrived almost to the minute. He heard the characteristic slam of the car door and tipped the beaten eggs into the pan.

'Come in,' he shouted as he heard the doorbell, then, 'Hi, Chris. This omelette will be ready in a few minutes. Can you toss the salad?' He nodded to the bowl on the kitchen table, 'and you can brief me while we eat.'

'No problem. Thanks, Boss. If you hadn't offered, I'd have been calling at the Macdonald's by Blofield. This is much better.'

She put the bowl of salad on the kitchen table as Greg brought two plates over, the giant omelette divided between them.

'Coke or water?' he asked. 'I know you won't drink and drive, but I hope you won't mind if I have a glass. It's been a bit of an evening.'

'Coke, please, and be my guest,' said Chris, waving her fork.

'So, what's bothering you?'

'That's the problem.' Chris replied. 'I'm not sure. I've spent most of the afternoon with the Agency HR team. They recruit and screen everyone below director level. Directors and the CEO are recruited by the parent department, so I've no information on them. For the rest of the staff, posts are always advertised either within the lab for an internal appointment or in the wider civil service or even publicly if the skill set needed is very specialist. Selection is competitive, and I've seen nothing that suggests a problem.

'Screening is thorough. Very thorough. The HR team have a checklist to work through for everyone – ID, addresses over the previous ten years, bank details, references and past employers, no gaps in the CV. All the normal stuff you'd expect to see. In addition, all of the staff on long-term contracts and anyone working in the animal unit is negatively vetted by the government security system. A few of those particularly sensitive posts are positively vetted too. As you know, that's even more thorough.

'I spoke to the HR director, the team leader and the HR

officer who deals with the animal unit. Their accounts of the processes were consistent. They were open and friendly, but something didn't sit right with me, and I can't put my finger on what it was.'

'Go back through your notes and your memory of what you learned,' recommended Greg. 'Try to identify the moment when you became concerned, then who you were speaking to at the time.'

'Concerned is a bit strong,' replied Chris, putting down her fork on the empty plate and picking up her notebook. 'But there was something that wasn't right.' She flicked pages while Greg cleared the plates away and produced a bowl of fruit.

'No pud I'm afraid, but I do have some fruit,' he said.

Chris wasn't paying attention. 'I think it was when the team leader was showing me the database and how it worked, but I don't think it was her that worried me. She seemed fine, if a bit inclined to let others do the work. Oh, that's it. That's what it was.' She paused a moment, obviously thinking hard.

'And?' prompted Greg.

'It was what I saw on the computer screen. The sign-offs for different parts of the screening process. They all went through one person. Or, at least, one digital ID.'

'Which means,' said Greg, catching on fast, 'there's no independent check. No counter balances.'

'That's right. Just one person, or possibly several people using one digital ID could authorise every part of the screening process for everyone being screened.'

'And you wouldn't set up an accounts system like that.'

'You wouldn't,' agreed Chris.

'Any idea who the ID belonged to?'

'No. We'd need to go back and check. And it may indeed be inefficient but innocent, but it is a flaw in their system.' Chris picked up an apple and sank her teeth into it. 'It's a relief to put my finger on what was bothering me. Thanks, Boss.'

'My pleasure. Actually,' he admitted, 'you did me a favour calling in this evening. I needed a work distraction.'

'Problem?'

Greg hesitated, then said, 'I saw Isabelle this evening. She's asked for a divorce. And she's pregnant.'

A silence fell, then Chris asked carefully, 'Tell me to butt out if I'm tramping in where angels fear to tread, but are you OK with that?'

Greg stood up and walked over to the big window with the view of the river. Bobby followed him. 'Yes and no,' he admitted. 'I knew there was no going back and that we both needed to move on. I thought I was OK with that. I am, sort of. The pregnancy, that's another thing. A bit of a shock if I'm honest.' He took a drink from the glass in his hand, still looking at the river, then discovered the glass was, somehow, empty. He looked into it for a moment, then came back to the table and refilled it.

'Last one for tonight,' he said, attempting a smile. 'I always thought I'd be the father of Isabelle's child. Thought I would be a few years ago, but she wasn't keen at the time. It seems my replacement has a more assertive approach to the subject.'

'I'm sorry,' said Chris, knowing as she spoke that anything she said would be inadequate. 'Let me know if I can do anything. Or any of us. You know we've got your back, Boss.'

'Yes, thanks.' This smile was more genuine. 'And you already did help. Giving me something else to think about. That was good. I shouldn't wish for it, I know, but a work crisis would be quite welcome at this point.'

'Can't help you there, Boss,' said Chris, rising to go. 'But if something does occur to me, I'll let you know.'

'One last thing,' said Greg, as he saw her to the door. 'We need to follow up with the lab.'

'I'm off on that blessed course tomorrow evening. I'll see what I can do before I go.'

In the car and driving towards Fleggburgh, Chris thought hard, then rang DI Henning. 'I'm sticking my neck out here,' she said, 'but you're a mate of his and I think you should know. He found out tonight that Isabelle's pregnant.' She listened in silence a moment then added, 'I'm sure he'd rather it wasn't gossiped about, but I thought it would help if you knew. He'll welcome being kept busy.'

'Do my best,' replied Jim. 'And thanks for letting me know.'

'I haven't told anyone else,' she warned. 'And I doubt he has. It was just I was there.'

'Understood.'

'I'll give some thought to distractions too.'

'Chris,' said Jim, knowing to whom he spoke. 'Don't do anything bonkers will you. He probably needs a bit of space.'

'Sure,' said Chris, an idea already bubbling in her head. 'I'm off on this blasted course for a day or two. I'll think about it.'


The following morning, a day in the office at Wymondham beckoned. Settled at his desk with a large black coffee, Greg started on the accrued paperwork. By lunchtime he had sore eyes and a sore back, as well as a pronounced desire to get outside for any reason whatsoever. He was heading for the door and at the least a leg stretch, when his phone rang. Trying not to sigh too audibly down the receiver he answered it and was rewarded by the bass tones of CPS from Norwich.

'Great news,' said the telephone. 'Convicted on all counts.'

Greg had to think quickly to catch up, dragging his mind from quarterly budget returns and data protection training courses to the case that had started with a dead body at a turkey cull and had, before it was finished, embraced modern slavery, wildlife and puppy smuggling, arson and a body count of three. That Ben Asheton had not been victim number four was largely down to good luck and the intervention of some burly mates from the Caister lifeboat crew.

'Oh,' and then, 'wow!' as his brain caught up with his ears. 'Metcalfe? On all counts?'

'Absolutely. The jury just came back. Guilty on all counts, even the joint enterprise to commit the murder of the poultry worker, Tomas.'

'Have you told the Chief Super?'

'Not yet. I wanted to let you know first.'

'Well, brilliant result, Roger. Especially as there was a lot of quite complex circumstantial evidence. I wasn't sure the jury would get it.'

'Well, they did. And that's partly down to your thorough prep of the case, Greg. Congratulations all round.'

'I'll let the rest of the team know.'

Greg found quite a few of them in the canteen, and hurried to share the good news. The conviction was worth a celebration.

The following morning, Greg was surprised when Chris's car pulled up in his drive, unannounced. He was even more surprised when she got out wearing a large grey parrot on her left shoulder.

'You look like Long John Silver,' he remarked. 'What on earth are you doing with a parrot? And what,' he added silently, 'are you doing bringing it here?' He noted with some concern that Chris was removing a box from the back of her car.

'She's an African Grey, and her name's Tallulah, or Tally for short. Can I come in, Boss? I don't want her to fly off and my hands are full.'

Following the pint-sized dynamo that was Chris in full flow, Greg wondered with some trepidation why her hands were full, and of what. They got to the conservatory where Chris put the box down and sat on the sofa facing the river. Tally waggled her wings to keep her balance, and looked around her.

'I was hoping you'd keep Tally for me while I go on this course you've sent me on. It's only a couple of days.'

'You mean the assertiveness training course I offered you a substantial bribe to skip, on the grounds that I didn't think I could handle any more assertiveness?' Greg was talking to avoid answering the question.

'That's the one. Well, I have to do it, like it or not, and it's residential so I'll be away overnight. Tally's used to being left during the day but she needs some company in the evening, and I thought you wouldn't mind.'

Greg didn't know where to start, and while he was thinking, Tally contributed, 'Pieces of eight' in a conversational tone.

'Oh God, it talks as well,' exclaimed Greg.

Offended, Tally added, 'Bollocks, balls,' and after a moment, more reflectively, 'Tits.'

'And swears.'

'Only a bit,' said Chris defensively. 'And you were rude to her. She's she, not it.'

'Piss,' added Tally, then 'Ffff', as Chris took a firm grip on her beak. The bird swivelled an eye to look at Chris and added 'Pffft' through the muffled beak.

'You're not helping, Tally,' admonished Chris. 'Be nice.'

'Nice Tally,' said the bird in a very good imitation of Chris's voice.

'So how about it?' asked Chris breezily.

'What about Bobby?' asked Greg, seizing at straws.

'Oh, Tally will be fine, don't worry. She can see off a cat, no problem.'

'That's my worry,' said Greg, eyeing the powerful beak. 'It's Bobby I'm concerned about, not that foul-mouthed bird brain.' Tally took off from Chris's shoulder and landed on Greg's, then took his ear gently in her beak. Greg froze.

'There, she likes you,' said Chris with satisfaction.

'And if she doesn't?' asked Greg with great care. 'All those years of rugby with no cauliflower ears, and you introduce a parrot that's likely to turn me into Van Gogh with one tweak of her beak.'

'Rubbish. That's her way of showing affection. She wouldn't go to you at all, if she didn't like you.'

'Nice Tally,' said the parrot in an ingratiating tone, then 'Nice cat,' as Bobby entered the room. Bobby took in the bird, the size of its claws and beak at a glance, and sat down to wash her face.

Greg was open mouthed. 'I know they're meant to be intelligent,' he said, 'but how…?'

'Oh, the first cat we had was just called Cat,' explained

Chris. 'So she calls all cats Cat. She is bright, but not that bright. Anyway, will you have her until tomorrow? Her food's in the box, I've got a perch in the car boot, and she uses a litter tray like Bobby. In fact she'll probably use Bobby's given half a chance. All you have to do is put food and water out and keep her company in the evening. Oh, and keep the windows closed.'

Tally let go of his ear and sidled along his shoulder a few inches, then rubbed her head on his.

'She hasn't got fleas has she,' asked Greg, hanging on to his common sense but aware he had, somehow, lost the debate.

'Of course not. I told you, she just likes you. That's OK then. I'd better get off. I'll just get the perch out of the car and leave you to it. It needs a little assembly,' she added.

Some half an hour later – Bobby relaxing in her bed and apparently quite chilled about the new arrival, Tally dozing on the back of the sofa with her head under her wing – Greg decided that the worst part of the whole thing, apart from being steamrollered by his sergeant, was undoubtedly the evil, knuckle-severing self-assembly perch with the incomprehensible Chinese instructions.

# 7

## Next steps for Jack

A week later, Jack got his further instructions. The following day, he was to arrive at work early and park his car in the space designated as K14, leave it there for the morning, then go out for lunch at 1320 precisely. They were emphatic he was to be neither late nor early leaving the car park. That afternoon, he walked to his car via row K and glanced at space K14. There seemed nothing unusual about it. It was a couple of spaces across the car park from the perimeter buildings. That afternoon there was a small blue Peugeot with a missing wing mirror parked in that area. He walked past without deviating from his route and without pausing. Then went home.

Friday morning dawned bright and clear. As ever when it was important to hear his alarm, he had woken multiple times during the night, apparently for the express purpose of checking his alarm clock. As a result, by the time it did go off at six thirty he felt as though he'd been through a mangle. Nonetheless, he got up, showered and drove to work a whole ninety minutes earlier than normal. The approaches were quiet and the security guard had time for a chat, remarking on the surprise of seeing him before seven thirty. He replied with some anodyne comment, then drove through to the car park. There were very few cars in it at that time, and he had no difficulty leaving his car in the space designated K14.

At 1310 precisely, he got up from his work bench, took off his white lab coat and left it over the back of his chair. Someone called to him as he left the lab, but mindful of his instructions he took no notice. Pretending he hadn't heard, he headed for the exit and the car park, pulling his keys from his pocket as he went. Just as he approached his car, his mobile phone rang. Typically, when you're in a rush, it caught on the edge of his pocket as he tried to pull it out to see if it was a call he needed to take. His mother! Oh God, this would be a long one and he was now running a few minutes late. As he got into his car, he saw the silver Ford Focus come round the corner and into the lane leading to K14. Hurriedly, he dropped the phone on the passenger seat and started his car. The silver Focus was already waiting a few yards away as he pulled out of the parking space. A man he didn't know gave him a very cold stare, then looked over his shoulder to reverse into K14. Looking in his rear view mirror, Jack saw him get out of the car, close the driver door and walk away towards the main entrance to the site. At this point, the phone connected to his car loudspeaker system and his mother became audible.

'Jack, can you hear me? Jack, I asked whether you would be able to come up for your Gran's birthday party next week? You know she's eighty, and would really love to have you.'

Distracted, Jack turned his attention away from the man

walking briskly down the drive and concentrated on the squawking phone. 'Hi, Mum,' he replied. 'I've told you, I don't know yet.'

He was interrupted by an overwhelming noise, more roar than bang, and his car was propelled violently forward into the car in front.

# 8

## Silver to gold

Delayed by waiting for Chris to collect her parrot, Greg was late into the office that morning. The hand-over had gone smoothly, except for a small hiccup when the (painfully) constructed perch had refused to deconstruct, presenting a challenge when attempting to put it in Chris's small runabout. In the end, Chris had driven off with the parrot occupying the passenger seat and the end of the perch resting on her left shoulder. She hadn't been impressed by his DIY, pointing out somewhat acerbically that he had clearly stripped the thread on a vital screw. Greg had ignored the comments, just relieved he had surmounted the challenge of parrot sitting without losing any digits or acquiring piles of guano in his sitting room. Bobby, sitting in the windowsill, looked mildly relieved too.

Greg had just consumed his tuna sandwich at his desk, having heroically passed on the bag of crisps for the benefit of his waistline, when his phone rang. As he picked it up, he noticed that almost every phone in the outer office beyond his glass walls was also ringing.

'Greg,' said Margaret, 'a bomb has gone off in the Science Park. No details yet, except that it's at NASA. Looks like their threat was real. The local uniforms have called in for back up. I'd like you to deal as SIO, at least for the moment. If it's terrorism, we may get some interference before long, but for now, you're it.'

'I'll get over there straightaway. Any casualties?'

'No confirmation, but it seems likely. The Norfolk and Norwich Hospital has been alerted. Fire service and ambulances are on their way.'

Greg left his office, grabbing phone and bag as he went. 'Chris, I assume you've heard. With me, please. Jill, contact Jim and have him meet us there. Also alert Ned to get his team over ASAP.'

As he ran to his car, Chris hot on his heels, he was aware she was on her phone. Scrambling into the passenger seat she said, 'Two local uniforms, Constables Brown and Deelan, were first on the scene. They say the fire brigade are in attendance and ambulances are arriving to take away the injured. It seems there's a lot of casualties and some of the buildings are on fire. A lot of people still unaccounted for.'

'Christ.' Greg concentrated on the traffic as he pulled onto the A11. 'No warning?'

'It seems not.'

By the time they turned west on the A47 they could see a glow in the sky and plumes of black smoke. All access roads to the Science Park were blocked by police officers and tape. Greg showed his warrant card and they were waved through. By the time they got to the NASA site perimeter, both Greg and Chris were bereft of words. Two of the three perimeter buildings set around the car park in a horse shoe arrangement were burning fiercely. The third, for the moment, appeared to be safe and hoses were playing on it. The car park was a shambles in both the new and the old senses of the word. Cars were strewn at odd angles. At what appeared to be ground zero there was a large pit in the tarmac, and in the immediate vicinity Greg could see body parts. He swallowed hard and as he turned away there was another bang and a sheet of flame flapped off into the sky behind him. The background roar was such that he found it hard to make himself heard.

'We need to find who's in charge,' he shouted to Chris, and the two of them backed away.

Just inside the main entrance gate, control was being exercised by fire officers in full protective clothing. 'Geldard, senior investigating officer,' Greg introduced himself to the man with the tabard reading Incident Commander.

'Fisher,' replied the man. 'Silver Command.'

'Yes. I understand you have operational control here. Obviously we'll need to get on site as soon as you say it's safe for us, but the immediate priority is to help where we can, and avoid getting in your way.'

'Thank you,' said the man with some relief. 'I understand they're setting up Gold Command at the police station in the city. But for the time being, it rests with me.'

'What's the position now?' asked Greg.

'In summary, a car bomb went off in the car park at 1325. You can see where it was parked. There was no warning. We reckon there were at least three casualties in the immediate vicinity of the blast, but it's hard to be sure for reasons that must be apparent.

'Immediately after the blast, staff followed their bomb alarm procedure, which essentially involves taking shelter in places that are less vulnerable to blast in case there is a further explosion. However, a fire followed very swiftly after the blast, so staff switched to evacuating the buildings where possible. That initial delay in evacuation has probably cost lives.

'The fire spread very rapidly, assisted by several further blasts, which were probably caused by their own hydrogen supplies going up. We still have concerns about flammable materials within the labs. Witnesses vary in their accounts of how many blasts there were.

'We have around twenty or thirty burn and blast casualties being taken to the Norfolk and Norwich. There are probably another fifteen walking wounded who've been triaged, treated by paramedics and will be taken to hospital when possible. Unhurt staff have been evacuated to the food lab across the way. As best we can tell, there are at least 100 people unaccounted for.' He looked bleak. 'The casualty figure is likely to rise.'

They were interrupted by the clatter of the Air Ambulance, approaching circumspectly from a direction away from the smoke. It landed on a lawn behind them and paramedics headed over to the burning buildings at a run.

'The fire seems to have taken hold very rapidly,' Greg's eyes followed the paramedics' progress. 'I would've thought it would have started in the car park then spread to the nearer buildings, but both the two alight seem to be equally devastated.'

'Yes. According to eye witnesses, the fire seems to have spread almost instantaneously to both those blocks, assisted by the flammable gas supplies and the failure of all the protective systems.'

Greg turned sharply. 'No sprinklers, no auto shutdowns?'

'No nothing! They have all those things in place but all rely on a power supply. Both the main supply and the emergency back-up seem to have failed simultaneously. So the fire started and then burnt completely out of control until we arrived. And by then, there wasn't much we could do except stop it spreading further.'

A couple of fire fighters rushed up to Fisher to report and seek instructions. Harassed, he said to Greg, 'That'll have to do for now. OK?'

'OK. I'll leave officers here to liaise with your team. For now, I'll get over to the food lab and have a chat with survivors while their memories are fresh. Chris, get Phil and Steve up here, but warn them to stay out of the way unless they are asked for help.'

Chris looked up from her phone.

'Just had a couple of messages, Boss. Jim has diverted direct to the food lab, and Chief Super Tayler is heading into the city to act as Gold Command. She'll be in touch.'

# 9

## Flashbacks

Dazed by the explosion and the blast, for several moments Jack was incapable of coherent thought. He pushed himself back in his seat and realised that the amorphous cloud in front of him was the airbag. The collision with the car in front had obviously been hard enough to set it off. He scratched an itch on the side of his face and his fingers came away red. He looked at them, confused, puzzled as to what had happened and how it had happened. Looking in the rear view mirror he found he had a shallow cut on his forehead that, as head wounds will, was bleeding profusely. Clutching at a train of thought, he decided the airbag cover must have hit him. As he felt in his pocket for a hanky, he became aware of returning sounds: a roaring and crackling behind him, and more squawking from the phone now in the passenger footwell as his panicking mother tried to find out what was happening. Still trying to mop at the blood and keep it out of his eye, he felt for the door catch with his other hand. As the door opened, he glanced again into the mirror and saw a horror behind him.

Getting out into the roadway, he turned slowly. Behind him was his worst nightmare, the one he saw regularly, had seen so many times day and night since that day on the farm when his heifer, Blossom, had been slaughtered for no reason.

In the middle distance, he was convinced he could see the familiar long bank of burning bodies and the glow that lit up the sky. Somewhere amongst that tangle of legs and heads was his Blossom. Dead like all the rest. He started to run towards the pyre, determined this time to save her. There were shouts, and a large powerful man ran after him. When he didn't stop, the other man powered into him and brought him to his knees.

'You can't help,' the man repeated. 'Leave it to the experts. You'll just get in the way.' As he spoke, the sound of sirens added to the cacophony, and the first of many fire engines arrived at speed. The security guard from the gate dragged Jack to one side. Other folk from cars at the entrance gathered round.

'I'm OK, Jack said. 'Sorry. I'm OK.' And he started to walk with the crowd towards the site entrance and away from the burning building behind him. The guard shepherded them firmly through the gate and away from their damaged cars.

'Don't stop for anything,' he said. 'Get clear. You can't know whether there'll be more explosions. Go over there,' and he pointed to a grassy bank between the NASA site and the adjacent Food Laboratory. As he spoke, there were people rushing over from the food lab, just as personnel from the fire brigade arrived to take control and the first police car screeched to a halt followed closely by a couple of ambulances. The security guard relinquished control with evident relief and after a quick word the police took charge of the perimeter while first aiders from the food lab put arms round survivors and ushered them into their reception hall. Jack just…went along. At the door to the food lab he turned and looked again at the long, low pyre glowing red and sending huge clouds of smoke into the wide Norfolk sky. For the first time since the blast, he realised he had played a part in this. He was sick in the flowerbed by the door; then, giving way to the pushing of the small crowd, he wiped his mouth on his sleeve and went in.

# 10

## Aftermath

By the time Greg and Chris arrived over at the Norwich Food Laboratory, shocked staff were providing a commendably well-organised emergency service. Incoming survivors, triaged by paramedics and judged to be reasonably fit, were being shepherded into the main reception area and from there into hurriedly freed up space in adjacent meeting rooms. Catering staff, assisted by absolutely anyone including several visiting dignitaries who had been participating in meetings when the bomb went off, were passing round tea, coffee, water and biscuits. Anyone with cuts and bruises, and a few who had discovered mild burns once they had chance to think about it, were redirected to the occupational health nurse, who'd set up an impromptu first aid corner by the reception desk. Considering the circumstances, there was an impressive air of calm and control.

In the centre of reception, flanked by two uniformed police, was the fulcrum of this emergency response. Greg was flabbergasted to realise that he knew the lady in question. The trademark tidy French pleat was still in place. As before, she was clad in an immaculate skirt suit, today with a white shirt that was only slightly smudged with dust. And as on every occasion when he had met her previously, even at a poultry farm with a dead human body in amongst the culled turkeys, she conveyed an imperturbable air of calm and efficiency. Mrs Pritchard, it seemed, could take a terrorist bomb in her stride.

'Mrs Pritchard,' said Greg, as he joined the small group around her. 'What a surprise to see you here!'

'Why, hello, Detective Chief Inspector Geldard, Detective Sergeant Mathews,' she replied with her usual precision. 'I'd say it was a pleasure, but not under these circumstances.'

'What are you doing here?' he asked, startled at seeing in this world the secretary permanently associated for him with Stalham Poultry and his last big case.

'I started work here last year,' she replied, 'and I'll happily bring you up to date when we have a moment, but I imagine you have more pressing matters to attend to at this time. Suffice it to say, I am the lab secretary. As you see, we're doing our best to assist survivors with refreshments and first aid where needed. Those who arrived first,' she waved at a room behind her, 'are in Conference Room A. I believe they're mainly people who were leaving the car park when the bomb went off. As people have arrived, we've guided them into the remaining conference rooms except for those needing first aid who are either with the nurse or in the reception area over there,' she pointed, 'where we can keep an eye on them in case there should be any deterioration.

'We've tried to keep a register of names, but I think we may have missed a few right at the start before I came down to take charge. If so, they should be in Room A, but I haven't had time to check yet. Would you like me to print you a copy?'

'Yes, please. And thank you, Mrs Pritchard. Very impressive.'

'We've done our best,' she replied. 'Now, if you'll excuse me, I'll get you that list.'

Greg was joined by Jim and Constable Jill Hayes as he turned to survey the scene.

'You've met Mrs P again I see,' Jim remarked.

'Yes, quite a surprise. But is that woman organised!'

'Does a one-legged duck swim in a circle?'

'What've you established so far, Jim?'

'Not much. Mrs P has done the important work for us in collecting names. Given there are no medical issues with this lot, with the possible exception of those over there,' he nodded at the group who had been on the receiving end of Mrs P's pointing finger, 'I guess it's a long slog of collecting first impressions, addresses and contact details to go with the names, and then let them go home.'

'Agreed. I suggest we prioritise those with injuries, in case they need further treatment, and those in Conference Room A, as it seems they include the ones who were in the car park. They may have seen something before the bomb went off, possibly even the arrival of the car. Do you agree?'

'Yes, absolutely.'

'Then you and Jill deal with the casualties, while Chris and I start in A. Make sure you get the OK from the nurse before you send anyone home.'

'Focus of questions?' asked Jim.

'Name, contact details, where do they work, where were they when the bomb went off, what did they see before and subsequently. Unless you can think of anything else, that's a good place to start.'

'OK. On it.'

'Let's share data in say, an hour, and we can modify our approach then if need be. Otherwise, if either of us turns up anything important, we check in immediately.'

'Got it.'

'There'll be a heap of follow-up interviews to do later, but that'll give us a start.'

Jim moved purposefully across the atrium, Jill in his wake. Greg turned to Chris, and the two of them headed for Conference Room A. Pushing the door open, Greg noticed through the glass panel that most of the occupants were gathered round the big boardroom table in the middle. The leather and chrome chairs looked more comfortable than they probably were, and were mainly occupied by shocked and silent people in their thirties or forties. Chris took over the list of names, and they started clockwise round the table, asking for a name, finding it on the list, then adding the contact details, work role, and recollections of events immediately prior to and after the bomb going off. No one had much of detail to contribute. No one had particularly noticed anything prior to the explosion, and after it everyone had been preoccupied with picking themselves up and checking for immediate injuries. Several had attempted to return to the laboratories but been dissuaded by the security guards on the gate. The security guards were present too, torn between shock, excitement and guilt that such a thing had happened on their watch.

It seemed there had been two guards on the gate when the bomb went off. The older man was in better shape: less shocked and more concerned about how to help the police. The younger man couldn't get his mind away from a missing colleague whom it seemed had headed into the car park shortly before the blast, and wasn't yet accounted for.

The older man looked at Greg meaningfully, as he said to his partner, 'Could you get me another coffee, Dave? Over there,' and nodded to a trolley in the corner. Greg and Chris watched him walk away without comment, then looked back at the other guard.

'I think our friend is one of the casualties in the car park,' he said. 'I haven't had a very close look. At first we were too busy trying to get people clear, and then the fire brigade wouldn't let us in, but I've seen the results of car bombs before and I think I recognised a watch on an arm near ground zero. I was in Helmand,' he added. 'I'm Pete Brooke. Ex Sergeant Brooke.'

Greg pulled up a chair and Chris perched on the edge of the table to take notes. 'Any ideas about the car that brought the bomb in?'

'There's not much of it left to make an ID,' Pete said. 'What's left is shredded and burnt out. But I can help narrow down the options. Between us, we log all visiting cars to the site, and they'll also be on the CCTV at the entrance. Assuming it was a stranger's car, we logged four visitors in the hour and a half prior to the blast. The details will be in the database, but from memory there were two Fords, a Peugeot and a Fiat. It shouldn't be difficult to work out which it was. If it came in aboard a staff car, then that's a different matter. But you can cross reference between the staff lists and the remaining cars in the car park. They'll be on the CCTV too.'

'You're tending to rule out the staff option,' commented Chris.

'Because of the vetting they get before appointment, yes. But I suppose you can't ignore the possibility.'

'Quite,' said Greg. 'We're keeping an open mind for the present. Chris, have we got the CCTV footage?'

'Just checking, Boss. And I've asked Silver Command what intelligence we have about the car. We should have some answers soon.'

Behind them, there was a sudden commotion. Cries of alarm rose above the quieter conversations, and as Greg turned, someone dashed though the doors into reception. One of the staff members was on the floor and appeared to be fitting. Greg and Chris both rushed across.

'Can we help? asked Greg dropping to his knees beside the casualty as he spoke. A girl in a smudged lab coat looked up from where she was holding the youngish man's head steady.

'I think he's coming out of it,' she said. 'It was so sudden. One moment he was sitting there, the next he was on the floor and having a fit.'

'Do you know him?'

'A little. He works in analytical chem like me, but in a different team. His name's Jack Haigh. He was very quiet when he came in from the car park, but I didn't notice anything else.'

The lab nurse rushed in, closely followed by Mrs P. As the nurse also dropped to her knees on the floor, Mrs P said, 'I've rung for an ambulance. If they can, they'll redirect one here from the main site.'

'Any history of fits? Or epilepsy?' asked the nurse.

'I don't know him well enough to know,' answered the girl. 'Never heard of anything.'

'OK. Seems to be stabilising now. I'll stay with him while

we wait for the ambulance.'

Pete had followed the police across the room.

'He's one of the ones I had to stop from going back. He wanted to get into the labs, but that was insane. He was very upset and quite out of control.'

'OK, thank you,' said Greg, automatically dusting the knees of his trousers as he stood up. 'We'll have to catch up with him at the hospital later.'

Pete seemed to have more to say. Greg paused and looked at him, raising an eyebrow.

'I've been keeping an eye on him,' Pete said slowly. 'He was in his car near the gate when the bomb went off. The car was blown into the car in front, and he had a cut head, but otherwise he seemed unhurt. But he was very shocked. He turned and ran towards the burning building and I had to rugby-tackle him to bring him down. He took some persuading to come away. There was something about his eyes that looked familiar.'

'Presumably you've seen him every day if he works here,' commented Greg.

'No, not that. I mean, yes, of course I've seen him before. But that wasn't what I meant. He reminded me of something in Helmand. A look I've seen before. For example, in someone who has PTSD.'

'Surely you don't get PTSD in seconds,' interrupted Chris.

'No, but if you already had it, I can't think off hand of a better trigger than a bomb and a burning building.'

By 1545, the two teams of Jim and Jill, Greg and Chris had between them spoken at least once to all the survivors in the food lab. The flow of incomers had slowed to a trickle and then stopped. A steady stream of taxis and relatives had begun to arrive to take them home, picking up from the rear gate, well away from the more distressing events over on the adjoining campus. Comparing notes, the four concluded that between them they were in a position to compile a list for priority follow up, when they were interrupted by a phone call from Gold Command and a demand for a sitrep. Greg marshalled his thoughts, and rang back on the appointed minute from the now peaceful Conference Room A.

# 11

## Sitreps

Prompted by a computer, Greg gave his name and shortly after:

'Thank you all for dialling in,' said Margaret's voice over a slightly echoey speaker phone. 'We have present at this bird-table.' Greg grinned a little as he recognised the army-derived terminology from his emergency training, 'Commander Fisher of the fire brigade, currently on site at NASA; here in the room, Professor Craig Bennington, deputy CEO of NASA, Angus Crawford, CEO of the Norfolk and Norwich Hospital; and telephoning in, DCI Geldard, Senior Investigating Officer, Norfolk Police. There are others present who will identify themselves if needed, but those four are the key personnel I have asked for sitreps. We will follow a standard agenda for this meeting and any subsequent meetings, for as long as they are needed, as follows: report from site by Commander Fisher; casualties, from Mr Crawford and Professor Bennington; investigation, DCI Geldard. Keep it snappy, gentlemen. None of us have time to spare. All we need at this point is key points and issues that need resolution. Right. Over to Commander Fisher.'

'Thank you, Chief Superintendent. You've all had the preliminary report we delivered shortly after arrival on site so I'll go straight to the update.' The voice was firm but tired. Greg brought to mind the calm face of the Silver Commander he had met what felt like many hours ago. 'There've been no further explosions and the fires in blocks B and C are now under control. Personnel should be able to access parts of the buildings, under our supervision, later tomorrow. Army explosives experts have checked Block A and the parts of the car parks currently accessible. No further devices have been discovered. They judge the car bomb to have been constructed largely of ammonium nitrate explosive with additional material to ensure detonation. Remains of the car suggest it was a silver Ford, but there's not much left of it. Searches have been conducted of Block A and all outbuildings. There are no personnel currently in any of them. Blocks B and C are still largely inaccessible. It is possible they contain further casualties.'

'Thank you. Mr Crawford?'

'Thirty-three casualties have been received at the N&N. Five are critical. As for persons found dead at the scene, the latest report I have is that there were seven. All but one have been identified. Most injuries are burns or blast related. One casualty has been admitted having apparently suffered a seizure and possibly a panic attack.'

'Professor Bennington?'

There was a rustle of paper as the professor took over the mike.

'Thanks to the fire officers and also the staff at the food

lab, we have accounted for 276 of our 292 staff. This figure sadly includes the known seven fatalities at the site, which leaves sixteen staff believed to have been on site unaccounted for. It's possible that in the confusion they have left the site without signing in. We must hope so, as otherwise they must be assumed to be part of the death toll. Amongst those missing is the head of analytical chemistry, Professor Lai. Some of my admin staff are currently ringing round, trying to establish their whereabouts.'

'And finally, Chief Inspector Geldard.'

Greg cleared his throat and picked up the piece of paper hurriedly thrust in front of him by Chris. He scowled at her scruffy writing and began:

'We've carried out preliminary interviews with the 232 staff available to us at the Food Laboratory. Four apparently left for their homes without authorisation shortly after our arrival. We're following them up as a matter of urgency. We'll shortly be transferring to the N&N to interview any other casualties that are fit enough to answer questions. I would also like to see Professor Bennington at an early opportunity.

'We have CCTV footage of the entrance to the site, the car parks and of the area surrounding the animal unit up to and immediately after the blast. At that point all cameras stopped recording owing to lack of power, either standard or emergency. The footage is being scrutinised as we speak. I can say that a car fitting the description given by Commander Fisher entered the site at 1318 and went in the direction of the car park.

'Crime scene officers are awaiting permission to enter the site from Commander Fisher and his team.'

'Any witnesses to the explosion?' asked Professor Bennington.

'None so far capable of responding to questions,' answered Greg. There was a silence.

'Thank you,' said Margaret. 'The only other fact worth reporting at this stage is that we can find no evidence of any warning being received. And so far, no one has claimed responsibility, although that may of course change. Thank you all. Anyone wish to add anything?'

Professor Bennington intervened with, 'I am heading to the N&N to see what staff I can. Perhaps we can meet there, Geldard?'

'Makes sense,' said Greg, and Bob Crawford interrupted with, 'We'll make a room available to you.'

'Anyone else?' asked Margaret, and after silence all round she said crisply, 'Next bird-table 2200.' And rang off.

Seconds later, Greg's phone rang again and Margaret's voice was back in his ear.

'Greg,' she said. 'You're clearly going to need all the help you can get. I'm getting Sarah back from Essex to lead on intelligence management. She can also liaise with Special Branch.'

'They're getting involved, are they?

'Inevitably! Expect a contact soon. They have your number.'

'When can I expect Sarah?'

'Tomorrow first thing. I've told her to report to you.'

Greg turned to Jim and Chris to communicate the news.

'We heard,' said Chris, a touch grimly.

Jim grinned. 'She'll be good in that role,' he said. 'Glad it's not me! I like to be out and about not getting red eyes over a screen. We off to the N&N now?'

'Yes. Jim, have Steve and Jill finish up their list of phone calls then send them home. Tomorrow will be a long day. Likewise, once we've spoken with Bennington and whatever patients are fit to speak at the hospital, we'll get off too. I'd like an early start on site, hopefully with Ned and his team able to get a proper look round.'

Greg and Chris got back in his car for the short drive across campus to the Norfolk and Norwich hospital.

'Straight to A&E I imagine,' he said.

'Head for car park G,' she replied. 'That's the handiest for A&E and they won't want us cluttering up the ambulance bays. Jim'll meet us there. He knows his way around OK.'

Greg looked around with interest at the mainly two- or three-storey buildings scattered around the gently sloping hill, as Chris directed him to the chosen car park.

'Looks more like a red brick uni than a hospital,' he remarked, as they swung into the car park and selected a parking bay near the entrance. 'Reminds me of York University.'

'What do you expect a hospital to look like,' enquired Chris with interest.

'Either grim ex-workhouse style, like most mental health hospitals, or all futuristic glass, like parts of Addenbrooke's. This one falls somewhere in the middle. I'm glad to say I haven't personally had a lot to do with hospitals,' he confessed, 'except when I broke my nose playing rugby, and that was a local London hospital. Professionally, it's been mainly cottage hospitals in Yorkshire or old city hospitals in London.'

Walking briskly, they were joined by Jim as they approached the A&E department. The place was filled with a purposeful bustle and Greg was impressed when they were swiftly intercepted by an official left in wait by the CEO.

'Bob said you'd be along,' commented this man, one of the few in the immediate vicinity not in scrubs. 'He's asked me to take you through to the trolley bay. That's where more seriously injured patients are normally taken, and today we've cleared it for victims of the explosion.'

There was a sitting area near the bay, currently occupied by worried-looking relatives and Professor Bennington. He stood up as they approached, but whatever he was about to say was pre-empted by a senior nurse.

'I understand you're the police,' she said. 'We'll do our best to meet your requirements but you must realise that the first priority is the wellbeing of our patients.'

'Absolutely,' replied Greg. 'But an update on how many you have and their current condition would be a good place to start.'

She referred to the tablet in her hand.

'We've had thirty-three casualties so far. Twenty-five have blast-type injuries, fractures, cuts from flying glass, soft tissue damage et cetera of varying degrees of severity. Two of those are in theatre, seven are waiting for surgery, the remainder are on a ward or were sufficiently lightly injured that they could be sent home. I have a list. Of the remaining eight, seven are burns victims of which five are in plastics and one has been sent to the specialist burns centre in Chelmsford. One has sadly succumbed to his injuries. The remaining casualty has no physical trauma that we can find but is very distressed and has fitted twice since admission to the bay. We think he's stabilised now, but psych are with him.'

'Who can we speak to?'

'Subject to the ward sister and registrar being happy, I would say you should be able to speak to any of those on the ward and, as I said, we have a list of those who have been sent home. The more serious casualties will have to wait until tomorrow.'

'And the person with psychological trauma?'

'I'll check with the psychiatric registrar when he appears.' Quiet footsteps attracted her attention. 'Oh, here he is. You can ask him yourself.'

Greg put the question to the small dark man with glasses. 'Obviously I'd prefer you didn't disturb him,' he replied, 'but I appreciate your problem too. I think a short chat would be OK provided I may be present as well.'

'No problem. I'd like a quick conversation with Professor Bennington first, if that's OK.'

'Good. You'll find me at the desk.'

Greg nodded his thanks and turned to Jim. 'Can you and Chris start on the ward?' he asked. 'The list of those who've gone home can be passed to Steve and Jill. I'll have a chat first with the Professor and with our chap with the possible PTSD, then I'll join you on the ward.'

Greg walked over to Professor Bennington, realising as he did so that the man looked dreadful. The smartly suited deputy CEO of a few days ago was dishevelled, his hair on end, his tie hanging limply from a torn pocket and his suit grubby. His eyes looked worst: red and shocked.

'Just a quick word,' he said, 'then I think you must go home. Tomorrow will be another hard day, and I think you've had it for today.'

'Just had a bit of a shock,' he replied. 'I'll be OK. You remember my PA, Ken? He's in theatre. They're amputating his right arm. It seems he was in the car park when the bomb went off and his arm was so badly shredded it can't be saved. He was lucky he didn't bleed to death. One of our first aiders got to him just in time.

'He's right handed,' he added bleakly.

Greg sat down with him, lost for words. 'That's awful,' he said inadequately. 'Is he going to be all right? I mean...'

'Yes. I know what you mean. It seems they expect him to live, but obviously he'll be facing life with a prosthesis. Yesterday he was talking about a badminton tournament. Today...' He shrugged.

'Have you heard any more about the numbers unaccounted for,' asked Greg, eager to change the subject but unable to get away from disaster whatever he said.

'Yes. Some good news there. We've found another nine, either at home or in their local pub, getting over the shock in whatever way suits them. I'm hopeful we may find a few more. God forbid they all died in the fire! Still no sign of Professor Lai though and I don't think that's a good sign. She was very conscientious. I keep thinking of captains and sinking ships!'

'I'll need to see you tomorrow to go through some staff data. Are the databases backed up off site?'

'Yes. And the last back-up was the end of the month, so they should be fairly well up to date.'

'And still no one claiming responsibility?'

'Not to me. But I imagine they'd probably make such a claim through the media now.'

'There was definitely no warning?'

'None that I'm aware of. I've spoken to the receptionists and the communications team. Nothing to any of them, and no calls on hold at the time the bomb went off. No warning at all.'

Right, thank you. That's all for now. I'll see you tomorrow, but for now, go home, man.'

'There's the bird-table at 2200.'

'You could call in from home. Get yourself off.'

Greg went back to the quiet man with the calm manner over at the nurses' station.

'Ready now?' he asked.

'Yes,' said the man, adding a final note to some records. 'I'm Dr Shah by the way.'

'And I'm DCI Geldard. Do you have a name for the casualty through there?'

'Yes. He's Jack Haigh. Works in analytical chemistry and it seems was in the car park when the bomb went off. But his immediate problem seems to be PTSD. Something about the explosion, or more specifically the fires, seems to have triggered memories dating back to a trauma in his childhood. If you could avoid dwelling on the fires too much, that would be helpful.'

'Noted, thanks.'

They had been walking into the area described as the trolley bay and Dr Shah ushered Greg to a curtained alcove halfway down. The man in the bed was staring blankly at the ceiling as they passed through the curtain, but turned his head when he realised he was no longer alone.

'Can I go home now?' he asked. 'I feel a bit of a fraud lying here.'

'Tomorrow maybe,' replied Dr Shah. 'We need to keep you under observation for tonight, but once we're happy you're stable you can go home provided you have someone with you for a day or two. In the meantime, DCI Geldard here has a few questions for you.' He nodded to Greg to sit down by the bedside, and went away to collect a spare chair, which he positioned at the end of the bed. Jack transferred his attention to Greg.

Taking out his notebook, Greg observed the man before him with care. He was young, in his late twenties or early thirties perhaps, and looked reasonably fit, like a weekend sportsman. The hands now tense on the top edge of the blanket covering him were coarsened by past hard work, although now well kept. The nails were short and clean, not battered and engrained with dirt or oil as the callouses might otherwise have led him to expect. He remembered that this man was a research chemist and wondered how he'd got the hard-worked hands. His blond hair was short and he was pale under a mild tan. There was a stitched cut on his forehead, and other bruising indicative of his recent experience.

'Just a few questions,' said Greg, 'then I'll leave you in peace. I gather you were in the car park when the explosion occurred. Where exactly were you?'

'Approaching the main gate,' replied Jack. 'Maybe twenty metres away from the security barrier.'

'On foot or in a car?'

'In my car. There was another car in front of me, and I think at least one other behind. It was lunchtime. There's usually a steady stream of traffic then.'

'What do you remember about what happened?'

'Just driving toward the gate, then a big bang that pushed my car into the one in front. The next thing I knew, I had blood trickling down my face and the airbag was floating about in front of me. That's how I got this,' he touched the cut and winced. 'I got out of the car and looked back.' He stopped short.

'Were there other people about? Near you I mean?'

I think there were a couple of folk getting out of the car in front. I don't remember about the car behind. There was a security guard too. He was shouting at me to come away. I remember I was looking back at the fire,' his voice trailed away, and Dr Shah shifted in his seat. Greg exchanged a glance with him, and took the hint.

'Can we go back to before the explosion?' he asked. 'Where were you working that morning?'

'In analytical chem, in Block C, as normal.'

'It was just a normal morning?'

'Yes, I'd got a series of tests set up, and I was going out to lunch while they ran.'

'Do you remember what time you left?'

'At 1310.'

'That's very precise. Is there a reason why you know the time so exactly?'

'I, I looked at my watch I suppose.' Jack seemed flustered. 'Then I walked to my car, and was driving out of the car park as I said.'

'Did you see anyone acting oddly in the car park? Any strangers, for example, hanging around?'

'No.'

'What about other cars moving around? Did you notice any cars manoeuvring as you left?'

'Not particularly.'

'What about a silver Ford? Did you notice a silver Ford coming into the car park at around that time?'

'No.'

# 12

## Evening

At 10pm Jack was still in the trolley bay, along with a few other of his fellow workers who had neither been sent home, nor found a space on a ward. Dr Shah had been along, apologised for the delay and promised a bed would soon be ready for him. The brisk nurse had popped her head round the corner and checked his vital signs again; then the nice care assistant in the lilac scrubs had brought him some tea and a sandwich.

'You'll have missed supper on the ward,' she said, 'so I hope this will keep you going until breakfast.' She'd patted his arm, smiled and whisked away to brighten someone else's evening. He gave the egg sandwich a try, but couldn't eat much of it. The tea was welcome.

He was just pushing the remains of what, harking back to his childhood, he would always think of as an 'egg butty', around his plate, when the curtain quivered and a face came through the gap. It was Pat. He had one arm bandaged and in a sling, but otherwise seemed unharmed until you looked into his eyes. Jack shuddered a little. The glazed look he saw there was mirrored in his own. Pat slipped through the curtain and came up to the bed.

'You shouldn't be here,' said Jack. 'We shouldn't be together.'

'Does it matter?' asked Pat. His face was twisted and his voice bitter. 'Does any of it matter now?' He sat in the chair by the bed. 'We were conned, Jack. No one would be hurt, they said. Property damage only. Warnings given. I've been watching the news on my phone.' He waved it vaguely in the air. 'It's all over the news. Terrorist attack at a Norfolk lab. Scores of casualties. No warnings given. No warnings!' He was breathing hard. 'That was us, Jack. I mixed the explosive. You provided the car. If they catch up with us we're going to prison for ever!' His voice was rising above a whisper.

'Hush,' said Jack sharply. 'Don't draw attention to us. Shut up.'

'Don't you care?' asked Pat, but more quietly. 'Do you really not care? Those were our colleagues. Our friends. And some of them burnt. D'you know Ken, Craig Bennington's PA? He's lost an arm. I heard them talking. He's only twenty-four.'

'Shut up. Shut up.' Jack had his eyes closed and now he was breathing hard, his hands clutching the edge of the blanket again. 'Don't say any more.' He took a deep breath. 'Look, I need to think. I can't think in here. They say they'll let me home tomorrow. What about you?' He opened his eyes again and looked at Pat.

'I'm going as soon as my taxi turns up.'

'Then I'll see you tomorrow. I promise. We can talk then.

For now, please go away. I'll see you tomorrow,' he repeated.

'How do I contact you?'

'Give me your phone.' Jack took it from Pat and put his mobile number in the contacts. 'I don't think we should use WhatsApp any more,' he said. 'Delete it. But you can ring me on this number. Just say you want to come to see me and we'll meet as colleagues.'

'OK.' Pat got up just as the curtain rustled again and the care assistant came bustling through.

'What are you doing here?' she exclaimed. 'You shouldn't be here. Your taxi's waiting. Get yourself off home.' She pushed Pat towards the exit and turned back to Jack. 'Not eaten much of your nice sandwich,' she said. 'Oh well. Perhaps you'll feel more like your breakfast in the morning. They're coming to take you to the ward now.'

The 2200 bird-table was short and sweet. Commander Fisher confirmed the police could have access to the site in the morning.

'Why not now?' asked the new voice from Special Branch, introduced as DI Newton.

'Because there are still hot spots.' Fisher was short with him. 'We're still damping down and even with floodlights, access isn't safe in the dark. The morning is the earliest I can let you in.'

'Thank you,' said Greg, thinking it was time he asserted his control. 'We'll be on site at 0530 with a forensic team. What about pathology? I assume we still have some staff unaccounted for.'

'Five,' said Bennington, and Margaret interrupted, 'I've been in touch with forensic anthropology. It's obvious we're going to need specialist help with ID.'

Greg wasn't the only one who swallowed hard.

'We'll have a forensic pathologist on hand in the morning, but we'll also have some help from Bradford. I'm promised a team of two anthropologists by mid-morning. I believe you've come across them before, DCI Geldard.'

Even amongst the overwhelming disaster, Greg was having an awful presentiment.

'Not,' he started.

'Yes,' said Margaret brightly, 'I believe they have a nickname. George and Mildred? Is that right?'

'They're very good,' agreed Greg hollowly.

DI Newton chimed in, 'See you at 0530 then, on site.'

Chris was looking at Greg quizzically as he terminated the call on the speakerphone loaned by the N&N.

'Do I gather you're not 100 per cent thrilled by this news?' she asked. Jim snorted.

'If what you told me about the Yorkshire skeleton case is true, they do seem a little,' he hesitated, 'idiosyncratic?'

'Let's just say they have a rich interior world,' said Greg, 'and leave it at that for now. Home, if you want any sleep at all before we start again in the morning. I'll drop you off, Chris.'

'I'll do that,' said Jim. 'It's on my way. See you at dawn.'

He whisked a not entirely thrilled Chris away. Yet another ambulance was arriving as they left the hospital.

# 13

## Recriminations

By nine the following morning, Jack was champing at the bit to go home. By ten, he was on the verge of discharging himself. By eleven, he was convinced that if he stayed there any longer his blood pressure would blow his head off, and he was guiltily snappy with the innocent nursing and care staff who kept answering his questions with, 'When the doctor does his rounds.'

At 11.11 precisely, a harassed doctor with a relatively short comet-tail of students behind her, rushed to his bed, asked how he felt, consulted his notes while he answered, then applied a squiggle to the page and dashed off. The sister, catching his eye, picked up his notes and confirmed, 'You can go. You just need to wait for the pharmacy to supply the painkillers the doctor has prescribed.'

Jack, his mouth open in amazement, shut it hurriedly and asked, 'What for?'

'The bruising and cuts I imagine,' said the sister, flicking through the notes.

'If I need anything, I'll take a paracetamol,' said Jack firmly. 'I've had worse from a bolshy sheep. I'm going home now.'

The nurse looked at him, shook her head, then smiled and asked, 'Do you have anyone at home?'

'My mother's coming to stay,' lied Jack. 'Look, I'll sign whatever you want then I'm off.'

An hour later he was paying the taxi and letting himself into his apartment with a sigh of relief. The first task was a mug of tea, then he sank into his reclining armchair with another huge sigh. For the moment he just held the comforting warmth in his hands, looking round the familiar space. It wasn't elegant, but it was home. Elderly Chinese rugs thrown out by his grandma covered most of the fitted carpet. His three comfortable chairs formed a circle round the mock wood burner with the TV on the wall above. Three of the walls were covered with bookcases, one of them recovered from a skip. The books and the wood insulated him from the outside world. He thought, as he often had before, that the only things missing were a partner and a dog, not necessarily in that order. Now, of all days, he missed being greeted at the door.

He leaned back, put his feet up and sipped at the tea, wondering how long he had to enjoy the peace, and what he should do next. His mind kept returning to the blast and the casualties, but he found it impossible to grasp any train of thought. Memories and ideas both shied away, faded and grew confused every time he tried to get a grip. The enormity of what he had done was overwhelming.

There was no knock on the door, no shout through the letter box. The first Jack knew that Pat had arrived was his appearance round the corner of the door.

'Bloody hell,' exclaimed Jack, and his hand jerked so hard, hot tea went all over his legs and his armchair. 'Shit!' He leapt to his feet, shaking his trouser legs and hopping about as the near-boiling liquid stung. 'What the devil are you doing, Pat? Never heard of doorbells? And how did you get in?'

'Pushed your backdoor latch off with my credit card,' replied Jack. 'You should get that replaced. It's not secure.' Then he laughed hollowly as he sat himself down. 'Not that that will matter much soon. Not once the police come calling.'

Jack sat down too, with a half-hearted scrub at the tea stains on the carpet with his slipper. 'Why should they come here?'

'Because they'll trace the car to you,' said Pat. 'Just how long do you think it'll take them? I give us twenty-four hours, perhaps forty-eight max, then you and me are on the frontline and we've nothing to tell them.

'You do realise,' he went on, 'that apart from each other and Jan, we know no one. And I'll bet you Jan's disappeared. We're the patsies, Jack. You ran the gauntlet of God knows how many cameras when you procured the car and my DNA must be all over that barn.'

'But we were promised that no one would get hurt,' said Jack. 'We never meant to hurt anything other than property.'

'Oh for God's sake, Jack! How d'you think that's going to sound in court? Either terminally stupid or terminally naive. In fact, I can't think how we fell for it.'

'Because we trusted them,' said Jack, misery written over his face. 'We thought we were on the same side. I'd never have got involved if I'd known what they planned.'

'But we did. And we don't even know who *they* are.'

There was a silence. Jack's tea, what remained of it, sat ignored and steaming gently on a side table.

'What're you going to do?'

'Run for it,' said Pat tersely, running his hand over his chin, as though testing the length of his stubble. Jack recognised the mannerism as familiar, and realised belatedly just how much it irritated him.

'Have you got any cash?'

'Cash,' asked Jack stupidly. 'What? No! Who has cash these days? I always use cards.'

'Well anything we can turn into cash? Gold? Valuable watch? Jewellery?'

'No. Nothing. Anyway, I'm not running for it. You're panicking, Pat. I'm going to sit tight.'

'Too right I'm panicking. And you're mad if you think they won't trace the car. OK, you stay put if you like, but I'm off. And I think you owe me.'

'Me owe you? How do you work that out?'

Pat ignored the question and, looking round, snatched a small silver cup off the mantelpiece. 'This'll do for starters. I imagine I can pawn it for something.'

Jack snatched back and the cup was in his ownership again, Pat nursing a wrenched finger.

'There's no need to get violent,' he whined. 'We're in this together.'

'No, we're not,' started Jack, but was interrupted by a bang on the front door, and then the doorbell rang for good measure.

'Cops,' said Pat, and in seconds was through the back door and down the long narrow garden. Another bang on the front door, louder this time. Jack reached for the latch with a shaking hand.

# 14

## Tomorrow is another day

Climbing out of his car at the Science Park at 0520, Greg reflected that very little had changed except for the state of the fires. Where yesterday had been sheets of flame and towering mountains of smoke, today there was the usual wide Norfolk sky and peaceful cloud. Ground level, however, was far from peaceful. Fire engines still stood guard in places, and fire officials stood ready to warn of hot spots. Greg, Jim, Chris and Ned all donned white overalls, blue shoe covers, hoods and masks.

'We'll keep the numbers to just us four for the present,' said Greg, his words muffled through the mask, 'until we have a better idea of priority areas. Then I'd like you, Chris, to work with Sarah on the databases available in the lab's off-site storage, while Jim and I keep an eye on pathology and our friends from Bradford.' As Chris glowered, Greg added, 'I'd like you to start from what you discovered about personnel checks and see if there are any leads within the staff at NASA.'

The four moved carefully over the car park towards the burnt-out remains that flagged ground zero. The bomb-conveying car and those immediately adjacent to it were burnt and shredded wrecks. There was a crater in the surface of the car park and damage over a wide area both to vehicles and the buildings.

'One of the things that's been puzzling me,' remarked Ned, 'is why the fire spread so swiftly to both Blocks B and C. Even with the sprinkler systems and so on knocked out, I might have expected a spread from C here,' he waved, 'over to Block B. But the fire brigade and the witness statements both say the fires started in both blocks almost simultaneously. Why was that?'

'We need to talk to someone from the lab facilities management,' said Greg, making a note. 'I'll ask Craig Bennington to suggest someone.'

Ned began a cautious poking about around the wrecked cars. 'What was it you said about cars on the CCTV?' he asked.

'A silver Ford Focus belonging to a visitor came onto the site only a matter of minutes before the explosions,' replied Chris.

'That's what I thought you said.' Ned bent and looked closely at a piece of metal on the ground near his feet. 'Greg, I need my team on here and particularly the photographer. We need pictures of this whole area before we start bagging exhibits, but I'm pretty sure this is from the roof of a silver Ford Focus and it's in the right place for it to be our suspect vehicle. That would be a good place to start.'

Greg turned, as another overalled and masked figure approached. 'Newton,' he introduced himself. 'I've some intelligence on terrorist organisations I need to share with you.' He turned to survey the devastation, giving his head a quick jerk to shake the hair out of his eyes.

'Anything specific to this site?' asked Greg.

'No. Nothing other than the recent threat that you were consulted on.'

Greg winced. 'Yes, noted. Can you liaise with DI Sarah Laurence. She'll be in the ops room in Wymondham by now. And DS Mathews here will be joining her to follow up some leads in NASA HR files and so on.'

Newton hesitated, obviously reluctant to leave the more exciting environs of the laboratory, then nodded to Chris and turned to go.

'Wait,' said Greg, 'before you go, is there anything I need to know urgently? Particularly, have there been any claims of responsibility yet?'

'Thought you'd never ask,' said Newton with a touch of smugness in his masked voice, shaking his head. The wayward lock of hair flew back again and Greg reflected that, even masked, Newton would not be difficult to ID if that mannerism was as ingrained as it seemed.

'There's been a call to the BBC. London not Norwich. A group calling themselves Animal Action UK have claimed responsibility. They said they were "striking a blow for farmed animals everywhere".'

'What the hell does that mean?'

'No idea.' The hair flew again. 'But it seems their objection is to the use of animals on farms and hence to the research being done here. They claim we are in breach of farm animals' rights as sentient beings by using them for any purpose, whether that be wool, hide, food or research. I'll email you the full text.'

'Is it a genuine claim or just a climb onto a bandwagon?'

'Probability is that it's genuine, albeit not proven as yet.

They've been on our radar in the past, but usually for fairly low level activity around intensive units or abattoirs. This is a departure if it is them.'

'Any other suspects?'

'Several, but no one clearly at the front of the queue.' Newton waved, and headed for the perimeter gate. 'See you in Wymondham,' he shouted over his shoulder.

As he approached his car, Greg saw the first of the media vans arrive from where they had been held in the food lab car park, and amongst them a small car from which emerged two figures he recognised.

Following his gaze, Jim asked, 'Are those your old anthropologist friends, George and Mildred?'

'That's right. Ned, are you OK to carry on and get whoever you need from your team here?' Ned waved agreement.

'Come on, Jim. Let's go and say hello.'

George and Mollie, aka Mildred, were struggling into the white coveralls when Greg and Jim approached. They were exactly as Greg remembered. The small and wizened George seemed to be having an easier time with the overalls but was, nonetheless, complaining about his difficulties in a voice to which Greg's mum would have responded with, 'Can't hear you. I'm deaf to whines.' Mildred appeared to have put on a little weight since Greg had last seen her and her reluctance to be separated from a hand-knitted cardigan in a fetching shade of calf-squitter brown made the wriggling even more painful. She was breathing heavily by the time she stood up, and just before she donned the hood Greg noted that her hair colour had also changed, from vivid auburn to brassy yellow – presumably because she was still worth it.

'Good morning,' he said, noting as he did so that no matter how irritating the twosome, he couldn't fault their professionalism. To be there at that hour they must have set off from Bradford before four in the morning. 'Thank you for coming so promptly.'

'Important we're here at the start,' replied George. 'Otherwise God knows what sort of a mess we'd find. OK then. Where are the bodies?'

'Don't we know you?' intervened Mildred accusingly. 'Aren't you DI Geldard from North Yorkshire?'

'DCI Geldard now, and from Norfolk,' he said. 'This way please. Commander Fisher tells me the remains are in Block C. If there are more in Block B, then they're not yet safely accessible, so this is all we have for the moment.'

'How many?'

'Three found so far. Badly burnt as you can imagine. On the basis of witness accounts and the staff database, we believe they are the bodies of two young lab assistants, one male, one female, and one older female member of staff.'

'Shouldn't have too much trouble confirming or denying those theories,' grunted George.

'You haven't seen them yet,' remarked Commander Fisher, joining the party.

'No, but we've seen the results of fierce fire damage many times. Just leave it to us.'

With a photographer tagging along behind Greg, George and Mildred followed Fisher through the battered remains of what had been analytical chemistry. The fire had gone through the building so fast, and burnt so intensely, that little was left other than metal and concrete. They were careful to follow Fisher's instructions to the letter, and soon came upon the two sets of remains found close together quite near the exit. Both exhibited the 'pugilistic' stance to be expected when intense heat has drawn up muscle and tissues. Despite the heat, a surprising amount of soft tissue still remained. George paused by the bodies and said, with an unexpected gentleness, 'You won't need us for these. There'll be sufficient tissue in these remains for a DNA match.'

'Yes,' agreed Fisher. 'That was the view of our fire scene investigator too. The hydrogen-driven fire burnt through this area very quickly, so although the deaths would have been very fast, the remains are substantial. It's the body in here we thought you might help with.'

He pushed on into the building, negotiating the waste-strewn ground with extreme care. In the corner was what appeared to have been a store room with a metal door. And inside were some remains that, unlike those already seen, were little more than carbonised bone. George and Mildred pushed to the fore to observe the bones closely, taking immense care not to touch them.

'Look at the pelvis,' commented Mildred, and George nodded, still trying to get a better look at the skull, which was disarticulated from the spine and face down.

'Were the remains like this when you found them?' he asked.

'Pretty much,' said Fisher. 'I think the skull rolled away when the fire investigator tried to get a closer look, but otherwise nothing has been moved.'

'Yes, the small bones will be very brittle. Indeed, all the bones will be very brittle,' said George. 'We can expect a lot of breakage when we start to move them, so let's get some photos first. Then Mollie and I will crate them up for removal to the morgue.'

'We think these may be the remains of Professor Lai,' added Fisher. 'She's not accounted for, and worked in this area. I'm told she was a small slight woman, around five foot four in height. Could this be her?'

'Too soon to be definitive,' replied George, 'but it is possible. These are the remains of a woman. I can tell you that by the shape of the pelvis. But without careful measurements we can't confirm anything else yet.'

They all stood back while the photographer went to work, then retraced their steps carefully to the fresh air.

Pulling his mask off Greg asked, 'How soon before we get an ID?'

'Depends how difficult it is,' replied Mildred unhelpfully, but added, 'We'll let you know when we have anything to share.'

'In the meantime,' said Greg, 'we'll assume the probability is that this is Professor Lai.'

As he walked back towards his car, he was stopped by a hail from Commander Fisher. 'Something you need to be aware of,' he said. 'The preliminary view from our fire investigator is that the reason the fire spread so fast, in the pattern it did, was dictated by the location of the car bomb. It seems it was parked directly over a nexus of laboratory services, located under the car park. These included lab gas supplies and energy supplies.'

'Which explains why both the electricity and water were cut.'

'And the huge flashovers. The lab gases include hydrogen.'

'Christ! But was that a lucky strike or a deliberate siting?'

'What do you think?'

'I think we have some pointed questions to ask about who knew the location of the nexus.'

'And why so much of the blast went down instead of up and out.'

'Quite. It'll be interesting to see what Ned and his team turn up.'

By lunchtime, the chief super was on the phone again. 'Greg, we've decided to stand Gold Command down. With the fires out and the remaining staff accounted for except for the bodies requiring identification, this is now primarily a police investigation and firmly in our court. I'd like a catch-up this afternoon, prior to a press conference. 1500 please, here in Wymondham.'

'OK, ma'am,' replied Greg. 'I'll let the team know. It would be helpful to have the fire service investigator as well.'

As it happened, the three o clock conference consisted of Greg, Jim, Chris and Sarah, plus Newton from Special Branch, a stockily built fire officer Greg hadn't met before and Ned. When Margaret bustled in, Greg was in the midst of a forensic catch-up. Seeing them arguing excitedly by the whiteboard, Margaret commented, 'Seems like forensics might be a good place to start.'

Ned looked up from his notes. 'Three key facts and a logical supposition,' he replied. 'First, the bomb was a good old-fashioned ammonium nitrate mix, bolstered and triggered with Semtex. Second, the delivery vehicle was the silver Ford Focus caught on CCTV at the entrance and subsequently in the car park. Third, the bomb had been located in the base of the car just above the chassis, and above it was a heavy lead plate. The logical supposition is that this was an attempt, partially successful, to force the explosion downwards, and hence that the positioning of the bomb in that precise location in the car park was deliberate.'

Margaret switched her gaze to Greg.

'We're still following that up,' he said. 'But the initial reaction from Craig Bennington is that the location of the nexus was known to only a few. The list includes board members who were involved in the design of the laboratory, ie himself, the past CEO and Professor Lai, plus the head of facilities management and maybe a few of his team. We're checking them out now.'

'And the car?'

Chris piped up. 'We're currently looking for it on CCTV and also in car sales etc. But the immediately interesting fact is that, according to the site CCTV, that spot in the car park was occupied by another car just a few minutes before the arrival of the Focus. And that car belongs to Jack Haigh.'

'The PTSD victim who says he didn't see the Focus?' asked Greg. 'The chap I spoke to at the hospital?'

'One and the same.'

'So, that could have been a coincidence, or it could have been the mechanism that freed up the space for the car bomb,' remarked Sarah.

'And I think it's the latter,' replied Chris. 'Watch!'

Looking to the chief super for permission, she picked up a remote control and pointed at a screen. They all watched as a rather blurry Ford Focus pulled into the car park, drove past a couple of empty spaces, then seemed to hesitate in row K. As they watched an odd-coloured Mini pulled out of space number

14 and, as it drove away, the Focus reversed into the newly vacated slot.

'And look,' said Chris, breaking the silence and freezing the screen. 'Look how low the car seems to be on the suspension. Isn't that what you'd expect to see, if it was weighed down with ammonium nitrate, Semtex and lead?'

At the end of the conference, Margaret pinned down Greg with a question. 'What do you want out of the press briefing?'

He hesitated, then, 'Information on the car is most likely to be helpful. Who handled it recently? Who sold it on and to whom? From where? Plus, maybe a general request for information on Animal Action UK, since they've claimed responsibility. But I'd rather we didn't share any other details.'

Margaret nodded. 'And for that reason, I'm planning to handle the press conference alone. Do you mind not being part of it?'

'Mind? You must be joking. I've got much more urgent tasks.' He caught himself. 'Sorry. I mean...'

'Don't worry, I know what you mean. Don't think you're off the hook for good. The press will need to see the SIO soon, but for the moment I can hold the line that you're busy with the immediate investigation. Speaking of which, what is your top priority?'

'Talking to Jack Haigh.'

Chris came over. 'Excuse me, but he's on the list of those sent home from the hospital and we have his home address on the list from the lab database.'

'Then let's try there first. You, me and Steve I think. Thanks, Chris,' said Greg.

*

When they pulled up outside the small house converted into flats in a Norwich suburb, there were two cars outside.

'That one's Jack's,' said Chris pointing. 'I recognise it from the CCTV. And look, it's got a dent in the front where he hit the other car at the gate when the bomb went off.'

'I've just asked them to run a check on the other,' chipped in Steve. 'It belongs to another worker from the lab, a Pat Nichols.'

'OK. Let's go in. But Steve, just in case, can you go round the back? Discreetly.'

Steve nodded and slipped out of the car without banging the door in his usual fashion, then followed the garden fence round the corner.

'We'll give him five minutes, then knock on the door,' said Greg. As he took his seat belt off he asked, 'How's Tallulah by the way?'

'Fine thanks, Boss,' answered Chris. 'Bit huffed she's having to spend more time on her own, but well.'

'Time I think,' said Greg, and they went up to the front door. There were two doorbells, apparently one for the ground floor and one for upstairs. The ground floor bell bore the name Haigh, so they rang it and then knocked on the door for good measure. The bell shrilled into the silence once, then again. After a pause the door opened and Jack stood in the hall.

'We've a few more questions, sir,' said Greg. 'May we come in?'

'Of course.' Jack stood to one side and waved them in. 'But I hope it won't take long. I find I'm feeling quite tired.'

He ushered them through the hall and into a kitchen diner of eccentric shape from which French windows opened onto a small garden. As they sat in armchairs either side of the fireplace the sounds of shouts and a scuffle broke out beyond the garden fence. Greg stood up again, and as he listened, a gate opened in the fence. Steve came through with his hands on the shoulders of a slight man in a duffel coat. Greg opened the French windows as Steve approached. Jack seemed frozen into place.

'I stopped this gentleman in the alley behind the garden,' said Steve. 'He seemed disinclined to stop and chat.'

Greg turned to Jack. 'Is he known to you, sir?' he asked formally.

# 15

## More questions

At the sight of Pat, Jack turned, went back into his small sitting room and sat down again in his armchair. The three police followed with Pat sandwiched between them, like the unlovely filling in a tired garage takeaway.

'Of course, I know him,' said Jack. 'He's a colleague. He came to see how I was.'

'So why was he away over your fence with his pants on fire?' asked Steve.

'I went through the garden gate,' responded Pat with an attempt at indignation, but it faded swiftly when Greg asked, 'Why were you so keen to avoid us?'

'No comment,' said Pat.

There was a silence during which Chris's phone rang and she stepped outside with a murmured apology to answer it.

Greg sat down without waiting to be asked. 'Why no comment?' he asked. 'We're not even down the station yet, and you're going with no comment. That's very curious. What do you think, Jack? Your colleague seems a little uneasy around us. Why would that be?'

Jack sighed heavily, seemed on the point of speaking then just shook his head. He sighed again, then said, 'I have no idea. You'll have to ask him.'

Pat glowered but seemed disinclined to say anything further. Greg regarded them both. Had it not been so serious he would have been half inclined to laugh. Each was so clearly put out at the other. And both were making a pig's ear of trying to appear unconcerned.

'I'll let you think about it for a moment,' he said, nodding to Steve to stay put, then left the room to find out what was keeping Chris. She came off the phone as he got outside.

'A witness has come forward in Great Yarmouth,' she said, her face alight with excitement. 'He says he sold the car a week or so ago and his description of the purchaser fits Jack Haigh.'

'What name?'

Ted Jones. And a fictitious address and the purchaser paid cash. We're checking CCTV and ANPR to see if we can find out where it went. But that's enough to bring Haigh in, don't you think?'

'Certainly worth a chat at the station. We'll bring them both in. Ideally voluntarily, but if they turn bolshy we'll arrest them.'

'What charge?'

'How about on suspicion of engaging in the preparation of an act of terrorism? I've always wanted to use that one, and it'll do for now.'

'What about Pat? We haven't anything on him.'

There was a scuffle behind them and Steve appeared in the doorway, again with his hands on Pat's collar.

'This one seems impatient to get away, sir,' puffed Steve, letting go as he spoke.

'Just a moment, sir,' said Greg. 'We'd like you to come down to the station with us to answer a few questions. Both you and Jack if you'd be so kind.'

Pat wasn't listening. He turned suddenly and, giving Steve a sharp shove, would have dashed off down the path to his car if Chris hadn't put her foot out. He came crashing to the ground as Greg said with considerable satisfaction, 'Patrick Nichols, I'm arresting you for assaulting a police officer. You do not have to say anything. But, it may harm your defence if you do not mention when questioned something which you later rely on in court. Anything you do say may be given in evidence. OK, Steve, put him in the car.'

In the shadows of the hall, Greg saw Jack observing events. 'What about you Mr Haigh? Are you going to come quietly?'

'Are you arresting me too?' asked Jack.

'Not yet. I just want to ask you a few questions at the station, but I will arrest you if I have to.'

'On what grounds?' Jack spread his hands. 'I've hit no one. Pat is always a bit of an idiot,' he added.

'The charge wouldn't be assault in your case,' said Greg. 'Probably something more connected with terrorism. But it's up to you, sir. You could just come to help us with our enquiries.'

'I'll come,' said Jack, picking up his phone and keys. 'I assume I can ring for a solicitor from the station, if I need one.'

At Wymondham they divided up, Pat and Steve to the custody

suite, Chris and Jack to an interview room.

'I'll be with you shortly,' said Greg to Jack. 'Just have a couple of things to check on, then we'll get this sorted. Chris will arrange you a cup of tea I'm sure.'

In the operations room, busy with the hum of phone calls and taps on laptops, Greg raised his voice to ask, 'Who can brief me on what we've got on the car and Jack Haigh?'

A hand went up in the corner and Greg saw, with some pleasure that it was Jenny – well known for her brevity and accuracy. 'OK, what've we got Jenny?' he said.

She shuffled her notes. 'First, Jack Haigh pulls his car out of car park space K14 just before the bomber's car pulled into it. He denied having seen it.

'Second, Mr Alan Grant of Grant's Motors Great Yarmouth claims he sold a silver Ford Focus to a Mr Ted Jones on 16 June for cash. His description of the purchaser fits Jack Haigh and he's picked a photo of Jack out of a selection. He's certain Jack was the purchaser.

'Third, ANPR and CCTV records show that car at several locations on the day of the purchase between Great Yarmouth and Aylsham, then one final ping on a camera near Blickling Hall. After that, nothing until the day of the explosions, when we can see it, again near Aylsham then en route to the Science Park.'

'What time?'

'First pick up is at 1215, then the final one is at the Science Park at 1311.'

'So, conclusions are?'

'That Jack Haigh delivered the car to some location near Aylsham where it was converted into an IED. But obviously someone else drove it to the Science Park as Jack was already in the lab by then. In fact, he clocked out pretty much as the car arrived at the main gate.'

'Have we picked up any other traffic of interest around Aylsham or Blickling?'

'Not yet.'

'Have a particular look for,' Greg flicked through his notes and read out two registration plates. 'The first is a blue and violet Mini that belongs to Jack Haigh. The second is an elderly white Peugeot belonging to Pat Nichols.'

'Will do, Boss.'

'Let me know straightaway if you find anything won't you?'

'Of course.'

Beckoning Chris out of the interview room, Greg shared what he had learnt from Jenny.

'So, I think we'll start with Jack Haigh as planned. But I'm very interested now in his link with Pat Nichols. Do we know what his discipline is, at the lab?'

Chris referred to her phone. 'I've got the staff list stored here,' she said, flicking through screens. 'There. Yes. He's a chemist.'

'Is he indeed! Right. Let's have a chat with Mr Haigh.'

Tape on and running and all present identified, Greg said, 'In light of recent information received, I think it best we carry out this interview under caution. So, Mr Haigh, you do not have to say anything. But, it may harm your defence if you do not mention when questioned something which you later rely on in court. Anything you do say may be given in evidence.'

'Are you arresting me?'

'Not yet, Mr Haigh, but depending on your answers

I should tell you that may be the outcome.'

'Then I want a solicitor present.'

'That is your right. Do you have one in mind or would you like us to arrange a duty solicitor?'

Jack hesitated, started to say something, then changed it to, 'A duty solicitor please.'

'Then Detective Sergeant Mathews will arrange that, and we'll reconvene as soon as one can be provided. Interview suspended.

Leaving Chris on the phone again, Greg hurried down to the custody suite and the irate Mr Nichols.

'Has he a solicitor?' he asked Steve.

'Yup. In there now. It's Phil Rule.'

'OK.' Greg was updating Steve as Chris came down the corridor. 'Let's have chat with him then.' Just as he put his hand on the door, his phone pinged with a text. 'Bingo,' he breathed. 'OK, his car was also in the Aylsham area, at least once during the relevant week. I think we'll re-arrest him and ask him about his experience of bomb making.'

A gruelling two hours later, Greg, Chris and Steve emerged to head for the interview suite.

'He's stonewalling,' remarked Chris. 'And he's been watching too much TV. All that "no comment" on matters we already know about. Things we've actually witnessed for God's sake.'

'Quite. Well, it'll do him no favours with the jury. But there's a couple of things we can use in our chat with Jack Haigh. Come on. Better luck with him.'

Jack had used his time with the duty solicitor productively. That much was evident when Greg and Chris started asking questions.

Yes, he had left the lab at around 1 o'clock and gone to pick up his car. He'd been planning on doing some shopping. No, he didn't remember seeing a silver Ford Focus. No, he didn't remember anything of the explosion. In fact he didn't remember anything between leaving the lab and sitting in the conference room at the food lab.

No he hadn't bought a car in Great Yarmouth. He already had a car. No he hadn't met Mr Grant. If he'd picked him out of a photo line-up then he must be mistaken. He thought he had a pretty ordinary British face. Hundreds of men would look like him in a smudgy photo.

No he hadn't driven to Blickling on 16 June nor any time as far as he could remember. No, he didn't remember what he was doing that particular evening. Not without checking his diary. But if it was an ordinary evening he was probably at home watching TV. No, there probably wouldn't have been anyone with him who could vouch for that. He hadn't realised, said sarcastically, that he'd be needing an alibi.

# 16

## Help from unexpected quarters

Heading back to his office, Greg was surprised to be stopped in the corridor with the words, 'There's a Mrs Pritchard asking to see you.'

He turned and looked at the civilian office worker chasing after him. 'I'm really sorry to bother you,' she gasped, out of breath with trotting, 'but she's very emphatic that you know her and that she has something important to tell you.'

'Can't Chris or Steve talk to her?' Greg was a bit impatient, turning away even as he spoke.

'I tried that,' said the girl, bravely standing her ground, 'but she's determined it has to be you.'

Even in his hurry, Greg smiled involuntarily, recalling Mrs P in forceful mode, running an entire poultry plant with a rod of iron.

'OK, where is she? I can spare a few minutes I suppose.'

'In interview room three.' The girl looked relieved.

'And you are?'

'Karen Phillips.'

'OK, Karen, thank you. I'll see Mrs P now.'

Interview room three was one of the less formal settings. There was a modernist mock leather sofa that was more uncomfortable than it looked, and a couple of chairs, ditto. Mrs Pritchard was sitting upright in one of the chairs, hair and skirt suit as immaculate as ever, perfectly composed. Unlike most folk left waiting, she was neither fiddling with a phone or iPad, nor pacing fretfully looking at her watch. As far as Greg could see she had simply been waiting, almost meditatively.

She looked up as he entered the room and held out a perfectly manicured hand. 'DCI Geldard, thank you for seeing me.'

Greg shook it and sat down. 'I think thanks are probably due from me. I gather there's something you want to tell me, and I'm guessing you think it's important to bring you all the way out here.'

She shifted slightly in her seat. 'Well, yes. I did consider ringing, but I wasn't sure I could explain it over the phone in a way that would persuade you to take me seriously. So difficult, isn't it, when you can't see the whites of the eyes, so to speak.'

'I would always take you seriously, Mrs P.' Greg realised as he spoke that he meant it. Then, 'I'm so sorry, that's how I always think of you.'

She smiled. 'Mrs P is fine. It's what they call me at the lab.'

'So what do you want to tell me?'

'I wanted to talk about what I saw just before the bomb went off.' She looked at Greg. 'You'll appreciate I'm sure that with everything that happened after, my memories got somewhat,' she hesitated, 'overwritten. But there's been something bothering me and I think it might be important.

'I might have told you I was outside behind the food lab. I often have my lunch there. There's a patch of garden and some picnic tables. It's quiet and I like to eat my sandwiches in peace in the fresh air. Anyway, the table I often sit at is slightly raised on the grassy bank and in the shade of a tree. It's not popular. Because of the shade,' she added, 'so I usually have the space to myself. I did that day. From there I have a view over the back road to the rear entrance of NASA.'

Although impatient to get to the nub, Greg let her talk, sensing he would get the story better if he let her tell it in her own way.

'Just before the big bang, a car pulled up at the NASA gate. It's unusual to see any traffic there unless livestock are being delivered, so I noticed particularly. Two people came through the gate and got into the car. Then it drove off.'

Disappointed, but assuming there was more, Greg asked, 'Did you know who they were?'

'Not for sure, no. I've rerun the images through my mind over and over again. One I definitely didn't know, but I think it was a man. He moved like a man. The other was short and slight and was wearing a hoody so I didn't see their face, but there was something about how they moved that looked familiar. I can't swear to it DCI Geldard, but I think it was Professor Lai.'

Greg looked up. 'It doesn't seem likely,' he said in a gentle tone. 'We think we've found Professor Lai's body in the lab.'

'Oh,' said Mrs P. 'You're sure of that are you? Because there was definitely something about how she got into the front of the car that looked familiar. Most people step in with one leg, then the other. Professor Lai always sat down first then swung both legs in together, regardless of whether she was wearing skirt or trousers. This woman in the hoody did that, and she was the right size and shape for Professor Lai too.'

'Which seat did she get into?' asked Greg.

'The front passenger seat. And the man got into the back, behind her.'

'Which side of the car were you looking at?'

'The passenger side. The car pulled up at the gate facing towards the bypass, so the driver's side was towards the gate and the passenger side towards me. They both came round the car to get in it.'

'How many people were in the car?'

'I don't know. The driver obviously, but I don't remember whether there was someone in the back seat already. If anything I was focussed on the two who'd come through the gate. That was what was unusual. Then there was the explosion, and I dropped my lunch and ran to the front of our building.'

'What happened to the car.'

'I don't know. I mean, it drove off, but I wasn't watching it after that. There's something else,' added Mrs P. 'The woman I think was Professor Lai, she locked the gate before she got into the car. I mean she locked it behind her. That's partly why I thought she was NASA staff. No one else would have a key.'

Still assimilating what he had been told, Greg walked into the main office to be hit by a wall of chatter.

'Whoa,' he said. 'One at a time folks. What's got you all excited?'

Jenny, the ANPR enthusiast, took the floor. 'I've been able to narrow down locations of interest to a couple of farms near Blickling,' she said. 'I've got both the silver Ford and Pat Nichols' car on camera on roads leading to here,' and she put her finger on the map on the wall. 'And we've got a taxi firm that says one of their chaps picked up a young man in Aylsham a week before the explosion and took him to Great Yarmouth, where he dropped him off near the magistrates' court. He picked Jack Haigh out of a photo line-up.'

'Bingo,' breathed Greg. 'OK, we need to get out there. Warn Ned we'll need his team. And speak to the army. We may need explosives specialists on standby.'

'OK, Boss.'

Greg looked round. 'Chris, with me. Let's get over there as quickly as we can.'

'Before we do,' said Chris, 'George and Mildred are downstairs with a report.'

'Oh God, I mean good,' said Greg. 'Look, can Jim see them? I really think we should get off to Aylsham ASAP.'

'I don't think they'll be pleased,' answered Chris.

'Too bad. I can't be in two places at once. Look, you get the car round, I'll ring Jim before we go.'

Jim sighed theatrically when asked, but went down to the meeting room cheerfully enough. If anything he was curious to see the apocryphal George and Mildred in full flow. When he entered the room they were sitting at the conference table, papers spread in front of them. In fact they appeared to be playing a form of forensic snap, with George snatching papers from Mildred and the cardigan-clad Mildred, today's offering in dung-coloured worsted drooping depressingly around her sturdy frame, snatching selected items back.

'I'd already put them in order, George,' she snapped, and plonked the latest recovered sheet of paper back on the pile in front of her.

George glared, then transferred his glare to Jim. 'Where's Geldard? Who're you?' he asked.

'DI Henning,' said Jim approaching with his hand held out. As neither of the forensic anthropologists seemed likely to take it he coughed, and put it in his pocket. 'Detective Chief Inspector Geldard has had to go out, so he sent me to you instead.'

'Oh, did he,' said George unpleasantly, and Mildred added, 'Too important for us now is he? Rude!'

'Not at all,' said Jim, as smoothly as he could manage. 'He had to follow up an urgent lead. I believe you had some results to report.'

George glowered some more, but was too professional to keep up the aggro. 'Quite. And I would have said this was important too. However,' he shrugged and Mildred followed suit, just slightly off the pace. 'Mollie, tell him what we found.'

Mildred picked up one of her recovered bits of paper and waved it about. 'To go straight to the point,' she said, 'the badly burnt body from the storage area in Block C that we were asked to examine – it's not Professor Lai.'

'Really!' exclaimed Jim. 'Are you sure? I mean,' he realised he was giving offence, 'I mean from what you said before, the measurements seemed to indicate a woman of around the right size.'

'Yes, and they still do,' said George. 'But we've had a closer look at the skull and it's vanishingly unlikely that it belonged to Professor Lai whom we've been assured was clearly ethnically Chinese. Had the skull been that of an ethnically Chinese woman, we would have expected to see round eye sockets, a heart-shaped nasal aperture and shovel-shaped upper incisors. In fact what we found was a skull with eye sockets of the "aviator sunglasses" shape typical of a European.' He indicated the quotation marks in the air with his fingers. 'The nasal aperture and teeth also indicate a European. So, in short, it is unlikely this skull and hence this body belonged to Professor Lai. Wherever she is, whether dead or alive, it is very unlikely she died in the storeroom of Block C.'

# 17

## Near Blickling

The two police cars and Forensic Service van pulled up at the entrance to an old farmyard. In the first, Greg had a large-scale Ordnance Survey map on his knee.

'So,' he said, stabbing at the badly folded paper with his finger, 'we're just over the boundary to the National Trust property here.'

'Which is what the satnav showed us,' said Chris with a degree of evident patience that bordered on the insolent. 'Are you just a teensy bit technophobic, Boss?'

'Not at all,' Greg defended himself. 'These large-scale maps show more detail. Anyway,' he folded it briskly, following the original folds with an accuracy born of long practice, 'this is the place that looks most promising, according to the ANPR data. It feels right too. Isolated, no farmhouse or other houses anywhere near by, buildings more than big enough to house a car or two and accessible by lorry. Something must have delivered the ammonium fertiliser here. On that – have we traced any deliveries here from local companies?'

'Not so far,' replied Chris. 'Are we going to have a look around then?'

'Let's have a chat with Ned. See how he wants to play it.'

Consulted, Ned was clearly torn between the need to protect the possible crime scene and the need to protect personnel.

'I suggest the drone first,' he said. 'Let's get a better picture of what the farmyard looks like, and see if anything shows on the infra-red camera too.'

'We won't see much on that,' objected Chris. 'Surely there's too much background radiation on a day like today.'

'Let's just take a look,' said Ned.

It was a bit blustery for the drone and the picture tended to wobble and slide as gusts of wind caught it. Nonetheless, they could see that the farm buildings were laid out in a sort of square, with an extra building attached to one side. The extension looked like a cattle shed. Two of the others were pole barns with open sides and the other two were big closed barns with corrugated iron sides and roofs. The pole barns were empty except for some big broken hay bales mouldering on the earth floor, a flat trailer with holes in its base and a battered old tractor.

'All looks derelict,' said Greg.

'Don't you believe it,' said Chris. 'That tractor will be the love of someone's life. It's a 1965 Fordson Major.'

Greg looked blank and so did everyone else.

Chris sighed. 'Just take it from me,' she said, 'it's probably still in working order and probably still used for some tasks around the farm. Like towing a trailer for instance.'

The drone was returned briskly to base and they all looked at Ned again.

'Clearly we need a look inside those barns,' he said, 'but I don't want you all trampling over everything en route. So, coveralls on, follow my team very closely, and mind where you put your clodhoppers. Let's see if the barns are secured.'

'But no one opens anything or steps anywhere without Ned's say so.' Greg reinforced the message. 'Let's not forget we might be dealing with explosives here. Anything suspect, and we back right off and call the army in.'

Several of the team looked at each other, and several nodded. It was with extreme caution that they left the farm entrance and followed Ned down the rutted track.

From ground level the enclosed barns looked bigger. One had its doors standing open. Ned wouldn't allow anyone to go in, but from the entrance it looked as though it had been used as a machinery store. There was a small concrete mixer at the back, tools on the wall and tyre marks on the dusty concrete floor. Some belonged to huge tyres set a very long way apart. Others looked more like car tyres.

'What's been in here?' asked one of the team looking closely at the larger marks. 'A tank? This looks like it was tracked.'

'A combine,' said Chris with authority. 'This looks like a tracked combine to me. A contractor probably used the barn for storage while he worked the land around here. When he was finished he'd have taken his kit away with him. We might find grain in the other barn. The one that's all closed up.' She went to walk towards the other barn, but Ned called her back.

'Not till we've had a first look,' he said. 'And I think you're right about the combine. Those are the older marks. These car tracks, now these are much more interesting.'

'And the concrete mixer,' called the forensic expert who

135

had ventured further into the barn. 'I'm pretty sure this's been used to mix the fertiliser and diesel to make the explosive.'

'OK, everyone out,' said Ned. 'This barn is now out of bounds to everyone except my team until we've done a thorough search and screen.'

Greg, Chris and Steve retreated to the farm track again and looked around them. As they did so Greg's phone rang.

'Two bars,' he muttered. 'That's all the signal I've got, even out here. Doesn't Norfolk's lack of mobile coverage really stink?' He moved away from the buildings in an effort to hear better and said, 'Yes, Jim, what was it they wanted?' There was a silence, then, 'So it looks as though Mrs P was right. Professor Lai did *not* die in the bomb attack, and must now be a person of interest. Thanks, Jim. And thank George and Mildred for me will you. Oh, and while you're on, can you ask that Special Branch chappie if he's got anything on Professor Lai? It's time he did something for his money!'

In answering the phone, Greg had moved steadily away from the masking effect of the farm buildings and into the shade of the dusty copse that lined the driveway. The sycamores were heavy with their winged seed and some were already spiralling downwards in the breeze. He turned in time to see Chris moving away from the Fordson Major she seemed to admire, and towards the closed barn with the big metal shutter door. She reached towards the handle of the pedestrian door to the left of the main entrance. Greg noted she was wearing the protective plastic gloves but nonetheless shouted, 'Hang on, Chris. Ned will want to go there first,' when there was a shattering roar.

# 18

## Professor Lai

The Special Branch connection had already occurred to Jim. Immediately on hearing George and Mildred confirm the impression left by Mrs P, he had hotfooted it to the ops room and demanded of Sarah the whereabouts of DI Newton.

'Gone for a bacon sarnie,' she said. 'He eats them all day. I've never seen anything like it.'

As she spoke, DI Newton, sandwich bag in hand, reappeared round the corner. He was also carrying a couple of coffees.

'One for you, Sarah,' he announced. 'Sorry, I didn't realise we'd got company.'

Sarah picked up the coffee and snapped the lid, looking at Jim through the steam. 'Jim has some questions for you,' she said.

As Newton perched on the edge of the conference table and took a big bite of his latest bacon butty, Jim brought him up to date with Mrs P's statement and the evidence from the forensic anthropologists.

'So, it seems highly probable that Professor Lai left the laboratory secretly just before the explosion and has kept out of sight ever since. As she was also one of the few who knew the location of the lab services nexus beneath the car park, that must put her squarely in the frame alongside that poor sap Jack Haigh and his dozy sidekick Pat Nichols. What do you know about her? Has she been in your sights?'

Newton took his time over finishing his bacon and wiped a smear of brown sauce from his lower lip. Jim waited patiently. He could spot a delaying tactic when he saw one.

'We may have some information,' said Newton at last. 'I'll need to refer your request upwards.'

'What? Why? This is an investigation of a terrorist attack resulting in multiple deaths. What could be more important than this?'

'It's above your pay grade. And mine,' Newton admitted. 'I'll get back to you with anything I can. As soon as I can.'

'And when will that be?'

'As soon as I can,' repeated Newton, looking awkward.

'Well, in the meantime, be sure we'll be doing our damnedest to find the missing professor, and to identify the body so conveniently similar to hers and burnt beyond recognition in Block C.

Turning his back on Newton and Sarah, Jim slammed over to the rank of desks currently accommodating Jenny and the civilian assistant Karen.

'Can you help?' he asked. 'I need you to go back through the lists of staff from the lab and identify precisely what happened to whom. Who have we spoken to, who is still in hospital or has been absolutely identified as one of the dead, either by DNA, teeth, or relative? I need to know who is still unaccounted for. Meanwhile, I'll go and have another chat with the anthropologists. See what else they can tell us about our mystery casualty.'

Setting the nasal whine and the cardi on one side (he decided that pond-slime green was a better description of the shade), George and Mildred were helpful.

'You're looking for a European woman, about five foot four in height, probably fairly slight in build, around thirty or forty years old. Could be a bit older, but not too much, I'd say. There's very little sign of any osteoarthritis.'

'Any chance of any DNA?'

'Very slight. The bones were very thoroughly carbonised. In bones burnt black like these, the chances of recovering DNA are not good. We might do better with mitochondrial DNA, but we won't know yet. We'll keep you posted.'

'Thank you,' said Jim sincerely, and went back to Jenny and Karen. 'You're looking for a thirty-to-forty-year-old European female,' he said. 'You can extend the age range a little to ensure we don't miss anyone, but what've you got so far?'

'Nothing,' said Jenny.

'Nothing?'

'Nothing. There's no one now unaccounted for, amongst the staff at least. And even amongst visitors we've only one logged in that day at the gate that we haven't found, and that's a male.'

'In fact, we were wondering if that was the driver of the car bomb,' added Karen. 'Especially given the statement from Mrs P that she saw a man accompanying Professor Lai out of the back gate before the blast.'

'OK. Let's park that one for the moment and turn your attention to Professor Lai. See what can you dig up on her from the lab records and anything else you can find. I'm going to have a chat with Craig Bennington.'

'And I'll have another look at the lab CCTV from the entrance gate,' offered Jenny. 'I might be able to find something more about the car driver.'

A few phone calls later and Jim had run Professor Bennington to ground at his home in Black Carr, a small and rather elegant hamlet not too far away. When called to the phone, he sounded tired.

'Sorry,' he said. 'I was in the garden. I was told to take a day at home, but it's hard to get the lab out of my mind.'

'How's your PA Ken,' asked Jim.

'About as well as you'd expect. He's putting a brave face on it, but he's a long way to go yet.'

'As you're quite near to us,' said Jim, 'may I come round for a chat? I need some information on one of your colleagues.'

'Yes, of course. I'll just let my wife know and I'm sure she'll find us coffee and biscuits.'

Mrs Bennington was, in reality, rather less welcoming than her husband had led Jim to expect. She surveyed him from the vantage point of the doorstep with a minatory air, and near as dammit asked him to remove his shoes. Jim wiped them on the mat, very thoroughly, and followed her meekly into the spacious conservatory added to the back of the half-timbered old house.

Professor Bennington was sitting by the open door, shaded by the roof blinds and apparently enjoying both the birdsong and the sun-warmed air.

Jim was shocked, but not surprised, at how wrecked the Professor looked, and nodded in answer to Mrs Bennington's, 'Don't keep him too long, will you.'

'Good morning, Professor,' he said, then corrected himself after a glance at the wall clock. 'Or rather, good afternoon.'

'Take a seat,' replied Craig Bennington, waving to a comfortably sagging sofa near him. 'How can I help?'

'It's about Professor Lai,' said Jim, then turned to accept a cup of coffee from Mrs Bennington. After she'd gone back into the kitchen, he went on, 'I'd like your impressions of her, please.'

'Poor woman,' replied the Professor. 'What's the problem? Are you struggling to find next of kin? I think all that information should be available in the staff records.'

'No, not that,' replied Jim. He paused, then went on, 'I want you to keep this confidential for the time being, Professor, but we've been told the remains we found in Block B that were assumed to be Professor Lai's in fact cannot be hers. Moreover, we have a witness who claims to have seen her leaving the site via the back entrance very shortly before the bomb went off. So you'll understand, we need to know a lot more about her.'

# 19

## After the blast

The boom seemed to stun the air. The wind dropped. Everything stood still, even the birds in the trees. For a few moments there was complete silence – no birdsong, no rustle of grasses. Greg couldn't hear even his own breathing or his heartbeat. Perhaps his heart had stopped? No. Gradually sounds started to reappear around the edges of awareness and as he ran towards the shape now lying motionless under the door that had blown off its hinges, he realised it was not the sounds that had been suspended, but his own hearing.

He reached Chris in a matter of seconds and, bending down, hurled the solid wood door away as though it had been a sheet of paper. As he dropped to his knees beside her he was simultaneously aware both of an ominous crackling sound coming from the barn and of shouts coming round the corner towards him.

Chris was lying on her back, arms curled over her body

as though in defence and legs splayed. She was out cold, her nose broken by the look of it, and blood pouring out of it down her face. Greg noted the active bleeding with some relief but nonetheless checked for pulse and respiration before looking round as Ned skidded to a halt beside him.

'Booby trap,' said Ned succinctly, as he dialled 999. 'Ambulance,' he said. 'One victim of a further bomb blast. Alive and breathing but not conscious. Concussion as a minimum.'

He paused to listen for a moment and as he did so Greg said, 'She's going to choke on her own blood if we leave her like this. I'm going to put her in the recovery position. Can you steady her head and neck?'

Ned also knelt, and between them the two men turned Chris onto her side as gently as they could.

'Control says there's a first responder and an ambulance on the way. Now we need to get the bomb disposal team here before anyone else is put at risk. I take it she touched the door?'

'Turned the handle, I think,' replied Greg. 'I was just shouting to her to wait when everything blew up in her face.'

'Never has been very patient,' grunted Ned, 'but she's got the luck of the devil.'

Greg looked up for a moment in astonishment.

'Well at least she landed soft.' Ned indicated the patch of yard where they had just turned Chris. It was covered in a thick coat of chaff. 'However, that's not so good,' added Ned. As they watched, a line of flame was beginning to creep from the doorway along the piles of chaff and grain dust. For the first time, Greg became aware of the heat beating on his face and the roaring coming from the barn. Ned kicked at the flame and it went out, but more were backing up behind it.

'We need to move her,' he said to Greg, and, as he seemed to take no notice, shook him by the shoulder. 'We need to move her, sir, and now,' he said. 'There may be other bombs and there's certainly a hell of a lot of flammables.'

Greg's eyes ran along his arm to where he was, almost without realising it, holding Chris's gloved hand in his. 'We might do more damage,' he said.

'And the fire might do more,' replied Ned.

'OK.' Greg made his mind up. 'You keep her head as steady as you can.' He slid his arms under Chris and lifted.

'You can't do it on your own. Oh, you have,' said Ned. And the little group of three retreated to a safe distance from the burning barn. As Greg laid Chris gently down on the grassy bank behind the police vehicles, there was a sound of sirens and bells. Almost simultaneously a car marked 'First Responder' pulled up beside them as the first of two fire engines made its lurching passage down the rutted track. Greg remained oblivious, as Chris choked, coughed and then moaned, her eyes fluttering for the first time since he'd seen her lying under the door.

'Oh, good. Looks like she's coming round,' said the familiar voice of Ben Asheton over his shoulder. 'Come on then, Greg. Let the dog see the rabbit.' Then, as he showed no signs of letting go of the hand he still held, Ben added, 'She's going nowhere just yet, mate. Let me check her over, eh?'

Greg let go reluctantly. As he stood up, Chris opened her eyes fully and squinted round her swollen nose and rapidly swelling eyes. 'That was one hell of a doorbell,' she said. And closed her eyes again.

For a moment Greg just stood, staring at Chris and Ben now taping monitors to her and asking questions she didn't seem very inclined to answer. Then he gave himself a physical shake and pulled himself together.

'Right,' he said to Ned. 'She's in good hands now.' Even as he spoke, two paramedics were jogging towards them across the yard. 'Are your team all accounted for, Ned?' As he spoke he was looking around and noted, with relief, that Steve had appointed himself traffic manager. Even as he watched, an army truck pulled up behind the fire engines.

'Yes. All safe and back in our van.'

'I need to have a word with the incident commander,' said Greg. 'Come with me? We need to share whatever intelligence we have.'

There was a familiar face under the helmet. 'Commander Fisher isn't it?' asked Greg.

'That's right. Found me another bomb have you?'

'So it seems.'

As they spoke, men were unrolling reels from the back of the first tender.

'What can you tell me?' asked Fisher.

Ned waved an arm. 'I'm confident the main farmyard is clear and also the open-sided barn over there. We've had a first look round those two, and while we need to take samples and so on when we can, and for what use they'll be now.' He sniffed, as yet more men ran across the area.

'Which was probably the point of the explosion, at least partly.' They had been joined by a slight man in fatigues. 'I recommend all personnel not directly involved in managing the fire pull back beyond our perimeter,' and he indicated a line somewhat beyond the boundary currently being controlled by Steve and a couple of Ned's colleagues. 'I also recommend that you concentrate on preventing the fire from spreading and let the main focus burn itself out.'

'My thoughts precisely,' responded Fisher.

'OK, we're agreed then. Everyone back behind our line except the men on the hoses.' 'Our casualty,' started Greg.

'Is already on her way to the hospital,' replied the army captain.

Greg swung round and, as he watched, Ben waved the ambulance off, then turned to Greg. 'She'll be fine,' he said. 'If you could just pause your single-handed attempts to keep the emergency services on permanent alert for a minute or two, I'll get back to work.' He got in his car with a smile and wave, then, head stuck out the window, he added, 'Make the most of the next couple of days. She won't be apologetic for long!'

Greg waved, then turned back to the army officer. 'Thank you. I'll leave a couple of my team here and we'd appreciate being kept in the loop.'

'I need to get in ASAP to see what we can find,' added Ned.

'No problem. It'll be a while though. First we need the fire out. Then I'll send in sniffer dogs and our robot to check for other IEDs. Then you can go in.'

'Understood.'

Greg was already talking to Steve. 'I need to report to the super,' he said, 'and get some bods over for crowd control. It can only be a matter of time before the vultures descend. Are you OK to stick around for a little while?'

'Sure, Boss. Is the sarge OK?'

'She'll be fine,' said Ben, from his car window. 'She'll have the devil of a hangover and eyes like a panda for a week or so.

Otherwise, I think she'll be fine. They'll set her nose at the hospital, then keep her in overnight at least, just to make sure there are no problems.'

'Right, now for the chief super and a catch-up with Jim,' said Greg. 'Ned, stand your folk down. It's going to be at least twenty-four hours before you can go back.'

# 20

## The roughest day

Jim was just leaving Professor Bennington when he got simultaneous calls on his car radio and his mobile. He fumbled with his phone as he picked up the radio call, then froze, aghast. The radio was quickly dealt with, and he turned back to his phone.

'Greg, how are you and how's Chris?'

'It seems she's going to be OK. We won't know for sure until the hospital have run more checks, but Ben seemed pretty confident. I thought she'd had it, Jim. I really did.'

'What about you and the rest of the team?'

'I'm fine. So's everyone else. They were all well clear when the booby trap went off. I have to say, Jim, that if Chris had followed instructions she'd be OK too. She was rushing in again. I'll have something to say about that when she's well enough to hear it.'

'Where are you now?'

'On my way to the hospital. Don't worry, I'll moderate my language for the moment.'

'I bet Chris doesn't. She'll be mortified she put her foot in it so badly.'

'Well, maybe. She gave me the fright of my life. I honestly thought she was dead for a few moments. It was only the blood flowing so freely that tipped me off she was still alive.'

'My God, where was she hurt?'

'No, it's OK, Jim. Sorry, I didn't mean to scare you. It was a broken nose. She'll have two lovely shiners as well! How about you, Jim? Any luck finding out more about our mystery skeleton?'

'Not yet. It doesn't seem there's anyone unaccounted for, so either there was a mystery guest, or someone's masquerading as someone else. I've spoken to Craig Bennington.'

'OK. Meet me at the hospital and update me there.'

'Will do. After that you should go home. Tomorrow will be another busy one.'

'Pots, kettles and black come to mind. See you shortly, Jim.'

By the time Jim got to the Norfolk and Norwich, Greg was already outside Chris's room, talking to a senior nurse. He turned as Jim approached. 'Apparently we can have a few minutes, then we're to make ourselves scarce and let the patient rest.'

'Good luck with that,' muttered Jim, as he smiled at the nurse and followed Greg through the door.

Chris was lying with the head of the bed raised. Her bruised eyes were closed when they entered and she attempted a smile. She raised a hand as Greg approached the bed. 'Before you say anything,' she whispered, 'I know I was out of line. Sorry.'

Greg sat down by the bed, half reached to take her hand,

then corrected himself and settled for patting it gently. 'I know,' he said. 'Let's forget it for now. Just remember the next time you scare me like that I'll nail you to the nearest available wall and sod HR's rules.'

Jim pulled over a spare chair and sat himself down. 'And if he doesn't, I will,' he said. 'So that's two careers in your hands, Chris. How're you feeling anyway? I hope the other bloke looks worse.'

The smile this time was more genuine. 'Thanks for the compliments, sirs. Can always rely on you two for a confidence boost. Never mind me – I'll be out of here by tomorrow. What's happening with the case?'

'Jim was just about to report,' said Greg. 'What about it, Jim? You can brief us both.'

Jim stared, startled, and Greg said, 'Go ahead. If madam here nods off in the middle, we can continue outside.'

Chris gave a thumbs up and whispered, 'In your dreams.' Nonetheless, Jim was barely two sentences in when her eyelids started to flutter and Greg indicated that they should tiptoe out.

'I thought that would happen,' he said, once they were safely outside the door. 'But that was easier than an argument. Let's find a quiet corner in the canteen and carry on there.'

Settled down with tea and cake, Greg said, 'OK, start over. What have we learned about Professor Lai and the casualty in the store room?'

Jim flicked though his notes. 'First, that it definitely isn't the professor but is a thirty-to-forty-year-old woman with European features. Second, that the professor is known to the funny buggers, and so far they've not yet shared what they know. I've pushed that up to the chief super to do some leaning.

Which all reinforces the impression that Mrs P was right when she said she saw Professor Lai leaving the site just before the bomb blast. Clearly, we need to find her urgently. And her male sidekick. I've got the camera team checking CCTV and ANPR to see what we can spot among vehicle movements near the site that afternoon.

'According to Craig Bennington, the Professor was also one of the few senior staff who were around when the lab was being built and had access to the plans and planning meetings. It's a short list, with just Craig Bennington, Professor Lai and the current head of site maintenance still in the picture. The previous CEO, now retired, was on the list and obviously some of the construction crew would have been aware. But only those three were both aware of the importance of the nexus *and* in a position to arrange for the car bomb to be parked there.'

'Speaking of which, we need to know who arranged for Jack Haigh to vacate the space at just the right moment,' remarked Greg.

'Precisely. But I assume he's still saying nothing.'

'At the moment. But what else does Craig say about Professor Lai?'

'Not a great deal about a colleague he has worked with for over seven years. He says she's quietly spoken, very determined, and more than capable of standing her ground on something that matters to her. When I asked what qualified as mattering, he could only say issues like funding for her laboratory. He said she was a very private person. As far as he knew, she was single. He had no idea about her politics or personal beliefs, and said he'd never known her socialise with anyone from the lab except on formal occasions. He described her as very professional with regard to the quality of her lab's work and very calm with customers. Other than that, he had very little to say.'

'What about our mystery body?'

'Nothing much yet, except that George thinks some mitochondrial DNA sequencing "may not be impossible". So we hope for the best.'

Greg sat in silence for a moment, pondering. 'Jim,' he said at last, 'I think the only way is good, old-fashioned, painstaking detection. We need to go through the staff list for female Europeans within the given age bracket, then check we know exactly where they are.'

'Already in hand,' said Jim triumphantly. 'Not turned anything up yet, but I'll keep you posted. The CCTV team have turned up a foggy picture of the man who may have delivered the bomb. Site security had a look and said it matches his recollection, so we're seeing whether we have matches to any known activists.'

'Thanks, Jim. Now home, I think, for both of us. Get yourself off, and I'll just check on Chris before I leave. Early start tomorrow at our new bomb site.'

Greg tiptoed back into the private room when the nurse's back was turned. Chris was still propped up, the remains of a sandwich on the table beside her. She turned her head as Greg came back.

'Don't think I didn't hear you go,' she said, but her voice was tired and she winced as she spoke.

'You don't need to keep the pretence up for me.' Greg took the seat by the bed again, and this time he did take her hand. 'How are you really?' he asked.

'Bit rough. Bit sore. Look, I *am* sorry, Boss.'

'Shh. I know. It doesn't matter just now. But don't give me a fright like that again will you?'

'No. I promise.' She squeezed his hand. 'I do remember you carrying me clear. Thank you, Boss.'

'I thought you were out of it then. And you could try calling me Greg, if you wanted. In private anyway.'

She opened her eyes again and said something he didn't quite catch.

'Come again?'

She looked up at him. 'I said "Come what come may, time and the hour runs through the roughest day." It's a quote.'

'I'll take your word for it. Good night, Chris. Stay safe. I'll see you tomorrow.'


When Greg got up the following morning he found a multiplicity of messages waiting for him on his phone and a very cross cat demanding a) breakfast and b) a game. He managed the tin of cat food one handed as he scrolled through the messages. One, from Margaret Tayler, requesting his presence in her office the moment he got in to Wymondham and, if that wasn't pronto, a phone call. One from Ned, reporting that the fire service had told them the earliest they could have access to the Aylsham barns was 1100, so no point rushing off there. And one from Jim, announcing that he'd got a message from George to say they'd managed to sequence some mitochondrial DNA but it was degraded. Even so, it might help with an ID. Greg looked at his watch. It was still only seven o'clock. Everyone seemed to have made a very early start that morning.

He placated Bobby with a game of catch the ball of wool while he dressed, then made tracks for Wymondham and what he feared was going to be a dressing-down from Margaret. On his way he used his hands-free to get an update from the hospital on Chris. She'd had a comfortable night he was told, which he interpreted as nurse-speak for not actually in agony, and would be discharged later that day. He gathered that she was only being kept in situ because she had no clothes, and even so was threatening to walk out in a blanket.

'Tell her that's theft,' he recommended. 'Who's going to collect her?'

'Her mother, we gather,' replied the nurse. 'Don't worry, we're used to bolshy patients. Shall I tell her you rang?'

'Yes please. And say I'll be in touch later.'


Parked, coffee collected and sitting in relative comfort in Margaret's office, Greg was somewhat relieved to discover that the dressing-down was comparatively mild.

'No, I know Sergeant Mathews can be headstrong,' she said. 'I'm sure you've had a word about rash behaviour. I wish I thought it wouldn't happen again, but Chris Mathews does have history in this area. I don't suppose anyone's told you about the incident on the Broads.'

'No,' said Greg. 'I don't believe so.'

'It happened long before your arrival here. We had a jumper off the bridge over the Bure in Great Yarmouth. Chris saw it happen from the bank near the White Lion. The tide was coming in at the time, so the man in the water was drifting upstream. Chris jumped in and saved his life, at considerable risk to her own. She got a commendation for that, and one hell of a telling off from her sergeant who saw her do it.

'No, the reason I wanted you to see me was because I want

you to have some counselling. It's no small thing to see one of your team caught up in an event like that. The consequences can come back to bite you later. I've already talked to Ned about his team. But I'm telling you, Greg, that I'm not accepting any excuses. I've already spoken to the counsellor and he'll make contact to agree a time.'

'But I'm rushed off my feet now,' protested Greg. 'Look, I appreciate the thought, but…'

'No you don't,' said Margaret with a grin. 'You think I'm being a busybody. But believe me, it's worth a little of your time to make sure you come out of this OK. Worth it to you and to me. So that's an end of it.

'Now, one other matter. I've been in touch with the anti-terrorist crowd. The funny buggers, as Jim calls them. I've got a report on Professor Lai. Don't get too excited. It doesn't say very much other than they've been keeping an eye on her.'

'Not very thoroughly judging from recent events,' grunted Greg.

'Well, yes, I think there are some red faces and it's not helping with transparency. I've not seen so much arse-covering since I toured a knicker factory. Here's the report, but I can summarise it for you in a few sentences. She came here from Hong Kong as a student in the 1980s. She got her first degree at Imperial College and her PhD at Reading. A range of academic posts followed then she transferred to the government science service and worked at Porton Down and the Food Science Laboratory before taking up a post at the precursor to NASA. She's always been in analytical chemistry.'

'So why were the funny buggers interested?'

'That's not clear. Presumably she was vetted before working

at Porton Down, but there's no record on this file of why they maintained an interest.'

'Have you asked why?'

'Of course.' Margaret gave him a look that suggested he was being impertinent. 'But all I'm told is that it's not in the public interest to release more.'

'Which usually means a witness protection scheme?'

'But they do deny that they have her, or know her whereabouts, so I'm afraid it's over to you, Greg. Find her, and then we can ask our own questions.'

Making his way back to the ops room before departing for Aylsham, Greg was way-layed by Jenny.

'I think we have something,' she said. Karen was jostling at her shoulder. 'Can you spare us a minute? We've narrowed down the possibilities to seven.'

'This is about the identity of the mystery body?'

'Yes. As I said, we've spoken to all but seven of our possibilities, but this one looks particularly interesting. She worked in analytical chemistry, but not normally in the lab where the body was found. She's not answering her phone, and no one seems to have seen her, but I've had the phone traced and up until yesterday it was moving around. Yesterday it went dead. And she's Jack Haigh's supervisor.'

'Where was the phone?'

'That's the thing. It was round and about Aylsham. I can't pinpoint it to the barn that blew up – the coverage out there is too poor.'

'Tell me about it,' said Greg with feeling.

'But it was in the area. Yet Jan Littleboys lived in Norwich.'

'OK. Get someone out to her place to check it over and collect something with her DNA on it, hairbrush or something. Then we can get it checked against the results George and Mildred got from their sample. Let me know what you find out. I'll be at the barn with Ned if anyone wants me.'

'Got it, Boss,' said Jenny.

In the ops room, Jim was deep in conversation with the team reviewing camera footage.

'We've managed to get the image of the driver cleaned up some more. I'm going to check it with Mrs P to see if she recognises it. Going on her rather vague description of the car that picked up two folk at the back gate, we've also got some possible vehicles to follow on ANPR.'

'Great. Jim, can I leave that with you? I'm just off to Aylsham to see what Ned can find there. Catch up later.'

Back in his car, his phone rang with an unknown number. A brisk voice with a north country accent took Greg, in memory, back to his previous posting in North Yorkshire.

'Hi. My name's Neil. I'm a counsellor with Norfolk Police. Your chief super, Margaret Tayler, asked me to get in touch. I believe she's spoken to you.'

'Yes. Look, thank you,' said Greg, looking both ways as he pulled out onto the main road. 'I don't want to start under any false pretences, so I should warn you I'm only doing this because Margaret made it plain I don't have a choice.'

'You and almost everyone else I talk to,' said the voice. 'It's no bother. Can we meet this afternoon?'

'Might be difficult. Would early evening be OK?'

'Six? OK, let's say six pm at the Wymondham offices.'

# 21

## Keeping pace

Between being charged and placed on remand, everything seemed to Jack to move at the speed of light. One moment he was consulting with his solicitor, next he was in front of the custody sergeant being deprived of various items of property before being consigned to a cell. Judging from a complaining voice heard in the corridor, Pat Nichols was not far away. Repeated pleas to be released on bail went unheeded. A request to speak to his solicitor was complied with, but all he did was explain that owing to the nature of the charge, Jack was unlikely to be granted bail, adding that he would be called into the Crown Court within a couple of days for a judge to make the decision. Then followed an uncomfortable trip to HM Prison, Norwich.

He arrived late in the evening, was processed swiftly as though he were a sack of spuds, and dumped into a shared cell with two other men, one tall and thin, the other short and fat. Had Jack been less stressed, Laurel and Hardy might have come to mind. Jack was still trying to get over the shock of the environment when the short, fat one introduced himself as Jack's 'mentor' and proceeded to explain what Jack could expect over the next few hours and days. As Jack wasn't listening, it was wasted effort. His main thought, as he pulled the blanket over his head in a vain attempt to shut out the background noise of shouts and cries, was that he'd seen lighter bars and less concrete in a bull pen. The mentor's voice eventually stopped.

The following day, he was surprised just how much of his time was spent in that room. On the other hand, his knowledge of prison procedures was based on the old TV programme *Porridge*, which he acknowledged, with a wry internal grin, was probably not a reliable guide. Conversation within the room was limited, which was mainly his choice. His mentor did his best, but after a series of short answers and silence, gave up on his well-meant efforts to ease the new inmate into his unfamiliar environment. His final words were depressing. 'Don't expect too much when you do get out there,' with a nod to the door. 'Folk don't much like a terrorist.'

In fact, when mixing with other prisoners for meals and so-called recreation, Jack did not have too much difficulty. He put that down to minding his own business, but in reality his size and evident fitness had something to do with it, together with the fact that his silence made him a difficult target to assess. In general the bullies found easier marks, of which one was Pat Nichols.

Jack had spotted him on the second day, and made a point of keeping clear as far as possible. He didn't trust Pat's discretion, and he didn't like him well enough to want to place himself between Pat and his persecutors. When he felt guilty about that, he reminded himself that much of the treatment Pat incurred was caused, if not justified by, his incessant complaining and whining. However, Pat cornered him at last near the canteen. By this time he was nursing a scalded wrist from hot coffee thrown over him, and his face was bruised.

'Heard anything?' he demanded.

'No. Why would I?'

'They're trying to track down the ringleaders. Surely once they do, they'll lose interest in us. All this,' he waved an arm, attracting stares from people Jack really didn't want attention from. 'All this is just to intimidate us into giving them some intelligence. They don't believe we know nothing.'

'Pat, if you believe that, you're stupider than you look. They've got evidence that ties you to bomb making. They think I was involved with the placement of it. No matter who else they catch, that's not going away.' Jack turned away sharply. There was some sort of response behind him, but he ignored it.

The day in court was over in a flash. Jack was taken to the Crown Court for what his solicitor had explained would be a 'pre-trial hearing'. The prosecution solicitor, a big man in every sense with a booming voice to match, made his argument that the offences with which Jack was charged were so serious that bail could not and should not be considered. Peering through the distorting glass around the dock, Jack noticed that DCI Geldard was in court for the hearing. He switched attention to his defence solicitor as he started to speak, making much of Jack's previously unblemished record, arguing that there was only circumstantial evidence linking Jack in any way to the explosion, and no evidence whatsoever that Jack had been involved in planning the attack. Jack saw DCI Geldard stir in his seat at this point, and slightly lost track of what was being said, which seemed to amount to a suggestion that he could not be regarded as a flight risk.

The judge took only a short while to consider his decision, during which Geldard stood, bowed to the court and left. The judge opened his mouth, and by the time he had pronounced that Jack was to be remanded into custody, the security guard behind him had the cuffs on his wrists. He was hustled out of the court and back to the holding cells to await his return journey to HMP Norwich.

Greg met Frank, the CPS solicitor in the corridor. 'Good result,' he congratulated him.

'I notice you felt the need to keep an eye on me,' said Frank with a twinkle. 'What's the problem? Did you think I was going to go soft on you?'

'Not that so much,' replied Greg, 'but I did want to make damn sure those two are held. You heard about the booby trap?'

'I heard there'd been another explosion. It wasn't an accident then?'

'No, but keep that to yourself for now. It was a deliberately laid trap and it was Chris who set it off.'

'My God! Is she OK?'

'Battered and bruised, but yes, she was lucky. It could have been a lot worse. You'll understand why I want those two secured. Especially the other one.'

'Whining Willy?'

'If you mean Pat Nichols, yes. There's really strong evidence he prepared the explosive. We need to know if he was involved with the trap too. Why "Whining Willy"?' he added.

'Apparently that's his nickname in the gaol, and after only two days. Right, this is the next bail hearing coming up. See you soon, and my best to Chris. You must have been beside yourself, seeing that happen to her.'

'Well, yes,' said Greg, a little puzzled by Frank's emphasis. Frank hesitated, seemed about to say something else, then waving a farewell turned to go back into court. 'Before you go,' said Greg suddenly, 'someone quoted something at me recently, and I didn't recognise it.' He repeated carefully 'Come what come may, time and the hour runs through the roughest day.'

'Shakespeare,' said Frank. 'The Scottish Play to be precise, so be careful how you quote it. It's supposed to be unlucky.'

'And what would you say it meant?' asked Greg.

'Well, the commonly accepted interpretation is that whatever is going to happen will happen. But personally, I think he meant that no matter how bad things get, they will come to an end eventually. Who quoted it?'

Greg didn't answer. 'I think I prefer your interpretation,' he said, and turned for the exit.

Between Margaret and the court hearing, short as it had been, it was midday by the time Greg joined Jim at the Aylsham barns. Ned and his team were just suiting up, preparatory to getting on site to continue collecting samples of everything. The fire team were putting away their final bits of kit and most of their vehicles had left. The whole area stank of smoke and water ran everywhere around the burnt-out barn and those still relatively undamaged.

'Best you leave this to us,' said Ned curtly. 'There's nothing much you can do at this stage. I'll report as soon as we have anything.'

'I just wanted an overview of the whole area,' replied Greg. 'I've seen the drone footage, but I don't really have a clear idea of how it all fits together.'

Ned waved an arm. 'OK, but you and you only,' he said. 'Keep to my duckboards. And I hope you've got some wellies this time. It's pretty wet.'

Greg retreated to his car, pulled on his wellies, blue overalls and foot covers, then looked around the site. Ned's folk were scattered about, photographing, bagging exhibits, and scrutinizing every inch of the farmyard. Picking his way carefully, Greg made his way over to the remains of the building that had housed the explosive trap. The roof had gone and much of the interior, but most of the walls still stood, water trickling down the corrugated metal and pooling on the ground. In a corner he could see the remains of an old tractor with, mounted on its three-point linkage, the skeleton of a concrete mixer.

'That's what they used to mix the explosive,' said Ned, materialising at his elbow. 'Even now there are still traces inside it. Over in the barn furthest from the centre of the fire, there are still some big bags of ammonium nitrate. What I think was the farm diesel tank went up in the flames.'

'Any sign of the other ingredients we know they used?'

'Not yet, but we've got an explosives dog arriving shortly. Speak of the devil,' he added, as a small van pulled up.

The explosives dog proved to have some attributes in common with his specialist subject. The black and white springer spaniel bounced out of the van with all the pent-up energy of a compressed steel spring, and proceeded to leap around his chauffeur until brought to a quivering heel by a quiet command. His eyes focussed solely on his human partner, the dog submitted quietly to having protective boots fitted to his paws, then sat, still alert in every cell, awaiting the next command.

'Don't know what might be lying around in there,' explained PC Fiona White, brushing short fair hair from her forehead. 'Warm day, isn't it? Right, we'll get going. Turbo, seek.'

The dog shot off, nose to the ground, quartering the space before him. He paused a couple of times in the farmyard, but then moved on. Fiona directed him into the burnt-out barn, and sure enough he signalled by the burnt-out tractor and at a couple of places in the barn.

'Too contaminated,' said Fiona briefly. 'I don't think he'll tell you anything in here you don't already know. OK, we'll do a sweep of the rest of the buildings.'

It was in the barn furthest from the fire remains that Turbo became excited. His speed of both sniffing and running accelerated. Zipping back and forth like a wasp trying to find its way out of a closed window, he hesitated several times then renewed his search.

The barn had clearly been used as housing for cattle. Multiple shoulder height partitions divided the space into cow cubicles, with old dirty straw piled in each. It made for a complex environment for Turbo's nose. With some quiet directions from Fiona, the dog patiently searched each cubicle in turn. At the higher end of the building his sniffing and tail wags intensified and he circled several times before indicating at the top of the passageway between the cubicles.

'There,' said Fiona. 'He's found something.'

'Are you sure?' asked Ned sceptically. 'We've searched in here several times.'

'He's sure,' said Fiona.

As if irritated that he wasn't being taken seriously, Turbo scraped diligently at the straw, which had spilled into the passageway, then sat again and panted at them. Greg moved forward and kicked at the straw, then stopped short.

'Ned, you need to look at this,' he said. 'There's a trapdoor.'

'Good boy, Turbo,' said Fiona, and threw him his reward – his favourite tennis ball.

Forensic exploration of the trapdoor revealed it gave access to a space under the cow shed. Those exploring recoiled from the smell that emanated when the hatch was lifted.

'It's a crawl space giving access to where the muck falls through the slats,' remarked Fiona. 'Maybe this barn was used for pigs once. Slurry would have fallen through and been collected from the lower end. But you wouldn't normally use straw on slats. It bungs them up. This bit of the building was probably out of use for a while. Yes,' she said, inspecting the floor of one of the cow cubicles. 'There's old felting covering the slats under this straw. Be careful of gasses,' she added. 'If there is a lot of fresh muck down there, it'll be releasing methane.'

Careful inspection revealed that, despite the smell, the space was largely empty except for the dry area at the higher end of the barn. There, a space had been cleared and a primitive bed or platform constructed out of pallets and an old sleeping bag. Lowered into the space, once it was checked for safety, Turbo froze and indicated the space at the highest and driest end of the cramped, smelly cavern. Fiona dropped in beside him, followed by Ned. Frustrated, Greg remained at the hatchway, peering in. There was no room for yet another body and the priority had to be preserving evidence, but he itched to be at the front end.

Another quiet command and Turbo rejoined Fiona, sneaking in a lick to her face as it was, now, down at his level. Ned inched forward and took some photos.

'Great dog, Fiona,' he complimented them both. 'I think he's found where the Semtex was stored.'

It was a cardboard box in the corner that was attracting the main force of Turbo's brown gaze. On the floor nearby were some scraps of waxed paper. One fragment was twisted together and secured by tape, for all the world like the bit you chop off a packaged loaf of bread in order to get to the slices.

'Many thanks to Turbo, but we need him out now. And everyone else. I'll get the team down here to see what we can recover.'

Stepping back from the hatchway to make room for Fiona to boost Turbo out, Greg heard a ping from his phone. Missed call. He moved out of the shelter of the barn's metal walls and, waving his phone around, scored a few bars of signal. Enough anyway, to return Margaret's call.

'I've made more progress with Jim's funny buggers,' she said. 'That chap Newton is here again and says he has some information to share. Can you get back here? He's refusing to send it by email. Says it has to be face to face and I'd like you to hear it straight from him.'

'On my way,' replied Greg.

# 22

## Secrets and lies

Dashing to the chief super's office, Greg was waylaid by George, with 'Mildred' as ever in tow. Despite his rush, Greg had time to notice that today's cardigan was an unpleasant shade of blush pink, distinctly reminiscent of the old-style ladies' underwear he remembered from shops even his granny would walk past with a disparaging sniff.

'Got you an answer,' said George, with the closest to a tone of triumph that Greg ever remembered hearing from him. 'It was tricky, but I won't bother you with the scientific details. I know you're not interested and you wouldn't understand them anyway.'

Swallowing this insult to his intelligence and education without a murmur, Greg waited for the punchline.

'Suffice it to say, we've identified the body found in the locked store room. It was a chemist named Jan Littleboys.'

'Hang on,' said Greg sharply. 'This is the first I've heard

about the store room being locked.'

George was offended. 'Take that up with your CSIs,' he snapped. 'The fact is, that beyond reasonable doubt we can identify this body as that of Jan Littleboys, and we're prepared to state that in court.' He snapped the file in his hands together. 'OK, we're done here. We'll be on our way back to Bradford. Come on M.' And they both bustled away.

'Thank you,' shouted Greg after them. 'Great work! I'm most grateful for your help.'

George waved the file without turning and kept going.

'Oh dear,' Greg said to his only audience, Phil Knight, who had popped out of the adjacent ops room. 'I think I've offended them again.'

'Wouldn't worry, Boss,' he said. 'That's their default state.'

'So what's this about the storeroom being locked?'

'That's what Forensics are saying. They've been taking a closer look at what's left of the door, which admittedly isn't much, and at the material surrounding it. Their report is that although the door is gone, much of the lock survived and the bolt was across. Moreover, they also think a metal-framed chair was wedged under the handle from the outside.'

'How sure are they?'

'I asked them that,' said Phil with some satisfaction. 'The lock, more than seventy per cent, the chair, more like fifty fifty, but taking the two elements together, it certainly looks like the poor woman was deliberately trapped in there.'

'And George has confirmed it was Jan Littleboys. Pass that on will you, Phil, and concentrate efforts on her now. We need to know why she was a target. Her past associations, friends, enemies. You know the deal.'

'I'll pass it on, Boss.'

'I'll be with you shortly. I have to meet with the chief super first.'

Greg wasn't surprised to find a frosty silence in the room. Margaret was ostentatiously consulting her online diary and DI Newton was sitting ignored in a corner. Sarah was also present, and flashed Greg a warm smile.

'Ah, DCI Geldard,' said Margaret, and Greg wasn't sure whether the acid in her tone was aimed at him for keeping her waiting, or Newton for being difficult. 'As DI Newton has apparently not yet moved into the twenty-first century with its digital facilities,' – Greg hid a smile as the source of her irritation became clear – 'perhaps he would now kindly share his information.'

Newton cleared his throat and, as so often before, ran a hand through his hair. 'This is strictly on a need-to-know basis,' he began. Greg shifted in his chair, but thought the better of interrupting and waited in silence. 'As you know, we've had Professor Lai under surveillance,' he began, paused as Margaret sniffed significantly, then went on, 'The reason for the surveillance was suspected involvement in animal rights activity.'

There was a pregnant pause then, 'And it didn't occur to you to mention this either before the attack when threats to the laboratory were reported, or even after? Jesus wept, which planet are you people on?' It was evident Margaret was definitely not happy.

Having anticipated this reaction, Newton continued calmly, 'When threats were reported, we stepped up surveillance, but there were good reasons why we couldn't release more information to you at that time.'

Margaret snorted and Greg asked, 'Which were?'

Newton hesitated. 'This can't go further than this room. We have an undercover agent embedded in the group involved. Too much information released at the wrong time would have put them at risk.'

'While too *little* information at the right time resulted in eight deaths and the destruction of a government laboratory,' almost snarled Margaret. 'Now is not the right time for a post mortem, but believe me when I say this, DI Newton, I *will* be insisting on a full enquiry. Someone ballsed this up and we in Norfolk have been playing catch-up ever since. So start cooperating now, or you will join your bosses on the firing line.

'Where is Professor Lai now? What precisely do you know about her involvement in animal rights, and what other information do you have, whether from your undercover agent or elsewhere, on other activists on the staff of the laboratory. Lai didn't do this on her own. What else do you know?'

Voices were rising, so when Greg chipped in quietly he immediately commanded attention. 'What do you know about Jack Haigh, Pat Nichols and Jan Littleboys? We already have sound evidence that the first two were involved in the bomb attack. The third has been identified as the victim found in C Block and seems to have been trapped there deliberately. All three worked in Professor Lai's team. So, what do you know?'

For the first time, Newton looked uncomfortable. 'All three have a history of animal rights activism. I can brief you further, with some limitations to protect our officer.'

Margaret slammed the file in her hands on the desk.

'I do not believe it,' she pronounced. 'And you let them carry on working at the lab without giving us any sort of heads up!'

Greg intervened again, although he too felt the anger rising as he spoke. 'Where is Lai now?'

'We don't know. We lost her when the bomb went off and it seems she hasn't been in touch with any of her usual contacts in the movement.'

'So she's loose and out of contact.'

'So it seems.'

'Does your officer have a way of contacting her?'

'No. At least, not one that is working. She, they have tried.'

Greg noted the slip without comment and Margaret's eyes glittered.

'OK. Back to good honest policing,' he said drily. And left the room.


Back in the Ops room, Greg glanced round and caught Phil's eye again. 'Bring me up to date with what we have on Jan Littleboys,' he said.

Phil picked up his note book and headed for the whiteboard. He pointed to a small photo taped to the top of the panel. It was cut from what looked like a group at a staff party. A slight woman of medium height was in the centre of the picture, raising what looked like a glass of cider to the camera. Sitting on the grass in front of her was a man Greg recognised as Jack Haigh.

'Jan Littleboys, aged forty-two, single, lived in a flat in Norwich. Worked at the lab for the past twelve years, the last three as head of section in analytical chemistry. The colleagues we've spoken to describe her as friendly but not warm. A bit of a loner. Liked, but not top of anyone's list for a night out. This photo is unusual in that there are very few of her around, and this is the only one depicting her at a social occasion. They say it was taken at a staff barbecue last summer.'

Greg studied the photo. 'It sounds a lonely life,' he commented. 'But perhaps she liked it like that.'

'She was known for working long hours and coming in at the weekend when necessary to process samples. She'd worked fairly closely with Lai for the past four years, but others describe the relationship as professional rather than cordial.'

Unnoticed by the two men, Sarah had followed Greg into the room and was standing behind them. 'Do we think it was Lai who locked her in the storage room?'

Greg jumped, taken by surprise. 'Sarah,' he exclaimed. 'I didn't realise you were there. It has to be a strong possibility. But if so, frankly it gives me the shivers.'

'Why?' Sarah looked puzzled.

'Because of what it implies about why she was chosen to die. How ruthless do you have to be to lock a colleague in a small room to burn alive, just because she's the right height and weight to provide you with a lookalike corpse?'

Sarah made no reply, and sat down at the nearest terminal to log on.

'Sarah,' said Greg, addressing the back of her head, 'what else have you managed to discover from our friend Newton.'

'Not much more than you know already,' she said, looking at her keyboard.

'Anything you can find out would be helpful,' he said. 'Particularly whatever intelligence they have about Lai.'

'I think he already told you all they're prepared to say.'

'But I need to know more. I need to know what sort of

a woman she is. What motivates her. What she feels strongly about. What she cares about. If we're going to find her, we need to know her better. She's out there on the run somewhere, and if we're going to intercept her, we need to know where to look. Surely none of that is going to be secret. Just ask him, Sarah.'

Greg went over to the team studying video footage and collating data from the laboratory HR systems.

Sarah looked round at Phil and raised an eyebrow. 'He's getting a bit touchy-feely, isn't he,' she remarked coolly.

'You don't agree the information would be useful?' asked Phil, surprised.

'I think we need to concentrate on hard data, mobile phone locations, ANPR and the like. Checks on airports and ports. Not how people feel and think.'

Phil shrugged and walked away to rejoin Greg.

'What's bothering Sarah,' asked Greg quietly.

'Well, if you don't know, I'm sure I don't, Boss,' said Phil with a grin. 'Take no notice. In the meantime, we get stuck into good, honest, old-style detection just like you said.'

Greg glanced at his watch and cursed. 'Damn it, I'm due with that counsellor any minute. I'll be back in an hour or so. After that, I hope we can all go home and start again fresh in the morning.' As he turned to leave, his phone rang.

'Chris,' he exclaimed. 'How are you? Where're you ringing from?' A pause and then, 'I hope you got properly signed off! Well, thank God for that anyway. Is your mum stopping?' Another pause, then as he reached the door he said, 'I'll drop in on my way home. See you then.'

As Greg left the room, Phil turned to look at Sarah. She sat rigidly at her terminal then turned and said, 'Let's get some proper work done then.'

Phil followed Greg from the room. Outside he walked straight into Jim Henning.

'I gather we're to have a quick catch up when the boss comes back from his counselling,' said Jim.

'That's right.'

Jim reached for the door and Phil stopped him with a hand on his arm.

'Sarah's in there,' he said.

'And Greg's put his foot in it again?'

'That's right,' said Phil again. 'When are you going to tell him?'

'Tell him what?'

'Come off it. You know what I mean. For a perceptive man he has a huge blind spot.'

Jim leaned on the door frame, idly using it to scratch an itch between his shoulder blades. 'Bit tricky,' he said.

'Will only get worse.'

'OK I'll think about it.'


About halfway into his counselling session, bored witless by looking into his own head, Greg decided to see if a change of subject might be more fruitful.

'Can I ask you some questions now?' he demanded.

Recognising a familiar side track, Neil smiled and leaned back in his chair. His grizzled curly beard was cut short, his hair likewise, the space between occupied by warm brown eyes and a hooked nose. The eyes were currently focussed very closely on Greg, who was lounging rather elaborately on the sofa opposite, one arm trailing along the back.

'OK, go ahead. Let's see where that takes us.'

'We have a key suspect on the run. For thirty-odd years she's been a respected scientist with an unblemished record and no history of activism, although for some reason currently not being disclosed to me, she did come to the attention of the funny buggers. Sorry, that's what we call…'

Neil waved a hand. 'Yes, I know who you mean by the funny buggers,' he said. 'I take it you're talking about Professor Lai?'

'That's right. I feel I know very little about her. Not least because the people who worked with her seem to know very little about her too, notwithstanding the years they're supposed to have known her. All anyone says is that she was quiet, firm when she needed to be, didn't socialise, didn't make friends, didn't express opinions.' Greg heaved a frustrated sigh. 'She's a blank. A conundrum. And I need to know something more about her if I'm going to find her. I can't work out where to look for her if I don't know her. I can't think like her if I can't get inside her head.' He looked up at Neil, who was thinking that this was the most interesting, most revealing comment Greg had made all session.

'Do you usually get inside their heads?' he asked.

'I try. But now you're answering a question with a question again.' Greg swung his arm off the back of the sofa and rested both elbows on his knees. 'How about an opinion?'

'The first thing that occurs to me,' replied Neil, 'is that you are describing a very isolated person. Possibly a lonely person. Not necessarily so. She may have a very rich inner world that more than compensates for her lack of human attachment, but isolation would seem to be a factor. If she were my client, I would be trying to answer three questions. Why does she choose isolation? What's happened in her life that makes her that way? And what gives her satisfaction or a sense of fulfilment?'

Greg sighed, frustrated. 'And those are just the questions I can't get the answers to.'

'I'd try the funny buggers again,' recommended Neil. 'Remember, they're not the enemy, although it may sometimes feel like it. Find a way to ask the questions that they *can* answer, and I think you'll find they're quite eager to help.' There was a pause and then Neil added, 'Don't think I can't recognise a distraction ploy when I see one, but if it helps I'll play along. Feel free to come back to me if you get some answers you'd like another view on.'

Greg grinned. 'OK. I'm not ungrateful,' he said. 'I just don't find navel gazing comes naturally.'

'Maybe not, and I think you have some pretty good coping mechanisms already, not least a network of friends who share a lot of experience. All I'd say is, don't be afraid to ask for help when you need it. You might also benefit from thinking through some of your feelings for your colleagues,' he added, almost as an afterthought.

'Meaning?'

'Meaning that feelings can creep up on you, and be none the worse for that. But sometimes it's wise to take stock. We all need someone to go to when things get tough. Well,' he amended, 'most of us anyway. It sounds as though your Professor Lai might be an exception. Setting that on one side, the difference between coping well and coping badly is sometimes as simple as knowing the right person to go to.'

Greg looked down at his hands. He nearly asked, 'Meaning?'

again, then thought better of it. He knew what Neil meant. What he didn't know was how he felt, and he wasn't ready to discuss that with anyone yet. 'I'll take your advice about going back to the funny buggers,' he said, as he headed for the door.

'And I'll see you again in a couple of days. Same sort of time?' asked Neil. Then, as Greg looked round with surprise on his face, he added, 'Don't come the naive with me, DCI Geldard. You didn't imagine this was a one session event I'm sure.'

Back in the ops room, Greg found the place empty except for Jim and Sarah.

'I told them all to go home,' said Jim.

'Good. I hoped you would. Before I sign off for tonight though, is Newton still around, Sarah?'

'I believe so,' she said without turning round.

'Then let's have another quick chat with him. Jim? Sarah? You OK to stick around a bit?'

They both nodded and Sarah added, 'I'll ask him to come in here, shall I?'

'Yes, please.'

While they waited, Greg occupied himself flicking through his emails and messages. Sarah watched him, went to speak a couple of times, then cleared her throat and said nothing. There was silence in the room when DI Newton joined them. He swung a chair into the space behind Sarah and sat across it wrong way round, leaning his arms on the back.

'What can I do for you?' he asked.

Greg looked up from his notes. 'Look,' he said. 'I think, no, I *know*, we got off on the wrong foot, and I'm sure you've got a very clear impression about how our chief super feels, but I'd like us to start over. We're all on the same side here, or should be, and we have a shared problem. Fact is, we've a key suspect loose in the wind. We urgently need to lay hands on her. I assume we agree so far. I have very little information on what she's like, as she seems to have been a major enigma as far as her colleagues are concerned, and she doesn't seem to have had any friends. You have information, some of which you don't want to share with me for whatever reason. I'll have to take it on trust that you have the balance of public interest right. I get that. But there must be information you *can* share and, to be blunt, I know so little I don't even know enough to ask the right questions. So, I'm trusting you to tell me whatever you can about Lai, whatever might help me lay hands on her.'

Newton looked away at the corner of the room, then back. 'OK, I'll do my best. I have a basic dossier I can share and I'll forward it to you. Born in 1964, she came to the UK from Hong Kong as a student in 1982. She studied chemistry at London. Then did a PhD in York and after that took a research post in London. You know she worked at Porton Down before coming to NASA here in Norwich.'

'Do we know anything about her family? Or relationships?'

'Parents dead. Father died in the late seventies, mother about ten years ago. No siblings. No significant others, at least not since the late nineties when it appears she was briefly engaged for a while to a Tom Bentley.'

'Has anyone spoken to him recently?'

'Not recently.'

'Then we need to,' said Greg to Jim. 'Can you put him on your list?'

'It's been a while,' protested Newton. 'His knowledge is not exactly current.'

'But he's the first person anyone has mentioned as having been close to Lai. He's worth a chat on that basis alone. What else can you tell me? For example, what about political affiliations, or radicalisation? Anything on that?'

'Only that she was part of a group involved in action against slaughterhouses a few years ago.'

'And that's the only inkling we have about her interests in animal rights?'

'Yes.'

'How do we know that?'

'And that's where you tread into questions I can't answer,' replied Newton.

'But it's good intelligence? She was definitely involved?'

'Yes.'

'What about Jack Haigh and Pat Nichols?' asked Jim. 'Were they part of the same group?'

'Haigh was. We don't know about the other.'

'How did she get involved?' asked Greg.

'I've no details. When she came to our attention she was already involved, although more as an organiser than as frontline activist.'

'We'll have another chat with Haigh too. OK, all jobs for tomorrow. Off home, folks. We'll pick this up in the morning. And if anything else occurs to you, please let us know. You can contact me via Sarah here.'

Sarah caught up with Greg as he walked briskly down the corridor towards the car park. 'Fancy a bite to eat before home?' she asked.

'Sorry, Sarah. I've got one other visit to make before home. See you in the morning,' and he dashed off, pulling car keys out of his pocket as he went.

As Sarah stopped following and stood irresolute, Newton caught her up. 'I'll take you up on that,' he said. 'I'm starving. Can you recommend anywhere?'

'What? Oh, yes.' She seemed a little distracted but pulled herself together. 'Yes, that would be nice. There's a pub in Wymondham. I'll show you the way.'

Almost an hour later Greg was pulling up outside a terraced cottage in Repps. On the edge of the village, it stood in a quiet cul de sac opposite a row of almost identical neighbours. There was no room outside, so he turned his car and left it slightly dubiously parked close to the corner. Walking back to the cottage he noted the colourful tubs surrounding Chris's car in the small front garden. He recognised, with a grin, Chris's distinctive colour sense in the choice of flowers.

The door opened as he raised his hand to knock. He was not surprised to see it was Chris behind it. 'Your mum gone home then?' he asked as he followed her through the door into the living room beyond.

'That's right. She's always keen to help out,' replied Chris, 'but we get on better if we take each other in small doses. And there's nothing wrong with me that won't mend in a day or so.'

She sat on one of a pair of grey leather sofas and indicated the one opposite to Greg. 'Take a seat. What's happening on the case?'

As Greg sat, there was flutter of substantial wings and Tally, the African Grey, arrived on the back of the sofa. She sidled along and took his ear gently in her beak.

'There, she's not forgotten you,' said Chris with satisfaction.

By now getting used to this attention, Greg turned his head only slightly cautiously and took in the room. To his surprise, it was a quiet blend of neutral colours, all tints of grey and white.

Chris, watching him, grinned suddenly. 'What's the matter, Greg?' she asked. 'Expecting everything to be orange and pink?'

'Well, yes,' he confessed. 'At least, more colourful than this. Don't get me wrong,' he added hastily. 'I like it. I like it very much. It's restful.' He turned his eyes from the decor and back to Chris. 'How do you get to be so surprising?' he asked.

'Don't ask me!' She leaned forward to the bottle of red wine already open on the table in front of her. 'Will you have a glass?' She waved the bottle.

Greg hesitated. 'Perhaps just a small one,' he said. 'I haven't eaten yet.'

'That's sorted too. Mum's best beef casserole is in the oven and she left a salad in the fridge. There's plenty for two. If you'd like some, Greg,' she added a little shyly.

'I'd love some,' he said, and a warm smile lit up his face. 'But can I bring you up to date on the case. I'd like your opinion on our missing professor.'

'I'd expect nothing less,' replied Chris. 'Tell me what we've got while I dish up the food. We'll eat in the kitchen.' As she passed behind his sofa, she rested a hand on the shoulder not currently occupied by her parrot. 'Then you're going home, Greg,' she said, 'or you'll be dead on your feet tomorrow.'

# 23

## Inside her head

The phone call came as Greg was driving to Wymondham.

'Found Tom Bentley,' said Jim succinctly. 'He works at King's, Cambridge.'

'That's handy,' said Greg. 'Is he there today?'

'Yes. And he's agreed to see us this morning.'

'In that case I'll go straight there. I'm on the A11 now. Can you meet me there?'

'Yes. And he says to park on the cobbles in front of the college and report to the Porter's Lodge. He'll warn them to expect us. Oh, and mind the rising bollards, Greg.'

'The what?'

'The bollards that leap out of the road to trap the unwary and rip their sumps off. They take their one-way street systems seriously in Cambridge.'

It was after nine by the time Greg was parking warily on the cobbles are per instructions. Somewhat to his relief, the feral bollards seemed to have been replaced by CCTV. No doubt also expensive if ignored, but less so than a lump of metal through your engine bay. The cobbles seemed a strange place to park, but Jim's car was already there and the porters were relaxed about it. Following their meticulous directions, Greg and Jim found Dr Tom Bentley's rooms without difficulty. The outer wooden door was standing open, which Jim said was known in Cambridge as an indication the occupant was happy to see visitors. The inner door was ajar too, and 'come in' shouted a tall, thin man sporting whiskers and a hairy tweed jacket. 'This lot are just finished,' he said, as three students continued picking up iPads and papers. 'Essays in by Friday,' he reminded them as they left with curious backward glances.

'DCI Geldard and DI Henning,' said Greg by way of introduction as they showed their warrant cards.

'And how can I help?' asked Dr Bentley, sitting down again at his desk and waving to the newly vacated chairs. 'As I told DI Henning when we spoke on the phone, it's a very long time since I had any contact with Lily Lai.'

'That's a good example of why we need to talk to you,' said Greg, getting a notebook out. 'You're the first person who's referred to her using her first name. Do you mind if we record our conversation by the way Dr Bentley?'

'Call me Tom. No, not at all. Strictly speaking it's her second name, of course. The Chinese give their family name first and their personal name second, and hers was Liling. But I always knew her as Lily Lai.'

'When was it you last saw her?'

'In the distance at a conference, it must have been five or six years ago. But I haven't seen her to speak to for much longer.'

'We understand you were engaged to her once?'

'Yes, but we broke it off in 1990.'

'We?' asked Jim.

'Well, she did, but it was pretty much consensual. We both knew we'd come to the end of the road.'

Greg looked at Jim. 'We're trying to understand Professor Lai a bit better,' he said. 'What sort of person was she? How would you characterise her?' he added as Tom Bentley appeared to be hesitating.

'Angry,' he said after a further pause. 'Mainly, angry. That's what broke us up in the end.'

'Angry about what?'

'Mostly, angry about how she was treated. She was a bright and beautiful girl, and she knew it. She could run rings round lots of her fellow students, but they didn't give her the respect she felt she deserved. Even in London back then, there were some sections of society that were pretty racist and sexist. I'll give you one stupid example. Quite a lot of the ethnic-minority students were non-drinkers. And, of course, many didn't have the same social networks as the rest of us, so a lot of them didn't patronise the student union bar, they mainly used one particular canteen.' He looked up at the police officers. 'I'm ashamed to say it was often referred to as 'WogSoc'. And I'm even more ashamed that I and others didn't challenge that attitude.

'Lily fell foul of both the racist and the sexist contingents and she wasn't one to turn the other cheek. And really, why should she have to? She was genuinely badly treated by some ignorant idiots, and instead of ignoring them she took it really personally. After a while everything that didn't go her way was, in her mind, because she was Chinese and a woman. She believed the world was tipped against her. Sometimes she may have been right. Other times, for example when she was beaten fair and square to a new appointment, she was wrong. But by then, she was convinced everything was because of prejudice. She was so angry it coloured everything she did or said, and I couldn't deal with it. When I suggested we should take a break from each other she instantly threw my ring at me and accused me too of being racist. I never saw her to speak to again.

'Look, I'm not the right person to talk to about this,' he added. 'I'm a privileged white male with a great job and a home in what's seen by many as a bastion of white privilege. Of course, I think I've earned my place here, but who's to say others wouldn't have been as well qualified if they'd had my chances? And I think that unless you've experienced prejudice you can have no real idea how corrosive even small slights can be.

'So, when I say Lily Lai was angry, it's because in my perception she was. Fuelled by anger and consumed by hate. But was she justified? I have no idea. I'm not in a position to judge.'

More questions and more conversation resulted in going over old ground. Disappointed, Greg and Jim retreated to a coffee bar for a chat.

'We need to talk to someone who's met her more recently,' fretted Jim.

'Absolutely, but don't discount what we've learned. It might be the beginning of understanding what made her who she is. Neil, the counsellor, said she sounded very isolated. That makes sense now. Maybe she isolated herself rather than risk more insults. And maybe the anger goes some way to explain why she did what she did. I read somewhere that for terrorism to exist you need three things: a supply of motivated offenders, an available target, and absence of someone minding the store.

'Well we had the target, there clearly was no one minding the store, for which we partly have the funny buggers to thank, and as for a motivated offender, hate would seem a pretty good motivator to me.'

'But that doesn't explain why this target, or why this cause.'

'No, it doesn't. Perhaps there was an element of hitting back at the establishment she felt slighted her, and animal rights was just an excuse. Perhaps there was an element, too, of look how clever I am. You had no idea I would do what I did, and so effectively.'

'But that's all guess work.'

'Yes, and will stay that way until we speak to the lady herself. Back to Norwich I think and a chat with Jack Haigh.' Greg looked round for the waiter and the bill.

'One other thing,' said Jim, looking as awkward as he felt. 'And please don't shoot the messenger on this.'

Greg turned back, amused. 'What on earth have you been deputed to tell me? Don't say it's BO and no one dared mention it.'

'No, but I couldn't be more embarrassed if it was,' confessed Jim. 'So please take this in the spirit it's meant. It's Sarah.'

'Has she got BO? No, sorry, Jim. Come on, tell me what's bothering you and I promise not to shoot.'

'She's carrying a torch for you, and I don't think you've noticed,' said Jim in a rush. 'But believe me when I say everyone else has. It's affecting her work and it's making her pretty snitty about Chris.'

'Because?'

'Come on, Greg, don't make me say it.'

Greg was silent. 'You're right,' he said at last. 'I hadn't really been paying attention to Sarah. I'm an idiot! But Jim, come on. I'm an ordinary bloke. I don't go around assuming everyone's got a crush on me.'

'I haven't, if that's any comfort,' replied Jim. Then, as Greg broke into a reluctant grin, 'As far as I know it's just the two of them, and the competition goes back to the naming of the kitten. From Sarah's point of view, Chris seems to be winning.'

There was another silence.

'Jim, this goes no further than us I hope.'

'Of course not.'

'Well, I'm not willing to talk about Chris. But I'll think about what you said about Sarah.' He looked up. 'Sorry Jim. I'm not being defensive. Or perhaps I am. Heavens, the dust hasn't settled yet on Isabelle. Also, as I'm sure you're thinking, Chris is a colleague, even a subordinate, although it's hard to think of her as subordinate to anyone.'

Jim smiled an answering smile. 'True,' he said, 'but...'

'Yes, but she is. Jim, will you trust me on this. If or when I think there's an issue, I'll talk to Margaret.'

'Of course I trust you. And sorry for raising it.'

'No. I'm grateful for your heads up on Sarah. Although how I address that without seeming to have the biggest head in Norfolk I do not know.'

'Happy to leave that with you, Boss,' grinned Jim. 'Now, if you're going to treat me to that coffee, you need to pay and we can get on.'

At HMP Norwich, Jack was finding time hung heavy. Moreover, his cell mates weren't pleased with him. The last few nights the old nightmare had returned. He'd woken sweating and shouting, terrified that his calf was going to be killed before his eyes again, and there was nothing he could do to stop it. There'd been muttering among his cell mates about broken sleep, and one of them had gone so far as to complain to a warder. As the only solution Jack could see was to stay awake as long as possible, he was now dog-tired and on edge, so much so that a chat with the police was almost a welcome break. Almost. He entered the interview room with some trepidation and was relieved to find his solicitor already there. On the police side of the table he recognised DCI Greg Geldard and DI Jim Henning.

'The big guns today I see,' he commented as he sat down.

For their part, Greg and Jim were interested to note that although Jack was clearly coping better than many in the prison environment, he still looked grey with exhaustion. Greg looked down at his notes. Nightmares. Not sleeping. Complaints from cell mates. All feedback from the prison officer he'd chatted to on the way in. There was an interesting resonance with the list of red flags Neil had given him. He tried to remember some of the others.

The silence was stretching out and the solicitor shifted in his seat. Greg took the cue, found the little video he was looking for on his iPad and turned it to face Jack. Jack looked, focussed and recoiled.

'For the sake of the tape,' said Greg in a conversational tone, 'I'm showing Mr Haigh the video of the explosion a few days ago at the bomb-making site near Aylsham.'

The solicitor craned to see the screen and asked, 'What has this to do with my client?'

Jack was looking sick, and his hand shook slightly as he

reached for his murky prison coffee.

Greg turned the iPad back towards him and tapped, then turned it back towards Jack. 'And this,' he added, 'was a video taken on a phone camera shortly after the car bomb went off at the NASA laboratory.'

Even on the small screen and through the shakes of the phone, the picture of a long low building well alight and flames leaping off into the sky stood out clearly. Whoever was holding the phone panned across the scene slowly. Jack made an inarticulate noise and retched.

'I must object,' said the solicitor, but Greg spoke over him.

'I'm sorry, Jack,' he said. 'I can see these scenes upset you.' He closed the iPad and leaned forward. 'But that being so,' he said, 'why won't you talk to me about what happened? We know you arranged for the car carrying the bomb to be parked in exactly the right place to do the most damage. But to be frank, I'm struggling to believe that you intended there to be casualties, at any level, let alone on the scale we saw here. It just doesn't fit with anything we know about you.'

There was a silence while Jack continued to stare at the table.

'Your mother agrees with me,' added Greg conversationally and as Jack looked up sharply he said, 'What was it she said, Jim?'

'As I recall,' said Jim, 'she said that, after what had happened to his pet calf, she wouldn't have been surprised if Jack had been arrested for attacking a slaughterhouse or making trouble outside a place using animals in their research, but she couldn't see him deliberately hurting people.'

'What did happen to your calf?' asked Greg. His voice

was quiet and after a long pause, Jack replied, as though from a distance, 'The government killed her.'

Another long pause, and after a glance at Greg, Jim went on, 'We now also have evidence that someone deliberately shut one of their colleagues in a locked storeroom and left them to burn, for no better reason than that they were a good match in physical type and might be misidentified. Thus throwing a red herring in our path. Clearly this can't have been you, Jack. No one would ever confuse a short, slight woman with a tall, well-muscled man. Not even when badly burned. Moreover, we think this must have happened after you left the laboratory.

'Who?' asked Jack.

'Well, there's the question.' Greg rejoined the chat. 'It seems the victim was Jan Littleboys, whom I think you knew. And we're pretty sure the perpetrator was a Professor Lai, whom you also knew.'

'But the Professor is Chinese,' protested Jack. 'No one would ever confuse her with Jan.'

'Not in the flesh,' replied Greg, 'but all we had left was a burned skeleton and, but for the sharp eyes of our forensic anthropologist, that would have passed as Professor Lai.'

As Jack looked sick again, Greg added, 'Think about it. I told you when we first met that you'd been used. Now we know you were used by a monster, a ruthless woman who would stop at nothing and cared nothing for her victims. Don't you think it's time you helped us catch her, before she does this again? She's already done it twice with eight dead already, to say nothing of those left mutilated and burned.'

To give him time to think, Jim said, 'Let's have more coffees. Everyone?' They all nodded and Jim went to the door and knocked. 'Any chance of more coffees?' he asked when the door opened, and a little while later a tray with four takeaway coffees appeared.

'Interview recommencing,' said Greg for the benefit of the tape. 'Jack, how well did you know Jan Littleboys?'

'She was my lab section leader,' replied Jack, looking at the table, 'and she was also my cell lead in the Movement.'

Greg looked up sharply as the solicitor choked on his coffee, and rising said, 'I need a private conversation with my client.'

'No you don't' said Jack. 'Enough is enough. I'll help where I can. It's the only way I'll get any peace.' Then looking at Greg and Jim he added, 'I genuinely don't know much that will help. But I will answer your questions.'

'The Movement?' asked Greg.

'That's what we called it. We started, at least I started as part of Compassion in World Farming, but they were too tame. Too passive. Not enough was happening quickly enough. So I was recruited into the Movement. It was their suggestion I came to work in the lab, and I was part of a cell that included Pat Nichols and Jan Littleboys. I didn't know anyone else.'

'Did you know Lily Lai was part of the Movement?'

'No. I told you, I only knew Pat and Jan.'

'What about the person who recruited you at the beginning?' asked Jim.

'That was a friend. Nothing to do with the lab.'

'We still need their name.' Jim had his pen poised.

'Meg. Meg Smith. But I don't know for sure it was her real name. Some of the Movement leaders had aliases. She may have had one too. But she had nothing to do with this,' insisted Jack. 'I haven't seen her since I started work here.'

'Who suggested you get a job here.'

Jack hesitated. 'That was Meg,' he admitted reluctantly, 'but she had nothing else to do with the lab. Nothing.'

A long interview, broken by toilet breaks (thanks to the coffee), elicited nothing much new. At last Greg and Jim had to admit defeat.

'He really doesn't know much else,' said Jim.

'No,' agreed Greg, 'and he hardly knew Lai at all. But we do at least have some confirmation about Jan Littleboys and the existence of the 'Movement'. Now we need to track down the original recruiter, Meg.'

'Something else occurs to me,' added Jim. 'Back before this all blew up, literally, Chris found a problem with their HR systems, remember? Maybe we should look into that. It might lead us to another cell.'

'Great idea. Thanks, Jim. I wish Chris was back. I miss her help.'

As they left the prison, Jack Haigh's solicitor was just getting into his car. 'Just give me a minute,' said Greg. 'I'll be with you in a sec.

'Hi,' he greeted the solicitor. 'Don't take this the wrong way, but have you considered seeking counselling for your client?'

The solicitor paused, one leg in the car, the rest of him somewhat awkwardly outside it. 'No,' he said. 'What do you have on your mind?'

'Well, I'm no expert, but I was wondering if he had PTSD. The specialist who saw him at the N&N thought so. It might be worth getting him checked over again.'

'What's in it for you?' asked the solicitor suspiciously.

'Nothing, except I suppose that anything that keeps folk

from reoffending saves us hassle in the long run. Look,' he said, 'I'm probably talking out of turn, but your Jack seems to me like someone led astray who was already vulnerable. What he did, well, it seems to me more likely stupid than evil. You don't need to comment,' he added in a hurry, 'but I do think he has a few problems.'

Back at Wymondham, Jim made a beeline for the ops room and the team that had been chasing down missing lab staff members.

'I've a new task for you,' he announced amid a torrent of, mostly mock, groans. He went on, 'I need you to look out that work Chris did before the bomb attack, on NASA HR systems. She found some dodgy processes and...'

'And it's probably worth following them up.' A woman brightly dressed in a lime green top and yellow jeans stood up at the far end of the room. 'I'm on it,' she said, with composure and an element of triumph.

Jim gaped for a second, then reached for his sunglasses. 'Glad I had these handy,' he said, putting them on with a flourish. 'What the devil are you doing here? I thought you were signed off for at least a week.'

'Oh ha bloody ha,' Chris responded to the sunglasses. 'There's only so much Australian soap a woman can take. Besides, there's nothing the matter with me time won't fix, and time's pretty much the same here as anywhere else.'

'Does Greg know you're back?'

'Probably not. I haven't seen him yet. Now, you were asking about what I found from the HR files before the explosion.' She beckoned him over to her screen. 'Essentially it was just this. All staff clearances, whether security, right to work, or even just standard references, were all signed off by this authority – known as HRAdmin2. The problem, as I saw it back then, was twofold. First, anyone could use that ID if they knew the password. And second, there was no second check. Provided HRAdmin2 signed off an appointment, it went ahead.'

'Can the IT forensic team find out who did use the password?'

'We're on the same page, Jim. I already asked them that very question. And the answer is, in normal circumstances no, because all the systems went up in smoke with the first bomb blast. But we're talking about a government lab here, and their files were backed up off site every month.'

'And the last back up was?' asked Jim, catching on fast.

'The last backup was only four days before the blast. So we have everything up to the last four days. The team are getting access now.'

'Is access a problem?'

'Apparently not. This isn't Porton Down we're talking about. Even the funny buggers aren't blocking this, so the only limiting factor at present is how fast they can narrow down the millions of pieces of data to the ones we want. The fact that access to HR files was strictly controlled does help.'

Pausing to lock his car, Greg had been a few yards behind Jim and was immediately distracted by a familiar figure with an already familiar beard.

'Neil,' he shouted, and speeded up down the corridor, pocketing the car keys as he went. 'Can I pick your brains for a moment? I need some specialist, psychological advice.'

Neil checked his watch as he replied. 'Yes, if you like. I've half an hour to spare if that's any use? Let's go in here,' turning back into the room he'd just left.

They sat down in the usual ersatz chairs and Neil smiled. 'I always boggle at how uncomfortable these can be,' he said. 'Now, how can I help?'

'I'm looking for some insight into anger and hate,' replied Greg, and Neil's bushy eyebrows rose. 'It's not something I have a lot of personal familiarity with,' went on Greg. 'In fact, while it's not hard to make a list of people I don't like much, or who irritate the hell out of me, I can't think of anyone I actually hate and very few who can make me angry. So when I'm told my probable perpetrator was full of anger and fuelled by hate, I'm at a bit of a loss.'

'You haven't come across it before,' asked Neil.

'Not much. Most criminals are greedy, selfish, narcissistic, and often a bit stupid. Not many of them are described as filled with hate. But then, I've never previously had a lot of contact with terrorists or terrorism and I'm coming to understand more fully that it's a different kind of crime. Not to say that terrorists aren't also greedy, narcissistic et cetera et cetera as well, but the hate is different.'

'It's interesting you link anger and hate in that way,' said Neil slowly. 'And very perceptive I'd say. I've read a few papers on the subject. They describe hate as a form of generalised anger, and as the most destructive phenomenon in the history of human nature, not least because it has the goal of eliminating its target. They also talk about us hating people or groups not because of what they do, but because of what they are and that hate can be both reassuring and self-protective, because it's simple and self-justifying.'

'You mean, because I hate them, they are by definition hateful, and I'm justified in ridding the world of them.'

'At its simplest, yes.'

'So what shifts irritation into anger and then hate?'

'Ah, now there I'd need to move from generalities to the specific. I can tell you that it's a well-observed phenomenon and not an unusual pattern, but I can't extrapolate from the general to the individual. Especially when I haven't even met them.'

'But a pattern of repeated, nasty slights and hurts, the sort of thing we'd call a hate crime today,' Greg paused. 'I'm back with hate again,' he said thoughtfully. 'Hate creating hate.'

'One thing I can add,' said Neil. 'Typically hate is not about change, it's about getting rid. Anger might instigate action to change something that created the anger. But hate perceives change as being impossible. So the angry person who has been assaulted might take action to make sure the assault can't happen again. The hater believes that nothing will change the behaviour of the people who hurt them. The only answer is to rid the world of them all.'

# 24

## Following the trail

To say Greg was surprised to see Chris back at work was an understatement. And it was no exaggeration to say that coming face to face with Chris and Sarah simultaneously, in view of his recent conversation with Jim, was one of the more embarrassing moments of his recent career. It need not have been, if he hadn't gone red, muttered something inarticulate about assuming she was still at home, and then dived into his office with a feeling of relief out of all proportion to the moment. The two women, who had been enjoying a somewhat stiff conversation in the corridor, were left confused and open mouthed.

'What was that about?' asked Sarah.

'No idea,' replied Chris, with a wicked sense that actually she probably did have a pretty good idea. Sarah, who shared the conviction but would never admit it, shrugged and moved away, leaving Chris in command of the field. Chris paused to give Greg a moment to cool down, then knocked and entered on the heels of the rap.

'Got something from the forensic IT folk,' she said.

Greg looked up from the papers he was studying slightly randomly. 'What? Oh good.' Then pulling himself together, he asked, 'What are you doing here anyway? You were supposed to be off for the week.'

'I know, but I'm going mad at home, Greg. And you need me. You need every hand on deck,' she added, leaving him in some doubt as to precisely how she reckoned he needed her.

'I've got you something anyway. So far forensics have identified four log-ons to HRAdmin2. Three of them were HR team members. We're chasing down their contact details now. The fourth was from a laptop in analytical chemistry.'

'Whose?'

'Well, that's the thing. It wasn't anyone's personal laptop. It seems to have been used in association with one of the PCR analysers and was also the spare that team members took with them to conferences when they were doing presentations.'

'Damn. So anyone could have used it?'

'Yes. That's the bad news. The good news is that it was linked to a mobile phone in order to access the internet off site, and it *has* been used since the explosion. We're trying to track the signal now.'

'That's great. Tell the team well done from me, Chris.'

'Will do.'

'Oh, and Chris, I should be mad at you for coming back to work too soon. But it's good to have you back.'

She turned at the door, and if he wasn't already dazzled by the lime green he could have sworn she flashed him a cheeky grin. 'I know,' she said, and closed the door behind her.

Greg had scarcely had a chance for a round-up with the team when Chris ran him to earth again, this time in the ops room, and this time she had Jenny in tow.

'Jenny's performed her miracle again,' she proclaimed. 'I'll let her tell you.'

Jenny went a little pink, having the attention of the entire room, but with an encouraging nod from Greg said, 'I've been looking again at the footage from CCTV cameras on and around the Science Park, and I think I've found what might be the car that picked up Professor Lai and her mysterious male associate from the back of the NASA site.' She looked round, then said, 'Shall I put it on the big screen?'

'Yes. Yes please,' said Greg. 'Show us what you've found.'

It only took Jenny a moment to pair her iPad to the main screen at the end of the room, and all gathered round to watch.

'First,' she said, 'I went through all the footage of cars leaving the site around and within an hour of the time of the explosion, and excluded all those I could identify as registered to staff or named visitors. That left me with half a dozen or so, and I eventually managed to exclude all but one. They mostly turned out to belong to friends of staff, or personnel from other Science Park agencies. That left me with this one.' She showed a blurry picture on the screen of a shadowy, pale car at the main Science Park entrance.

'I know you're thinking that doesn't tell us anything,' she said with a grin, 'but watch. This is the same image after the digital wizards at the UEA had their way with it. I know one of them socially,' she added. She then showed on screen a series of pictures with the images sharpened to the point that the number plate could be seen. Greg leaned forward.

'N62WES,' he read. 'And it's a Ford.'

'That's right. It matches the description given by Mrs P, although admittedly that was a bit vague. She did say she couldn't identify the make of a car unless she could read it on the bonnet! But I've got that car on multiple images. It arrived at the Science Park just thirty minutes before the explosion. I've then got it on the John Innes cameras passing their site on the way to the back road. I've picked it up again just before the explosion, heading off site and again a few minutes later on the cameras by the Norfolk and Norwich Hospital heading towards the centre of town. That's it,' she said. 'Except, the number's registered to a car of that make and colour and to an owner who lives in North Walsham.'

'They've made a mistake,' breathed Greg. 'Hallelujah, they've made a mistake. They've failed to use a false number plate. If it is them, of course,' he reminded himself with a sudden feeling of disappointment. 'It could be a perfectly innocent passer-by. Sorry Jenny.'

'It could,' said Chris, 'but there's a good chance it wasn't. We've saved the best to last.' She waved a bit of paper in the air. 'The digital team have come through. They've pinpointed the last transmissions from that mobile phone we were after, the one used to log in to HRAdmin2, and they're all from the same area. North Walsham.'

'Wow. Jenny, Chris, well done both of you. That's good work. And pass on my thanks to the digital team, Chris. How much can they narrow down the area in North Walsham?'

'For the phone, to within a couple of streets. It's an area of houses with gardens, near the cottage hospital, so that's not so many places. We were lucky there are three transmitters nearby, which gives us a rather good triangulation. And it fits with the address logged by DVLA for the car.'

'Then,' said Greg, 'I feel a visit to North Walsham coming on. Well done again, Jenny. You have the sharpest eyes for CCTV I've ever come across.'

'And some rather useful contacts,' added Chris.

'Chris, get Jim and ask him to meet us in the car park in ten minutes.'

Four of them gathered round the two cars: Chris, Jim, Bill Street and Greg.

'What's your thinking?' asked Jim.

'All we've got to go on is the car and the address from DVLA. While we're heading to North Walsham I thought we'd ask the local team for some help, a look round for the car, for example. Failing that, we might need to try a house to house. I've sent them a rather official-looking photo of Lai just in case they spot her.'

'And their instructions?'

'Low profile. If they spot the car, just keep it under surveillance and radio us the location. If they spot Lai, arrest her. On no account to enter any property, just in case there're more booby traps set up. Chris, you come with me. Jim and Bill in Jim's car? OK?'

Once on the A11, Greg snatched a sideways glance at Chris. 'How're you doing?' he asked. 'This is a lot on top of a recent...' He hesitated.

'Near death experience?' she offered.

'Well, I was going to say something about getting blown up and concussion, but your version will do. And while I'm on the subject, Chris, I'll swing for you if you ever do anything like that to me again.'

She smiled at him. 'I won't.'

'Promise?'

'Want me to cross my heart and hope to die?'

'Just a straight promise will do. I think I can trust your promise.'

'OK. I promise, Greg.'

'Thank you.' He realised he did trust her promise and that gave him a warm feeling he hadn't felt for a while. Perhaps something was changing for him. 'Chris,' he started, and the radio crackled.

'Base to Geldard,' it said.

'Geldard receiving, over.'

'Got an update for you from Jenny. She's cross referenced the location and the car owner's name to data from the lab. It's a staff member recorded as living at that address after all. Over.'

'Thank you. Text it to Chris and Jim Henning. Over.' Greg glanced at Chris again. 'Make sure Jim got the message, will you? And check the details on which staff member from what team. I didn't want it shared on air.'

'Just in case someone's listening?'

'Precisely. I don't want to get to North Walsham and find the EDP there before us.'

There was a pause while Greg negotiated the Thickthorn roundabout and joined the A47. He could see Jim in his rear view mirror as Chris said, 'Jim's got the message. And the staff member was from the utilities team. So no reason on the face of it that they should have been logging on to the HR systems. But every reason for Lai to find them useful.'

'OK. Tell Jim we'll head straight for that location. And tell the locals to keep their distance. But contact the dog team and get them on their way. A sniff around for explosives might be wise. No one's going in until I get there and give the OK.

# 25

## Journey's end

Navigating North Walsham one-way streets took concentration, so silence fell in the car. Just as they turned the corner into an avenue of mixed houses and bungalows, all with gardens as Chris had said, the radio crackled and the local team reported, 'Car not in sight. Maintaining distance as requested. ETA dog team, ten minutes.'

In fact, the two cars and the dog team van pulled up outside a small bungalow at more or less the same time. The bungalow was set back a little from the road with just a small lawn in front. It was clear from the view down the empty driveway that it was asymmetrically placed on its plot, with a much bigger garden behind. A small corrugated iron garage occupied the end of the drive, the rickety doors padlocked closed. On Greg's signal the dog team left their van and they all congregated on the pavement.

'The local chaps are in the avenue behind just in case

we get anyone making a dash for it,' he said. 'I'd like you to take a look around the property from the outside to check for explosives. Don't go into anything, just check the garden, doors, perimeter etc.'

Turbo bounced out of the van with his usual elan, and quivered to a sit. His handler, Fiona, took him round the perimeter of the property and then the bungalow, paying particular attention to doors. Nothing. Then, at a nod from Greg, she released him to quarter the garden more thoroughly.

'Clean,' she reported. 'Out here at least. Obviously I can't speak for the interior until we go inside, but not a hint of anything of concern out here or near any of the doors.'

Jim nodded. 'So let's have a look at what we can see,' he said. Peering through windows suggested the house was empty. There were only four rooms plus one with frosted glass that they assumed was a bathroom. One had vertical slatted blinds partly drawn, but even then they had a reasonable view into the room. No one in sight.

'Have we enough for a warrant to search?' asked Jim.

'Just about, perhaps,' said Greg. 'I'll give Margaret a ring and see if she got anywhere. In the meantime, can someone check out the garage, as far as we can, and see if the neighbours have any CCTV.'

Jim and Greg went to the garage. The windows were filthy but the doors so ill-fitting they got a pretty good view of the interior. It seemed to be empty except for some garden tools and an old freezer. Greg turned to see Chris still peering in through the bungalow windows, her hands shading her eyes from the sunlight behind her. As he watched, she stiffened, then adjusted her position and peered again.

'Boss,' she called. 'I think we need to get in here.'

'So do I,' he said, 'but…'

'No, I mean now. Look, am I seeing right?'

Greg joined her at the window overlooking the back garden and peered in where she indicated, shading his eyes too.

'See, through the open door to the hall?'

He peered again, then turned, shouting, 'Bill, bring the ram. We need to get in here ASAP. Jim, we both think there's a body lying in the hall.'

Jim took a quick look, then joined Bill with the ram. Two swings, and the door was open, its lock hanging loose from the door frame.

'Hang on,' said Greg, stopping the rush. 'Dog first, please.'

Fiona got Turbo back on his lead and entered slowly, with extreme caution. No signals for explosives in the porch or in the hall, but 'There's a casualty here,' she shouted.

'OK. Carry on and check the rest of the bungalow,' said Greg over her shoulder, then he went to the body lying in the hall. A quick check and, 'He's breathing. Get an ambulance ASAP. No one come any further than this until Turbo's given it the all clear.' Greg turned the man on the hall floor into the recovery position.

'It's OK, mate,' he said. 'We've got you now. Help's coming.' The man, brown hair mussed by lying on the floor and with vomit staining his tartan shirt, was breathing in gasps. His hands clenched and unclenched on the floor beside him and his bare feet twitched.

'Hazel,' he choked out between gasps. 'Where's Hazel?'

'There's someone else?' asked Greg. 'We haven't found anyone else yet. We'll keep looking.'

'Hazel's ill too,' said the man. 'Hazel...'

Greg raised his voice. 'We're looking for another casualty,' he shouted. 'Take a look around. How far off is the ambulance?'

'About five minutes, they say,' said Chris, arriving at his side. 'Any ID?'

'Not that I can see.' Greg turned his attention back to the man. 'Can you tell us what happened?' he asked gently. 'What was wrong with Hazel.'

'Lily,' gasped the man. 'I think Lily poisoned us. Hazel was worse.' Then his eyes rolled up and he shook in the effort to get his breath.

'OK, let us at him.' The paramedics had arrived. 'Any idea what's the problem?'

'He mentioned poison, but no idea what,' replied Greg. 'We'll let you know if we find anything.'

'Do you have a name?' asked the second paramedic, a slight girl with bushy brown hair tightly controlled in a bun.

'No.' Greg watched as the first green uniform, bearing the name Tom on a badge, put an oxygen mask on the man gasping for air. 'He's a suspect in the Science Park bombing.' Greg patted the man's chinos for anything that might identify him, but the pockets were empty. 'One of us will go with you to the hospital. We'll take his fingerprints and a DNA sample and see if that throws anything up.'

'Whatever he's taken or been given, it's playing hell with his respiration,' said Tom. 'We'll take him directly to the N&N. If someone's coming with him, they'd better get a shift on.'

'He mentioned the possibility of another casualty,' said Greg, 'but we haven't found anyone yet. I'll just check round and ask Constable Bill Street to come with you.'

As Tom and his colleague Fara got the man on a stretcher, Greg went into the garden to check progress.

'Bill,' he shouted across the garden again, 'you go in the ambulance with our first casualty.' Then to Jim, 'Any progress on finding the second?'

'Not so far,' replied Jim. 'No one in the house or garden, but we haven't checked the garage yet.' A splintering crash interrupted his words as Bill wielded the ram again, this time putting it straight through the flimsy garage door.

'Right, I'll make tracks to the ambulance,' he said, dusting his hands down. 'Don't forget the ram when you leave.' He trotted off round the corner.

A quick glance inside and it was clear the garage was empty, as it had appeared through the windows.

'Nothing here either,' were the words on Jim's lips, as he opened the deep freeze in the corner. 'Oh, bugger,' he said, as the curled and frosted body of a young girl fell out at his feet.

As Jim remarked later over a consoling pint with his wife, there was nothing like a stiff dropping at your feet to change the tone of the day. And a very stiff stiff at that. Even after all his years on the job, the sight of the frost-covered eyes staring up at him had nearly caused him to lose his breakfast, though by that time said breakfast was but a faded memory.

It was the work of moments to get the two local North Walsham constables from the back gate and on duty securing the scene. A couple more phone calls and Greg had Ned and the pathologist on the way. They occupied the waiting time checking, as best they could, for ID. Nothing on the body, which was not surprising since she seemed to be wearing nothing but skimpy pyjamas. A cautious look round the house, conscious all the time of the need to avoid contaminating the scene, suggested that their corpse lived there. A couple of photos featured a slim woman with long blonde hair in a ponytail that could have been a match for the icy remains they'd found in the freezer. Chris peered at one.

'She can't have been more than twenty or so in this one,' she said.

'Anyone found a wallet or anything with a name on it?' asked Greg.

'Nothing on this.' Chris picked up the photo in her gloved hand, then put it back carefully where it had come from. 'No name on the back. I haven't seen a handbag or purse.'

'No address book on the bookshelves either,' said Jim. 'Not that I've spotted anyway. Lots of books about conservation and animal welfare. No laptop or iPad, which seems odd. Especially as there is a printer.'

'Not so odd if the person who took it had reason to fear what might be on it,' replied Greg. He looked up as the throaty roar of a heavy van drew attention to the first reinforcements: the pathologist and the mortuary team.

A swift glance from Dr Sawston and, 'For God's sake, don't ask me how long since she died,' she said. 'The first thing I need to do is get her back to the lab and defrosted before I can tell you anything.'

'How long will that take?' asked Greg, and wished he hadn't when the reply was, 'Ever defrosted a turkey? Well, a lot longer than that. It takes several days, maybe a week to defrost a body in a refrigerator. And no, I can't hurry it up. If I tried, the outside would start to decompose while the inner organs were still frozen.'

Aware that his Christmas turkey would never taste the same again, Greg said, 'She's quite a small woman. Will that make things any faster?'

'A bit. But assume days not hours. Come on,' said the doctor to the mortuary team hovering behind her, 'let's get her home before there's any more deterioration.'

'Before you go, any obvious causes of death?'

'You really are pushing your luck, DCI Geldard,' replied the doctor, but with a small smile. 'No, sorry. No obvious major trauma, no unexplained holes or breaks. I won't be able to tell you anything else until I have her thawed and on my table.'

'The other casualty,' said Greg tentatively, 'said he thought they'd been poisoned.'

'That's useful to know,' said the doctor with a sharpened glance. 'I might need a look at that other casualty too, or at least a chat with his medical team. Is he at the N&N? OK. And obviously if you turn up a likely candidate for the toxin, let me know. It's always easier to find something when you know what you're looking for'

Greg watched thoughtfully as the van drove away. 'While we're waiting for Ned, let's get on with some house to house. This isn't a long roadway. With luck we might find some neighbours in.

'Priorities – do they have CCTV? How well did they know the inhabitants here?' Greg waved at the bungalow. 'Ideally get a description and see if it matches the girl in the freezer. A name would help and if we get really lucky, details of a next of kin.'

Unfortunately, it seemed the small estate was largely occupied by workers rather than the retired. Three of the nearest houses were empty, although, as Jim reported, at least one seemed to have the sort of doorbell that incorporated a camera. There was a possibility it might have some images of visitors to the bungalow opposite. Greg was the only one of them who struck lucky, in his case a retired couple living next door but one to the establishment currently festooned in crime scene tape. They were consumed with curiosity.

'Come in, come in.' Greg was greeted by an elderly but sprightly lady in jeans and spotted shirt. Her, he presumed, husband was sitting in a chair between an unlit gas fire and the bay window, with a good view of the crime scene. The chair looked worn with much sitting and greasy marks on the arms where hands had rubbed the upholstery. Greg's hopes rose. Today's paper had fallen, disregarded, on the floor by the chair.

'Coffee or tea? And I just made some shortbread,' said the lady. I'm May, and this is my husband, Ted. We thought you might be round soon, so I whipped up some shortbread just in case. It's the police, Ted, come about the trouble down the road.'

Ted looked up at Greg with some difficulty, the curvature of his spine meaning that he had a natural tendency to look at knee level.

'How can we help?' he asked, then added with a youthful grin belying his apparent years, 'We're a nosy old pair and we do have a good view down the road.'

May returned with a tray of coffee mugs, the shortbread, milk and sugar, and waved Greg to the other chair in the window.

'Just black please,' said Greg, accepting the coffee. 'If you sit here very often, you might be a great help to us. First, do you know who lived at number five?'

'Lived?' said May alertly. 'Past tense?'

'Yes. I'm afraid there has been a fatality. But I'll come to that. Do you know the people at number five?'

'Usually just the one girl,' replied Ted, picking up the dropped paper and folding it tidily away. 'Older than she looked, I think. Mid thirties. Name of Hazel Partner. Civil servant of some kind. We only knew her to say hello to. But we'd taken in mail for her from time to time when she went away, and she did the same for us. Nice girl. Bit of an activist on stuff like conservation and so on. Last time we spoke she was trying to persuade us to get solar panels.'

'And when was that?'

'Oh, about a month ago I should think. You remember, May?'

'Yes. You'd been moaning about the electricity bill again, so it would have been about a month ago.'

'You said usually just one girl. Have there been more recently?'

'I saw an older bloke. Been there a week or more. I wondered if it was her father but I don't think so. Then yesterday there was a Chinese lady hanging around as well.'

'So you haven't met her parents? Do you have any contact details for them?'

'No. Afraid not. As I said, Hazel tended to keep herself to herself.'

'Why do you want her parents,' asked May suddenly. 'Don't tell me it's Hazel who's died?' She looked upset.

'Can you give me a description of Hazel,' asked Greg, dodging the question again.

'As I said,' replied Ted, 'mid thirties, younger looking' and May chipped in, 'About my height, five foot five, probably a size ten, blonde hair, usually in a ponytail, sharp featured, you know, big nose.'

Greg put his notebook down and finished his coffee. 'Then I'm sorry to say that it does seem likely that the body we've found is that of Hazel Partner,' he said. 'Please don't say anything to anyone until we've found and notified her next of kin. And on that theme, I'm afraid the press will probably descend on you later today. I'll arrange for a family liaison officer to help you out.'

Back with Jim and Chris, Greg said shortly, 'It's the utilities team staff member. The name her neighbour knew her by matches, and they have a good description too. Get on to Jenny for the next-of-kin details. They should be on the lab database.'

At least the hurried departure of the mortuary team had left the landscape clear for Ned and his lot. Waiting in his car, to avoid getting in their way, Greg reflected that a lot of his time over the last few days had involved climbing in and out of paper suits. Briefed by phone, Margaret was relatively philosophical about this latest pressure on her budget.

'Any idea what the poison was, if any?'

'No. The male casualty had been sick and we found him collapsed on the floor. He could hardly raise his head, he was gasping for air, and his heart was beating very fast when I felt for a pulse, but a lot of materials cause symptoms like that.'

'The doc say anything?'

'No. Just a reference to frozen turkeys that's put me off Christmas for life, and she disappeared with the poor girl from the freezer to start the long process of thawing her out. We needn't expect much from her for around a week apparently. We might have more data from the N&N if they can work out what their patient's problem is.'

'OK. Keep me posted if Ned finds anything.'

'I'm just waiting for the next-of-kin details. We'll inform them and organise the identification once the body is in a fit state. Failing next of kin, we might be able to use a colleague from the lab.'

While team members photographed, logged, dusted, fingerprinted and sampled, Ned took it upon himself to have a careful search for potential toxins. Dirty dishes from the dishwasher were retrieved and bagged for later study. Packets, jars and bottles were sampled. After an hour or so he came out to the car where Greg, Chris and Jim were sitting waiting with varying degrees of patience.

'Not much to say for sure,' he reported, 'and we'll be here a while yet, so you might as well go home and I'll ring when I have anything to report. In general this household has fewer toxins around than most. No weed killers, no ant sprays, no fly papers even. The occupier seems to have been living in harmony with nature. Which does make this a bit of an oddity.' He held up a plastic bag containing a small bottle that looked as though it had held lemonade. In the bottom was a few millilitres of a pale yellow, slightly viscous liquid.

'I don't know what it is, but it's not what you would expect to find in this type of bottle. And something about the look and smell is making me suspicious.'

'Can I have a closer look?' asked Chris from the back seat.

He handed it to her and she held it up to the light. 'What sort of a smell does it have?' she asked. 'Like petrol perhaps?'

'No. Very little smell at all.'

'To me, it looks like an agricultural pesticide in concentrate form,' she said. 'But most of the more toxic have dyes and stenching agents added, in Europe at least.'

'Given the link with NASA,' said Ned, 'a pesticide is my guess as well. I'll send it in for analysis and let you know what they find. Knowing what poisoned him might be crucial in saving the life of your male suspect.'

As Ned left them, Chris's phone rang again.

'We have the next of kin,' she reported. 'Parents, living in Ashton-under-Lyme. I'll get the local uniforms to break the news, shall I, then arrange for them to come here if possible?'

'Yes, thank you, Chris,' replied Greg. 'Just make sure they understand that the parents probably won't be able to see their daughter's body for a few days.'

'I don't envy them communicating that,' remarked Jim. There was a silence, broken by Greg.

'I'll just make sure the local chaps understand the importance of securing the site, and then I think it's home for us,' he said.

'No, I'll do that,' said Chris. 'I'm probably better at putting the fear of God into them than you are.'

The car door slammed behind her as she got out and Jim remarked, 'She probably is at that. She seems to be coping OK.'

'Yes,' said Greg watching her in his rear view mirror. 'Made of steel wire that one.'

Jim grinned privately and got out of the car. 'Where do you want me tomorrow, Greg?'

'I already checked with the N&N and our suspect is in an induced coma, so nothing we can do there except keep him safe. Bill will be relieved for the night shift and then go back in the morning. As soon as he's awake and communicating, we need a chat. Otherwise, as so often, we're in Ned's hands. So see you at Wymondham unless we have any news in the meantime,' he replied.

'Do you want me to drop Chris home?'

'No, thank you, Jim. I'll do that.'

The return journey was conducted largely in silence, but it was a good, comfortable silence. At one point Greg glanced over and, judging from the closed eyes and slightly open mouth, Chris had nodded off. He smiled to himself and tried to drive extra smoothly. She woke with a bit of a snort as he approached Rollesby and turned off down the back road towards Repps.

'Oh lord, have I been dribbling?' she asked.

'Not so I'd noticed. Although you did manage the odd snore.'

'I don't snore,' she said indignantly. 'It's like sweating. Horses sweat, men perspire (and snore), ladies glow and breathe heavily.'

'Well, you were breathing very heavily then,' he said equably. 'Bit like a horse since you mentioned it. Don't let it worry you. I'd much rather you breathed heavily than not at all, and it's not so long ago I thought you'd breathed your last!'

She snorted again, only this time deliberately, and when he glanced over she was smiling.

'Chris,' he said carefully, eyes firmly on the road, 'can I ask you something?'

'Ask away,' she said, still smiling.

'Please stop me if I'm stepping out of line, and believe me, it won't affect our professional relationship, not one jot, but I'm not very good at picking up signals I think, and I'm not sure whether I should be saying this at all.' He paused, aware that somehow the sentence seemed to have got away from him.

'You haven't actually asked me anything yet,' she pointed out, as he seemed to be waiting for an answer.

'Oh, sod it. I'll just spit it out then,' he said, as he pulled up outside her house. 'Would you like to come out for dinner? With me I mean. When this case is sorted obviously, and I didn't mean in a group, I meant…' He paused, as another sentence showed signs of taking on a life of its own.

'I know what you mean,' she said, 'and yes, I would like that, very much.'

'Really?' he asked, as though amazed.

'Really. And for God's sake, kiss me, Greg, before you change your mind.'

She leaned over and, even allowing for the central console in the way, he was very glad she did.

'Really,' she said again, as he smoothed her hair back from her face. 'And don't worry that I'll step over the line when we're at work. Work is work and this is, different.' She got out of the car and blew him another kiss before closing the door.

'Wait,' he said suddenly. 'We need to arrange me picking you up in the morning. Your car's still at Wymondham.'

'So it is. Is that OK, me coming in with you, or should I get Jim to pick me up on his way past?'

'Given that, on this occasion at least, my conscience is clear,' he emphasized 'this' with voice and air-drawn punctuation, 'I'll pick you up.'

'And when your conscience isn't clear, you'll get Jim to do it?'

He laughed aloud and put his car in gear.

'Bugger off and give my regards to your parrot. I'll pick you up at seven thirty.'

'Strange,' he thought as he drove the few miles to Acle and his cottage by the Bure, that the evening sun seemed brighter and anything seemed possible. Even the photo of Isabelle and her newborn on his Twitter feed didn't dent his new-found happiness.

# 26

## Complications

The good mood lasted right through the night and into the morning. Greg woke feeling so good he whistled as he got Bobby's breakfast, and was still whistling when he got into his car and turned north towards Billockby to pick up Chris. Admittedly it was pretty tuneless, but neither Greg nor Bobby were fussy.

The radio woke into life as he drew up outside Chris's cottage and was still rattling on when the vision in pink and navy got into the car. She would have looked unusually conventional, he noted, but for the bright green tote bag.

'We're going via the N&N,' he said by way of greeting. 'Our casualty of yesterday is awake and we can have a word.'

'And good morning to you too,' she said composedly.

He snatched a glance across at her and the answering smile warmed him right down to his toes. He had to clear his throat for a moment, before he could say, 'Looking very fetching, Chris.'

Then added, 'Am I allowed to say that sort of thing now?'

'Not just allowed, required,' she replied. 'In private obviously.'

'Obviously. Then, Chris we do need a private chat.'

'Later,' she said. 'This evening? Let's keep work for work.'

'Yes. Agreed.'

At the hospital they were directed to a suite of private rooms and found Bill already standing guard outside one.

'You're early, Bill,' Greg greeted him. 'What news?'

'He's awake, and as I understand it, has asked to see you. But the doctors want a word first.'

Showing them into a crowded office, the registrar wasted no time. Exhausted by a night on duty he perched on his desk and announced, without preamble, 'Whatever questions you want to ask Mr Atkinson, you need to ask him now. He isn't going to make it.'

Shocked, Greg asked, 'How long?'

'Days, probably not more. I'd be reluctant to let you question him except it's his wish and frankly it isn't going to make much difference.'

'Was he poisoned?'

'Yes. We're not absolutely sure, but it looks very like paraquat and a hefty dose at that. There's no antidote and no cure. All we can do is treat symptoms, but his organs are failing one by one. His lungs are shot, hence the gasping, and his kidneys are switching off too.'

'Can he speak?'

'A little. And he can type too. You might need to use both approaches.'

Ushered in to the private room, Greg and Chris sat either side the bed. The man they now knew as Nigel Atkinson was propped up and covered in a face mask. Tubes led in every direction. He turned his head as they entered.

'We understand you want to make a statement,' said Greg, then as the man went to remove his oxygen mask, he added, 'Just nod for now. Let's save speaking for when it's really needed.'

The man nodded and raised a thumb.

'Good. You understand that, as you are a suspect, this will need to be an interview under caution. Is that clear?'

The thumb went up again.

'And as such, you should have a legal adviser present.'

This time the mask did come off and, 'No time,' he said.

Greg hesitated. It was going to be difficult enough to arrive at a statement that would be admissible in court. No legal advice would make things worse. He made his mind up.

'OK, I understand. We'll take a preliminary statement and Sergeant Mathews here will record it on her phone.' Chris nodded and held it up. 'We may need to return for a further statement when a legal adviser can be present. Is that understood?'

'Understood. But good luck with that,' the man whispered. 'I don't think I'm going to be around for too long.'

Greg administered the caution then started to ask a question but was interrupted. 'Can I tell it my way,' the man asked. 'Then you ask questions and I'll answer if I can.'

He proceeded in a terrible guttural whisper and Chris leaned forward to make sure the recording got every word.

'My name's Nigel Atkinson. I was recruited to the Movement and given the job of placing the car bomb in a specific slot in the car park. I drove the car from a farmyard near Blickling and parked it as instructed.' He paused for a sip of water. 'I left it there and joined Professor Lai at the back gate of the site. We got into another car driven by a girl from the lab, Hazel Partner. Hazel drove us to the house where you found me in North Walsham. It was Hazel's car and Hazel's house.' Another sip of water.

'Neither of us had expected casualties. We didn't find out until we saw the news. Hazel was very upset, but Lai said there'd been a terrible mistake, that the timer must have been mis-set and I was lucky to be alive. Then there was the second bomb.

'That time Hazel was distraught. It was obvious to us both that something else was going on, but I was wary of Lai. Hazel said she'd had enough and she was going to the police before more lives were lost. Lai cooked that night. Something spicy. She persuaded Hazel to eat before going to the police, and Hazel was taken ill almost immediately. Then me. I never saw Hazel again. Lai helped her out of the bathroom and I never saw her again. Then I heard the car drive off. That's all,' he said. 'Lai planned everything. She planned both explosions and she poisoned us both. If you don't stop her more will die.'

Atkinson closed his eyes and tried to replace his oxygen mask, but fumbled it. Greg helped him get it in place. 'Can you see to read?' he asked gently.

The thumb went up again.

'Then we'll get your statement transcribed and we'll need you to sign it. We'll come back with the statement and a lawyer for you. Will you answer a few more questions?'

'If I can,' said Atkinson through the mask, and closed his eyes.

In the corridor, the registrar was waiting. He shook his head. 'You'll be lucky if you get anymore,' he said.

'Is there somewhere I can get the recording transcribed?' asked Chris.

'You can use my office and my laptop.'

'Then let's at least get a signature on this statement,' replied Greg. 'Thanks, Chris. I'll pass the news on and line up a duty solicitor.'

Less than thirty minutes later, typed statement and duty solicitor ready, they returned to Atkinson. It was immediately obvious that he had deteriorated rapidly, but also that he was determined to sign his statement. With Chris again recording, the solicitor established that he was happy with his statement and it was duly signed with a shaky hand.

'One question,' said Greg, guessing correctly that was all he would have. 'Why are you so confident it was Professor Lai who set up the bombing?'

'Because she provided the Semtex,' was the reply. 'I saw her hand it over. It came from Ireland I think.' He was interrupted by a bout of coughing and the nurse at the life support machines shook her head. 'Enough,' she said. And they left.

Outside, the duty solicitor looked at them, not unsympathetically. 'You do realise you'll be lucky to get any of that into court,' he asked.

'So, we just have to find the evidence to support it.'

An hour later and they were back in Wymondham.

'Chris, can you see what progress's been made on finding that car?' Greg asked. 'I just want a word with Jim.' But he was interrupted as they walked down the corridor by raised voices emanating from the room Sarah was using as an office. The voices got louder and there was a bang, as of a hand smashed into a table. Greg flung the door open and walked in.

'What the devil is going on?' he demanded. 'I can hear you all over the building.'

The door bounced off the wall and, to Chris's disappointment, slammed closed behind him. She waited a moment, listening, then shrugged and returned to the ops room.

In the office were two red faces and one ice-cold, angry Greg. 'I can't and won't have two DIs making a spectacle of themselves, even if one of them is not under my command,' he said. 'I ask again, what's going on?'

Newton went to push past him but was stopped by Greg's arm on the door. 'Unless you want a formal complaint made to your seniors,' Greg said softly, 'I suggest you have second thoughts. Don't make me ask again. I want an answer from one of you. Or both.' There was a controlled force about Greg that neither had seen before.

Sarah tightened her ponytail and sat down at her desk, attempting composure. 'I just found out that the undercover cop being run by DI Newton had knowledge of a planned bomb attack and of the sourcing of Semtex from Ireland. I was asking for their ID and contact details so they can be interviewed.'

'Reasonable request,' agreed Greg. 'So why did that involve shouting?'

'Because I refused,' said Newton. 'And she didn't like it.'

There was a long pause, while Greg made sure his voice was level. 'I don't like it either,' he said. 'I don't like it on several counts. First, she had information about a dangerous development in the organisation's plans. Second, she knew they had access to explosives. She should have reported both and you should have reported the risks to us. Or did she?' he asked, 'and you just sat on the intelligence?'

'Who says the operative is female,' asked Newton in a vain attempt to regain the upper hand.

'You did. You let it slip when you were talking to the chief super a few days ago.'

Newton looked abashed and started to bluster, but Greg cut him off short. 'Enough,' he said. 'I'm taking this up the line. As far as I can see, the lives lost here in Norfolk can be laid at least partly at your door. And I want a proper investigation into what happened, including your undercover cop taking the witness box.'

Newton shouldered past him, face ablaze, and left.

Sarah looked up. 'So you do agree with me,' she started, but Greg interrupted her.

'I agree with your conclusion but not with your method,' he said coldly. 'Losing your temper in the office! It was unprofessional, Sarah, and I expect better of you.' He left the room, closing the door quietly behind him.

When he reported to Margaret she was equally enraged, and equally cold. In fact, if anything, Greg thought there was an element of satisfaction in her response.

'Right,' she said reaching for her phone. 'This is where I involve the chief constable, and we really lay it on the line. That undercover cop is going to give evidence if it's the last thing I do. And she can start by showing up here and being interviewed under caution. By you.'

He managed precisely an hour of peace and quiet before someone was knocking on his door. It was Jim. It was obvious the news of the row, and Greg's reading of the riot act, had spread through the building like wildfire.

'I'm afraid things are going to get worse before they get better,' he said. 'I've been in contact with Hazel Partner's parents. They're on their way here and want to see you, or at least, they said "the detective in charge" and I guess that's you.'

'Get me a family liaison officer will you, Jim, and ask them to stand by. Are we booking them into a hotel?'

'We've got a room arranged, but they say they want to go to Hazel's bungalow as soon as we release it.'

'OK. I'll talk to them about that too.'

The conversation with Mr and Mrs Partner was fraught. Both were weeping, both clutching photos of their lost daughter, both totally uncomprehending of why they could neither see her body nor go to her home. They were touchingly proud of their daughter and her achievements.

'She was so good at anything techy,' said Mr Partner, a short and stocky man with his daughter's pale hair and sharp nose. He wiped his eyes again on his sleeve. 'She could make computers jump through hoops. Her boss told us she pretty well kept the whole lab IT systems running single handed when they had problems with a hacker.'

Greg's interest sharpened. 'When was that?' he asked.

'About a year ago,' was the answer.

Greg made a note to ask Craig Bennington about the incident and tried again to explain why they could not yet see their daughter. In the end he was forced to be blunt.

'You must take my word for it,' he said to them firmly but kindly. 'You don't want to have your memories of your daughter forever marred by seeing her as she is now. The hospital staff,' – he thought it best not to mention the mortuary – 'will be very respectful of Hazel and as soon as the circumstances are right, I do promise you that I will personally make sure that you can see her.

'As for the bungalow, I'll ring the forensic team right now and see whether it can be released to you.' A quick word with Ned, and he turned back to the sad parents before him. 'I can give you a choice,' he said. 'You can go to the bungalow right now, but you need to understand that it will show signs of the forensics team having been there. Surfaces have been dusted for fingerprints. Everywhere's been searched. We've left no stone unturned to make sure we can find out who did this to Hazel and obviously that does leave a mark. Or you can wait until tomorrow and I can get a team in to clean up before you see it all. What would you prefer?'

They looked at each other and then Mrs Partner spoke for them both. 'We'll go straight there,' she said. 'We'll clear up. It's the last thing we can do for Hazel, to make her home nice again.'

'I think that's very brave of you,' he said and held out his card. 'If you need anything, don't hesitate to give me a ring at any time.'

Greg had barely seen them out, accompanied by the family liaison officer, when Margaret was on the phone.

'You can interview the undercover cop,' she said, 'but not here. They're worried about her cover. But they have agreed to you meeting her at one of their safe houses. They've promised all the usual recording equipment so the interview and statement is PACE compliant.'

'Where?' asked Greg.

'Outskirts of Cambridge. Here's the postcode.' She held out a yellow Post-it note.

'OK. I'll take Jim with me.'

Greg looked at his watch and sighed, realising that a trip to Cambridge and back was going to swallow up the rest of his day. He caught Jim in the canteen and agreed they would go in separate cars, so each could go straight home after, then ran Chris to earth in the ops room. Swiftly he explained his revised schedule then looked at her hopefully, his back to the rest of the room.

'Would you like supper tonight, in Acle?' he asked quietly. 'I could ring when I leave Cambridge to arrange a time to meet. There's quite a nice Greek restaurant, nothing fancy but the cooking's good.'

'I'd like that,' she said quietly. 'Meanwhile I'll see what I can find out about that car!'

'Oh, that reminds me, I've another job for you,' said Greg turning back. 'Can you ask Craig Bennington about a hacking problem they had a year ago and Hazel Partner's involvement in solving it. I have this cynical suspicion she may have set it up then miraculously put it right in order to get access to the whole system.'

'Interesting,' she commented. 'I'll get on it straightaway. Till later then.' She turned away with just the slightest suspicion of a wink.

They met in the car park. Jim had a map open on the bonnet of his VW. 'I've looked it up,' he said. 'It's on a housing estate between Addenbrooke's and Trumpington. Quickest way for us will be down the A11, across on the A505 to Whittlesford and then back up the M11.' He traced the route with a finger.

'OK,' said Greg and got in his car. 'See you there.'

Nonetheless, he put the postcode in his satnav and was reassured it came up with the same route. Ferreting in his car door pocket for some sweets in lieu of lunch, he came up with a part-eaten bag of wine gums and set off, chewing.

They arrived at their destination within a few moments of each other, and Greg silently congratulated his funny bugger opposite number for an excellent choice of location. It was the perfect environment for a safe house: a new and anonymous housing estate, full of young professionals with busy lives and zero curiosity about their neighbours. The address they'd been given was a house that looked exactly like a score of others – dull, bland and nondescript. The door opened as they reached it and they were beckoned in by an officer who was clearly armed. Jim and Greg exchanged a glance as they were shown into the back room. It was, as they had been promised, set out like an interview room with a table, four chairs and recording equipment.

Already seated on the far side of the table was a woman in her mid-thirties with shoulder-length, wavy hair. It was currently faintly auburn, but something about the rest of her colouring suggested to Greg that it was not her natural shade. He peered hard as he sat down, seeking to ascertain whether it was a wig.

'I think you'll recognise me again,' remarked the woman, and Greg realised he had been staring. He was not inclined to apologise. He took out his paperwork and iPad, but was told to put the latter away by the officer near the door.

'No photos,' he said. Greg complied.

The woman opposite was accompanied by an older man who introduced himself as her representative. He didn't say of what. Greg started to deliver the formal caution but was interrupted by said representative.

'Is that necessary?' he asked.

'I believe so,' replied Greg. 'We have information that...' and he paused for a name.

'You can call her Agent A,' said the representative.

'We have information that Agent A,' he paused sarcastically, 'had intelligence that a crime was being planned and that the organisation responsible was equipping itself for terrorist activity, yet it would appear that information was not shared in a way that would have assisted in thwarting the plot. This raises serious questions about Agent A's involvement and precise role in the plot, all of which require answers. If the answers are not satisfactory then Agent A may be charged with assisting a terrorist attack. So yes, interview under caution is necessary.'

That resolved, Greg and Jim settled down to their questions, but rapidly found that few of them were answered. After multiple responses along the lines of, 'I'm sorry, it's not in the public interest for me to answer that question,' Greg decided to regroup.

'So, to recap,' he said with a very moderate degree of sarcasm, considering the circumstances, 'you're not able to tell me when you began this work, what your role is within the Movement, how the Semtex was sourced from Ireland, nor how terrorists from the Movement found their jobs within NASA.'

'That's correct,' said Agent A composedly. 'Perhaps it might be quicker if I told you what I can say.'

Greg shook his head in exasperation and Jim, looking at

him, replied 'Well, let's start there, anyway.'

'I am able to tell you that I've been working within the Movement since it broke away from more conventional animal rights organisations. At first it was involved in the sort of direct action typical of a lot of animal rights activists – filming in slaughterhouses, releases of laboratory animals et cetera. But more recently the plans became more indiscriminate, more rash, and involved more violence against people. I became concerned that the violence was escalating and reported my concerns.'

'When?' asked Greg.

She pushed a file across the table to him. 'Dates and details are in here, only individual names redacted.'

'Does this file also cover when you found out about the Semtex?'

'Yes, it does.'

'And does it explain why, when there'd already been an explicit threat against NASA, no warning was given either to the laboratory or to Norfolk Police?' She hesitated, glanced at the rep beside her and said, 'No comment.'

'What about Professor Lai? When did you learn about her involvement?'

'I'm sorry, it's not in the public interest for me to answer that question.'

'But you did know she was involved.'

She nodded and Greg said, 'Aloud, for the tape please.'

'Yes. We had become aware of Professor Lai's involvement.'

'How?'

'We have signal data from GCHQ that showed her involvement both in the decision to target NASA and in sourcing the Semtex.'

'And you still didn't warn anybody.'

For the first time Agent A hesitated, then said, 'The decision was above my pay grade. But I do know it was hoped to trace more of the network before my involvement was exposed. That's still the hope.'

Greg looked at Jim, shuffled the files together and stated, 'Interview concluded at,' he looked at his watch, '1700.'

The tape off he looked again at Agent A. 'You're taking a huge risk, and not all the risk is yours. I hope it's worth it.'

Once outside he looked at Jim. 'What do you think?' he asked. Jim got into his car and rested his wrists on his steering wheel. 'I think I'll never understand the funny buggers,' he said. 'They seem to be completely bonkers. Totally divorced from reality. They always have very plausible justification for what they do, but they lose track of the basics. Sometimes it's better to collar some bad guys than none, and it's always better to prevent rather than mop up the blood after the event.'

'I'm sure they'd say that prevention was what they were all about,' said Greg with a terse irritation that just barely hid his growing rage and frustration.

'Then in this case, they failed badly.'

The Olive Tree was tucked away behind Acle high street. Small and cosy, the food was traditional Greek and excellent. Greg was waiting impatiently in a table near the window, bowls of olives, bread and oils in front of him, when Chris came through the door. He got to his feet so enthusiastically the table rocked dangerously for a moment and he had to stabilise it before leaning over to land a kiss on Chris's cheek. The proprietor nodded, smiled and held out her seat for her, as they both sat down.

Greg put a hand out and took up the one Chris had laid on the table, turning it and landing a kiss on the palm.

'So glad you're here,' he said.

'Me too. Me too.' Picking up the waiting glass of red wine she said, 'To us?'

'To us. Let's get the ordering out of the way, then we can chat.'

'Right.' She looked down at the menu somewhat at random and said, 'Taramasalata, then beef stifado with salad.'

'Houmous then grilled skate for me,' said Greg. The food ordered, Greg added, 'Look, Chris, there's something I need to say but...'

'Oh God, don't tell me you've changed your mind already,' said Chris and snatched her hand back.

'Have I heck! Don't be daft, woman,' said Greg, recapturing the hand with ease.

Chris smiled involuntarily at his rare descent into Yorkshire speak.

'It's just that we have to navigate working together and,' he hesitated, 'being together. I don't want to get you into difficulties with them upstairs.'

'Nor me you,' she interrupted. 'But can't we give ourselves a bit of leeway for a while? It does happen after all. Colleagues "*being together*",' she mimicked him gently.

'You're right, of course. But secrecy doesn't sit well with me. I guess it's OK for now, but I think there'll come a time when we need to come clean. Or when I'll have to speak to Margaret at least.'

'I see that,' she said slowly, 'and I like that you're looking to a future. But I don't want to lose working with you. Not just yet. So, can we let things lie for the moment?'

'For the moment,' he agreed. 'And I'll talk to you before I say anything, I promise.'

They were interrupted by the arrival of their starters.

'So now, tell me about the funny buggers,' she said.

'You don't mind us talking shop?'

'Of course not. Come on. I want to know what you found out.'

'I'll begin to think you're only after my mind,' he complained.

'One thing at a time,' she replied.

Supper passed so quickly with good food and conversation, both were surprised when the proprietor offered them coffee with a degree of enthusiasm that suggested they'd been there long enough. Greg paid, with some muttering from Chris, and they went out to their cars.

'Err, would you like to come back with me, for a nightcap or something,' asked Greg.

'Yes, I'd like that,' replied Chris, half in and half out of her car with Greg chivalrously holding the door open for her.

They drove in convoy to the cottage by the river, and were greeted by an ecstatic Bobby, twining figures of eight round their ankles and purring loudly. Chris picked her up and went into the cottage wearing her as an animated stole.

'Coffee, wine, liqueur?' asked Greg. 'Of course, if you drink any more you'll have to take a taxi home, or stop here?' He left the sentence hanging for a moment then added, 'You did say it wasn't just my mind you were after.'

Chris laughed. 'I didn't say it, but I did imply it.' She came up and put her arms round him, so she, Greg and the cat were one warm bundle. 'But I'll say it now. How about we take that bottle of red up to bed?'

With a bravado he didn't feel, Greg led the way upstairs. He contemplated saying something about being out of practice or not being very practiced, but however he phrased it, it was just too toe-curlingly awful to be said. As it happened, he needn't have worried. When he woke in the early hours of the morning, Chris curled, spoon-like, within his arms, he felt nothing but joy and a sense of coming home.

The morning was just as easy. Fitting old habits and new adjustments together seemed to come easily to them. Greg pottered about making coffee while Chris had a shower, then she shouted downstairs, 'Do me a favour, Greg. Could you get the small case out of the boot of my car?'

'Sure.' Then, as he brought it to the foot of the stairs, 'You came prepared then?'

'Don't look so smug,' she reproved him but he corrected her. 'This isn't smug. This is happy.'

His mobile ringing brought them crashing down to earth and the start of the working day. It was Mrs Partner.

'We've had an intruder,' she said.

# 27

## ...and developments

Mrs Partner sounded shaken.

'Are you all right,' asked Greg. 'Is your husband with you?'

'Yes. At least, he's looking round to see if anything seems to have been taken.'

'Is the intruder still there?'

'No. They left when I screamed.'

'OK. Tell me what happened and I'll get the local team to send someone round ASAP. I'll be with you as soon as I can. Chris,' he said in an aside, 'get uniform from North Walsham out to Hazel Partner's place. They've had an intruder.'

'Now Mrs Partner,' he said in the most reassuring tones he could muster, 'tell me exactly what happened.'

'I got up early this morning to go to the bathroom,' she said, 'and I heard something in the sitting room at the front of the house. I turned the hall lights on, and as I did I saw someone through the open sitting room door. I screamed, and they turned and ran out through the front door. They must have unlocked it because it was just on the latch and I know we locked it before we went to bed.'

'Did you see where they went next?'

'They ran up the street and then I didn't see anything else, but I did hear a car start.'

'Ok Mrs Partner. Hannah, isn't it? Do you mind if I call you Hannah?'

'No, not at all,' she said and then added, 'My husband's back now.'

Greg heard a scuffle as the phone changed hands and then Mr Partner's voice.

'I can't see anyone out there now, but whatever they were after, they had a good look round. They've even been through the dustbins. There's a right old mess out there now.'

'Don't touch anything if you can avoid it,' said Greg. 'We'll get forensics to see if they can pick up any fingerprints. I don't suppose you have any idea what they were after?'

'None,' said Mr Partner. 'Unless it was someone who knew Hazel had some valuable IT kit. Her laptop was top of the range. But, of course, you've got that.'

'No,' said Greg. 'No, we haven't. That must have been taken before we arrived at the property. But if that had already gone, what were they looking for now? Can you put your wife back on the line please?'

'Yes, of course. Hannah,' he called.

'Hannah,' said Greg, 'do you know whether the intruder was male or female?'

'Not for sure,' she said, 'but they weren't very big. Either a woman or a boy I'd have said.'

'What sort of height?' he asked.

'A bit shorter than me. Say about five foot three or thereabouts. And slight.'

'Any sight of their hair or skin colour?'

'No, sorry. They were in dark clothes with a hood, and the only light was from the hall and that's a bit dim. Oh, the police are here now,' she added.

'Good. My colleague is briefing them and they'll look after you until I get there. I'd have a nice cup of tea and a sit down if I were you, Hannah. We'll be there in less than an hour.'

While Chris dealt with their uniformed colleagues, Greg occupied himself feeding Bobby and getting ready to leave.

'Chris, are you OK to come with me?' he asked. We can pick up your car on our way back.'

'Of course. No problem. I'll just grab my bag.' The bright green tote made its reappearance and the two got into Greg's car.

'It seems that Hazel's laptop had disappeared before we got there,' he said. 'But if she had a top of the range laptop, why was she using the old lab kit anyway?'

'Perhaps it wasn't her using it? Or perhaps there was something she didn't want on her personal account.'

'Either way, it seems the intruder didn't find what they were looking for. I think we need to take a very careful look round again and see if we missed anything.'

'D'you think it was Lily Lai? The intruder I mean?' asked Chris.

'I think it could have been, from the description. But that's why I want Ned's team back. Just in case she left any fingerprints or DNA while she was breaking in and searching.'

'Come to that, how did she get in? She certainly seems to

have been pretty quiet about it.'

'So very likely a key.'

'While you were on the phone to Mrs Partner I left a message for Jenny too. Just in case Lily Lai is still driving round in Hazel Partner's car. I suggested she take a look at what the cameras in North Walsham can show us.'

The Partners, husband and wife, had calmed down a lot by the time Greg and Chris arrived. The presence of two burly uniformed constables had helped, and Chris commended one, PC Rob Bates, for his common sense approach. By the time the detective contingent got there, he'd already lined up a locksmith to change the locks the moment forensics gave him the go ahead, and had promised drive-bys during the night.

Greg and Chris spent an intensive and tedious hour searching the property again for anything that might have been missed first time around, but without success. Ned and his assistant were pretty gloomy about the chances of picking up prints, pointing out that Lily Lai was known to be intelligent and would surely have known enough to wear gloves, but duly paid attention nonetheless to any surface that looked remotely possible. The only thing of interest that they found was a partial print on the grey dustbin lid, but Ned was shaking his head over that. Rob Bates and his partner, Geoff Buxton, had by that time been sent off on another house to house, but were forced to report back empty handed. No one had seen anything or heard anything in the night, except a car driving off.

Greg and Chris were just about to head off back to Wymondham, when one of the neighbours suddenly reappeared carrying something flat and grey. Greg looked at it with rising interest.

'Just went to put some rubbish in my bin and found this,' puffed the somewhat overweight gentleman in tracksuit and trainers. 'It's not mine. I wondered if it might be anything to do with all the fuss going on here? I picked it up with these plastic bags, just in case,' he added.

'There you are,' said Ned. 'Everyone's an expert these days.' He took the laptop from the portly neighbour and, handling it gingerly by the edges, turned it over. 'Aha,' he said, as a label stating 'property of Hazel Partner' came into view. 'The missing high-end laptop of Hazel's. Now this should be interesting. We'll dust it and sample it, then drop it in with our IT team. Very interesting.'

Greg turned to the neighbour. 'That's very helpful,' he said. 'My sergeant here will take a statement, about how and where you found it, and if you'd show her where as well, we'll need to take a close look at your bin.'

'Quite exciting, isn't it' replied the portly one as he led the way back to his house and garden.

Some more concentrated dusting and photographing, and Ned was able to say, 'Doing a rough comparison, I'm pretty sure some of the fingerprints on this laptop and on the bin and entrance gate belonged to Hazel Partner, so it's looking likely she hid it in the bin, for whatever reason. But there are some other fingerprints as well. I'll have to get back to you on those.'

At long last, and way past lunch time, Greg and Chris set off again south towards Acle and then Wymondham.

'I don't think we're going to have time to stop for lunch,' he said. 'Are you OK with something like a sandwich from a garage?'

'No problem,' said Chris and looking ahead said, 'There's one just up the road. Shall I whip in and get something?'

'Yes, thanks,' said Greg, but Chris's phone rang just as she was getting out of the car. As it looked set to be a long conversation, he left her with phone pressed to her ear and went into the shop himself. Returning with sandwiches, crisps and cans of coke he was surprised to see her hopping about with excitement.

'Hurry up, Boss,' she said. 'The car's been spotted not far from here.'

'Hazel's car? Where?'

'In the Waitrose car park just up the Cromer road.'

'How on earth did they spot it there? asked Greg, getting back into his car in a hurry.

'Jenny found it caught on ANPR in this area, put out an APB and it was spotted by some uniforms.'

'Are they in a marked car?'

'Yes. I told them to keep a low profile but to keep an eye on the car and let us know if it moves off.'

'Good.' Tossing the food carelessly onto the back seat, he put the car in gear and they sped off back the way they'd come towards Cromer.

The radio crackled, and the team hanging about near Waitrose reported, 'Car on the move. Heading towards the junction with the A149. Are we to follow?'

'Tell them yes, but at a distance and no lights or sirens.'

Silence, and then, 'Car turned onto A149 heading south.'

'Great.' A glance up and down the road and Greg spun the car round and drew up in a layby on the southbound side of the A149.

'Give them our details, Chris, and say we'll pick up the car as it comes past. Then they can break off. Ask them for a heads up as it's getting near.'

A short wait and then, 'We reckon you'll see them coming round the corner in about two minutes,' announced the voice on the loudspeaker.

'Keep your eye on the road over my shoulder,' instructed Greg, then leaned over and embraced Chris, taking her by surprise. 'We don't want them to see us watching for them,' he added.

'Any excuse,' she muttered, but with a grin. 'I look forward to you explaining this to uniform later.'

A silver VW Golf went past, quite quickly but well within the speed limit.

'One driver, no passenger that I can see,' Chris reported. 'And it's round the corner now. Get going.'

As they joined the stream of traffic, they spotted a police car a couple of vehicles behind them.

'You can peel off at the next turning,' said Chris into the radio. 'And thank you.'

Just past Dilham, at the junction with the A1151, their subject turned left towards Stalham and Greg, to his frustration, found they slipped several cars behind as they waited their turn.

'Chris, get on to the radio and get us some help,' he said, 'or we risk losing them. Ideally get a car or two from Great Yarmouth or Caister and deploy them further south, on the A149 and the A47.'

'I'll try,' she replied. 'But you'll be lucky to get that much help. They're short handed out here remember.' Greg cursed, and pushed his luck slightly to move a car or two up the line, earning cold stares and a finger from one driver.

'One patrol car on the A47 heading down the Acle straight,' she said. 'That's the best they can do at short notice. It all depends which way they go now.'

Past Potter Heigham and through Bastwick and 'she's paying you a visit,' remarked Greg, as the silver Golf turned on to the side road leading to Billockby. Just then a slow-moving tractor pulled out into the road ahead, threatening to hold them up for some time and, taking a risk, Greg pulled round it at speed to follow the Golf. He was now immediately behind it and slowed down to drop back a little, but 'That's torn it,' said Chris, clinging to her seat, as the Golf took off like a bat out of hell.

'Damn. She's spotted us,' said Greg. 'OK. No point hiding any more. Lights and siren on, and ask the car on the A47 if it can get a move on and block the road over the Acle bridge. She's surely going to go that way. There's nowhere else to cross the river unless she ties herself up in Great Yarmouth.'

'Or uses the Reedham ferry,' remarked Chris, putting the radio down, 'and that's not exactly a high speed option.'

Both cars continued at speed past Clippesby, and Greg throttled back as far as he dared as they approached the Billockby junction.

'I don't want to push her too hard,' he said grimly, 'but we don't want to lose her either.'

'Oh my God,' gasped Chris as the Golf shot through the junction and turned towards Acle without pausing. Other vehicles heading in both directions were forced to pull up and take evasive action to avoid a collision. Slowing, but relying heavily on lights and siren, Greg also took the turning rather faster than normal and followed on.

'Have they closed the bridge?' he asked.

'Yes. That's why there's nothing coming the other way now.'

'Then provided she doesn't turn off to Stokesby, we've got her cornered.'

They passed the Stokesby turn without incident and Greg started to drop back again. As they came round the bend, the liveried police cars on the brow of the bridge came into sight, all lights flashing. Clearly the driver of the Golf spotted them too. With a wrenching turn, the car spun off the road onto a dirt track to the right, barely made the bend in the track, wheels spinning and dirt flying, and accelerated. Greg followed at a more sober pace, just in time to see the Golf fly straight between the riverside cafe and the shop taking a couple of light tables and chairs with it, as it bounced over the reinforced bank and into the river.

# 28

## The river

Brakes slammed on, Greg and Chris shot out of the car and ran to the bank. A gabble rose from shocked tourists at the cafe but Greg ignored them as he watched the silver Golf turn in the stream and start to sink. The driver turned to look at him, waved mockingly and opened the windows, thus accelerating the speed of sinking ten-fold. Greg kicked his shoes off and wrenched at his jacket, then glanced sideways at Chris to see her making similar moves.

'Don't you dare!' he shouted. 'You promised.' And as Chris hesitated, Greg jumped into the river and swam strongly to where the car was just disappearing below the murky water.

Within the first few seconds he was surprised by just how cold the water was, and how much it affected his ability to swim efficiently. Gritting his teeth and hyperventilating to fill his lungs and blood stream with oxygen, he dived after the car. He could see only a vague shape.

'Lucky it's pale,' he thought, and kept going after it, catching hold of the edge of the open window frame. He reached in and got his hands on someone's head. It twisted away and hands reached up to fight back. Trying again, with his lungs in agony and a desperate desire to take a breath, he got a grip on the hair and pulled.

'Lucky she's small too,' he thought as the driver popped out of the window, still struggling as they both rose towards the surface.

Chris wasn't wasting time. She ran along the bank to where a Broads Cruiser, ironically flying a skull and crossbones, had been preparing to moor.

'Police,' she shouted, holding out her warrant card. 'I'm commandeering this boat. Take her out into the middle of the river.'

The youngster at the helm looked startled but started to turn the wheel. The rest of the pirate crew, mostly lounging around on deck holding identical bottles of lager and with identically open mouths, sat around in shock for a moment. Then the more sober of them helped push the boat off from the bank and one, seizing the boat's lifebelt, stood ready at the stern. Chris, turning to look up river, spotted a figure she recognised on the bank.

'Jim,' she exclaimed in relief, and then, over the rumble of the boats engine, she shouted, 'Greg's gone in after her.'

'I know,' he shouted back. 'I saw from the bridge.' And kicking off his shoes in turn he too jumped into the river, heading for the two heads just surfacing in the centre of the quick-running current. Chris turned her attention back to her boat.

'Take her upstream of those two,' she said pointing, 'and get ready to haul them aboard.'

By the time Jim reached Greg he was tiring fast. The cold water and the struggles of his rescue were taking their toll. Twice she had dragged him under again, and after the second time Greg raised his hand and punched. She went limp and at that moment Jim arrived.

'Leave her to me,' he gasped. 'Head for the boat,' and with his last strength Greg did that. By the time he reached the side he knew he was beat. The cold had reached every part. Instead of floating horizontally he was trying to tread water and starting to slide beneath it, quite peacefully. Peacefully, that is, until a hand grabbed his and a very familiar voice shouted close to his ear, 'Grab my hand, you numpty, and if you give up now, so help me…'

There was no way Chris could haul Greg into the boat, but the lager-fuelled pirates were both young and fit. It took only two of them to get Greg over the side, while the others helped Jim and his semiconscious captive onto the pontoon. One of them even brought duvets from the cabin to wrap around the soaking and shivering rescues.

'Back to the bank,' said Chris, having satisfied herself that no one was likely to die in the next few minutes. Even the shape she assumed was Lily Lai was coughing as she came back to full consciousness.

'Is she OK?' asked Greg from where he was sitting enrobed like an Indian chief. 'That's the first time I've ever hit a woman,' he added. 'Unless you count Whining Wendy.'

'Who was Whining Wendy and why did you hit her?' enquired Chris. 'Didn't this come up at your recruitment interview?'

'I was only four at the time,' protested Greg. 'She'd been

bullying another child. I showed her what it felt like.'

He turned his attention back to Lily Lai. 'She'll need to go to hospital. When she does, I want one of us with her. Explain they're there for her own safety but make sure she doesn't disappear again. Arrest her if there's no other alternative. I'd like her in for questioning as soon as the hospital releases her.'

The boat arrived at the wharf by the Acle Bridge pub, where the car park was now filled with police cars and ambulances. One ambulance took Lily Lai with Phil Knight in attendance. A second checked Jim and Greg, and after much argument agreed to leave without them. Chris went to thank the pirate crew, and found they were having a whale of a time being feted by the pub staff, plied with free drinks and interviewed by *BBC Look East*. The captain broke away to speak to her.

'This is turning out to be the best ever stag do,' he enthused. 'D'you want to come to the wedding?'

Chris grinned back. 'No, thanks, I'm good,' she said. 'But thank you for the loan of your boat. And if you get any hassle from the hire company about the duvets, for example, please refer them to us.' She handed over her card. 'By the way,' she said, turning back, 'after all that hospitality, I hope you're staying here for the night.'

'I guess so,' he said. 'I think we've had enough excitement for one day,' and turned back to his memorable party.

Chris surveyed her two soaking colleagues, now wrapped in NHS blankets with the sodden duvets at their feet.

'Can I trust you to stay out of mischief while I fetch Greg's car?' she asked, in a minatory tone.

'Oh God, my car keys,' exclaimed Greg, clutching at a non-existent pocket.

'Don't worry, your jacket's safely on the bank in the care of one of the cafe waiters. I'll pick everything up and bring the car round. Just don't move!'

'My upholstery,' mourned Greg. 'It'll never be the same again.'

It was handy, Greg's cottage being so close. It meant both he and Jim could have a warming shower, although Jim had to roll the sleeves and trouser legs up on the sweatshirt and jeans loaned him by Greg.

'This is going to ruin my street cred,' he lamented, peering down at the rugby club logo on the sweatshirt.

'At least you're still around to be worrying about it,' replied Chris tartly. 'I know Greg has no sense around water, but what made you jump in a fast-flowing river, right next to a bridge, what's more?'

'The thought of what Margaret would say if we went back without him,' replied Jim. 'Anyway, you've no room to talk. You've history in this area. And I saw you taking your shoes off. Thank God Greg managed to exercise some control.'

Chris snorted eloquently. 'And...' she started, but Greg thought it best to intervene.

'There's just one thing I'd like to ask,' he said. 'Does it ever occur to you Norfolk folk that there's a sight too much damn water in this county?'

Chris set off for Wymondham, while Greg ran Jim back to his car at Acle Bridge.

'Out with it, Jim,' he said. 'All this tact with regard to Chris's car being at mine is just too painful. Spit it out, whatever you've got to say.'

Jim spread his hands in denial. 'Nothing,' he said. 'I've had my say and I'm pleased for you both. You know to be careful.'

Word had travelled fast. When Jim and Greg arrived at Wymondham, they were met by a mixture of applause and good-humoured leg pulling, and 'The Chief Super wants to see you both ASAP in her office.'

The two men exchanged glances, and went on up the stairs.

'Well,' said Margaret, coming from behind her desk. 'I don't know whether to clap you two on the back or clip you round the ears. What were you thinking of? By a bridge as well!'

'You all keep harping on about the bridge,' complained Greg.

'As well we might. Get your friends from the inshore lifeboat to brief you on what a bridge does to water flow and currents. Anyway, I'm glad you're both safe, and I'm glad we have our chief suspect in custody. Just don't ever do anything like that again.

'I gather the appropriate teams and cranes are standing by to raise the car from the water and I've got frogmen, or more correctly persons, looking to see if anything fell or was thrown out. We'll see what we can recover.'

Correctly assuming both the praise and the ticking off were now over and it was back to business as usual, both men relaxed and pulled out seats.

Margaret nodded. 'Yes, sit down by all means. And take an early one too. Tomorrow is going to be busy, so take a break while you can.'

Greg leaned forward. 'Amongst other things, I'm hoping

we can find the missing lab laptop. We found Hazel Partner's personal one, the one we think Lily went back for, but there may be incriminating material on either or both. As for an early knock-off, I was hoping we might be able to interview Lily Lai this evening.'

'Leave it to the morning,' advised Margaret. 'I've just been on the phone to the hospital. They don't think they'll need to keep her in after tonight, so tomorrow she can be taken into custody and interviewed here at the station. You'll be fresher, and the environment more suitable than round her hospital bed. So, off with you, Jim. Greg, I'd like a quick word before you go.'

Once they were alone, she sat down again and looked across at Greg.

'Well done for keeping Chris Mathews out of the river,' she said. 'I didn't think it possible. Incidentally, she'll be in line for a commendation too. That business with the boat was quick thinking and effective.'

'After that booby trap explosion I made her promise,' said Greg. 'And yes, the boat was great thinking. She saved my life.'

Margaret looked at him steadily, twiddling a pen. 'A promise sounds more personal than professional. Is there anything I need to know?'

Greg returned her look straight. 'Not yet. We are getting close,' he admitted, 'but I won't compromise efficiency.'

'That's good as far as it goes, but...'

'Yes, I understand the "but". I'm just asking for a bit of time. Both to see if there is anything to worry about, and to see if it has the potential to cause difficulties.'

Margaret thought a moment then leaned back. 'Thank you for being straight with me. And this stays between us, Greg.

And Jim I assume.'

'And Jim,' he agreed.

'OK. I'll keep a watching brief. You have enough to do without me destabilising an excellent team.'

Searching for Chris, Greg tried the ops room, various offices and the interview suite before running her to earth in the canteen. She was sitting in front of the biggest mug of coffee they could provide and looked exhausted.

He sat down in front of her. 'Are you OK to drive home?' he asked. 'You look washed out.'

'Yes, I'll be fine Greg, thank you.' She stirred the coffee. 'I don't suppose there's the remotest chance I can extract a promise from you too?'

'Not a chance,' he said cheerfully.

'And why not? Why shouldn't the gander and the goose play by the same rules?'

Greg glanced round and noted they had the place to themselves. 'Because the goose is strong – resilient as well as quick thinking, as she proved today. And she's a survivor. While the gander,' he looked down at the table top, 'the gander would really struggle to get by without her. You saved my life today, Chris,' he said softly. 'Thank you.

'Now,' he said more loudly before emotion threatened them both. 'Bugger off home before you fall asleep where you sit.'

'Yes, Boss,' she said.

# 29

## After effects

By the time Greg got home he was shaking with cold again – either that or delayed shock. He fed Bobby, pulled on a thick sweater and sat down with the cat on his lap, she purring with delight, turning and kneading his lap until she decided the correct position had been achieved for sleep. Unfortunately, Greg found himself unable to join her, as his mind also went round in circles and he found himself too weary and too irresolute to do anything about supper. He must have sat like that for more than an hour, unable to summon up the energy to move, when he was startled by a bang on the backdoor followed immediately by it opening and Ben Asheton's face coming round the corner.

'Heard what happened,' he announced. 'I've brought pizza and a listening ear. No don't move. I'll grab a couple of glasses from the kitchen and we can pig it in here with our fingers.'

He dropped the huge flat box on the coffee table and produced a couple of bottles of lager from his pockets.

'Is this normal service from a first responder?' asked Greg. 'I had no idea I could get pizza on the NHS.'

'Special prescription for friends, heroes and idiots who jump into rivers,' replied Ben over his shoulder. 'Back in a second.'

Wobbly slices of American-hot-one in hand, bubbles rising in the glasses, Ben said, 'Now, get it off your chest.'

Greg looked at him. 'How do you know there's anything on it?' he enquired.

'One,' Ben held up a finger. 'After our ups and downs over the last couple of years, I think I know you pretty well. Moreover, I've talked to survivors of this type of experience before. It always hits them harder than they think. Two, Chris rang me.'

'Looking out for me, is she?' asked Greg with a warm feeling somewhere under his shirt. 'I hope she's OK. She looked knackered when I sent her home.'

'She's fine. And just to be clear I was already on my way here when she rang. But the pizza was her idea, and a very good one,' he added, reaching for another slice. 'Come on, eat it while it's hot.'

Greg reached out, then said, 'I never expected nearly drowning to feel like that. Not that I'd given it a lot of thought, but I suppose I assumed it'd involve a lot of thrashing about and struggling. A more active sort of death I suppose. Whereas…'

'Whereas what?'

'Whereas I was just too cold and tired to think properly and I'd have just slid beneath the water if it hadn't been for Jim and Chris.'

'From what Jim says, you came close,' said Ben. 'You were

vertical in the water instead of floating horizontally. That's always a bad sign. No one ever realises just how different it is swimming in cold fresh water in England, compared to a heated swimming pool, or the sea on a Caribbean holiday. Have a chat with the lifeboat crew. They'll tell you how often they fish someone out just in time. And they're rarely kicking and waving. They just slip quietly under, as you described.'

Greg shivered again. 'Don't remind me,' he said. 'It's probably going to give me nightmares as it is.'

'In a sense, the odd nightmare is normal and healthy,' replied Ben. 'It's your mind sorting out the memories and filing them away. But if you get stuck in a rut of reliving it again and again, that's unhealthy and you should get some help. One thing that interests me,' he added, 'is why you were so determined to save her. Given how many deaths she's caused, wouldn't leaving her have been a neat solution?'

Greg looked up sharply. 'That's a very immoral suggestion from you, Ben Asheton,' he said. 'I'm surprised at you. In the first place, she's innocent until proven guilty. In the second, I want her to face justice. Sidling into the hereafter under her own steam would be too easy. She needs to face her victims and face what she's done. Not that I thought all that through on the river bank,' he added. 'In fact, in that moment I was mainly thinking, "Bugger me, she's not getting away like that!"'

Ben laughed. 'That sounds like you,' he commented. 'And do you think you can get justice?'

Greg leaned back with his glass of lager, the pizza now no more than crumbs in a greasy box. 'I think we've a good chance. There're some gaps in our evidence,' he admitted, 'but I'm hoping what we find in the car and on the laptops might fill some of those. But even without anything else, we've a pretty good case already.'

'Job for tomorrow,' announced Ben, getting up and clearing away the remains of their meal. 'Bed for you my friend. And if you do wake in the night, I prescribe a chamomile tea, a walk in the garden and back to bed.'

'Will do,' said Greg, getting up and disturbing an indignant cat. 'And thanks, Ben. You're a mate.'

A reasonable night with only one disturbing dream, and the morning brought new energy along with a voicemail from Chris saying she'd see him at work and hoping he'd slept well.

He rang her from the car. 'Thanks for Ben and the pizza,' he said. 'Both were just what I needed. Are you OK after all that happened yesterday?'

'I'm fine,' she said, her warm voice filling the car. 'I'll see you at the office? I'll be there shortly. I want to chase up the IT guys. At the least they should have something from the laptop found in the neighbour's bin.'

'I'm on my way in but a little behind you,' he admitted. 'I agree, top priority is that laptop and whatever they've managed to recover from the car. Then it's prep for the interview with Professor Lai. See you in about twenty minutes.'

The drive to Wymondham suffered the usual hold-ups around Postwick and at the junction with the A11, but the day was intermittently sunny, the clouds scudded fast in the brisk breeze and it felt good to be alive. In his mind, Greg was going over all the evidence they had against their various suspects, and concluded that the first, the very first thing he needed was a thorough round-up with the whole team. Instinctively he felt they were close to convincing the CPS to go ahead, but knew that he didn't have a full grasp of all the detail. Certainly not enough to face Lily Lai across a table. The general effect of his arrival at HQ was therefore of a whirlwind, as he swept in issuing orders that everyone, and he meant everyone, gather in the ops room.

It was quite a crowd that faced him. Ned was there along with the core team of Jim, Sarah, Chris, Jenny and Steve. In addition, Greg noticed as he swivelled round to bring everyone into view, he had representatives from the forensic IT team.

'Great. Welcome all,' said Greg. 'I think we're all here except Turbo, and hopefully we won't need his help this morning.' There were grins as he went on to say, 'And thank you to you all. This has been a supreme team effort, and all the stronger for it. Before we get into the nitty gritty, let's establish what our day is going to look like. Anyone know when Lily Lai is arriving from the hospital?'

Chris spoke up. 'Heard from Phil at the hospital,' she said. 'She's on the way and should be here in less than thirty minutes.'

'And a brief?'

'Also on the way. It seems she's hired a barrister from London but the solicitor is local, from the city. It's a Mr Leavenham, of Parkes and Leavenham, so possibly a partner.'

'Anyone know him?'

Heads were shaken until Phil contributed, 'I think I came across a Mr Leavenham some years ago, but that would probably be this chap's father or uncle, as he was getting on even then.'

'OK. Let's start the review of where we're at. I'd like to do this suspect by suspect, starting with Jack Haigh. Sarah, you've been collating data. Would you like to go first?'

She looked up, apparently startled, then flicked through her iPad screens and cleared her throat. 'Case against Jack Haigh,' she started. 'One, we have a witness and CCTV footage tying him to the acquisition of the car used to carry the bomb and its journey to the bomb-making factory near Aylsham. Two, we have evidence from a police undercover agent that he was specifically recruited to work at the NASA in order to be part of a bomb plot. Three, we have his confession that he was involved in all those activities and that he was material to ensuring that the car bomb could be parked in exactly the right location to cause maximum damage.'

'Anyone want to add anything?' asked Greg.

Ned looked up. 'Some fingerprint evidence confirming his presence at the bomb-making site.'

'OK,' said Greg. 'I think we're home and dry on Jack Haigh. As to his claim he'd been assured there'd be no casualties. I'm inclined to believe him, but it doesn't invalidate the rest of the evidence. No doubt his brief will make the most of it in mitigation.

'Next, Pat Nichols. What do we have on him?'

'Nothing from the undercover agent,' remarked Sarah.

'Fingerprints and DNA at the bomb-making site, and his car on CCTV at various locations travelling to and from the bomb-making factory,' said Ned.

'Plus Jack Haigh's statement describing both the terrorist cell comprising Pat, Jan Littleboys and himself, and Pat's involvement in mixing the explosive,' added Chris.

'Good. That's another one in the bag. Noting also that, courtesy of the evidence provided by George and Mildred, Jan

Littleboys was the casualty in the fire who appears to have been locked in the storeroom by Professor Lily Lai. Which brings us to Professor Lai.'

'There we do have more evidence from undercover,' interrupted Sarah. 'Relating to the acquisition of the Semtex and the planning of the attack.'

Jaws dropped around the room as those who hadn't heard this before assimilated the implications.

'They knew?' asked Steve incredulously. 'They knew and they didn't say anything?'

'They were hoping to round up the whole organisation,' said Sarah. That she was feeling defensive was obvious both from her tone and from the way she tightened her ponytail to the point of stretching her eyebrows into her forehead.

'That's likely to be the subject of a different investigation,' said Greg repressively. 'And it won't be us doing the investigating, although some of us may need to give evidence. For today, it's enough that we have a credible witness that can state Professor Lai was involved in the procurement of the Semtex and the planning of the attack. We also have a statement from the man who was picked up with her from the back of the lab just before the bomb went off, that he saw her hand the Semtex over to Jan Littleboys at the bomb-making site. Unfortunately, that witness, Nigel Atkinson, has since died, so whether his statement will be admissible in court is somewhat moot.

'But we're getting ahead of ourselves. Back to Lily Lai. We have evidence that ties her in to the bomb attack. We have Mrs P's statement that she left the lab just before the bomb went off, and reason to believe that Lai left Jan Littleboys to die in her place, although I think we'll struggle to prove that. Nigel

Atkinson himself also accused her of poisoning him and Hazel Partner. What do we have on that? Ned?'

'Both Partner and Atkinson died of paraquat poisoning. The final pathology and lab reports came through this morning,' replied Ned. 'The material in the bottle I showed you was paraquat concentrate. Lethal dose roughly two teaspoons full.'

'And that's available to farmers?' asked Jim. 'Nasty stuff!'

'Not now and not for a long time in the form we have here,' replied Ned. 'Commercial paraquat contained a stenching agent and an emetic from the seventies onward, precisely to reduce the risks of accidental ingestion. And it's been banned since 2007. This stuff is laboratory-synthesised pure active ingredient. It can only have been held for research purposes, which points towards the chem lab at NASA, and Lily Lai again.'

'We need to see if there're any records of such work at the lab. Can you check with Craig Bennington please, Jim.' Jim made a note. 'OK, what else? Anything from IT yet?' Greg looked over at the relevant expert.

'We're still working on it,' he said. 'But we do have some interesting material on the laptop recovered from the waste bin in North Walsham. We've some way to go yet, but it definitely shows links between Hazel Partner and Lily Lai. In particular, it seems Partner engineered the hack that resulted in her having access to almost all lab systems, and she did it on instruction from an IP address linked to Lai. Later in the time line, she seems to have initiated some creative hacking of that IP address itself, almost certainly against Lai's wishes and possibly without her knowledge – at least in the beginning. It looks as though she was starting to worry about Lai. There was a spate of activity after the bombing at the lab.

'Possibly Jack Haigh wasn't the only one promised a no-casualties action. Either way, those links are of considerable interest to our friends in antiterrorism. With luck, they might provide evidence of actors further up the chain even than Lai.'

'And the laptop in the car?' asked Greg.

'Nothing yet. The soaking it got didn't do it a lot of good. We should find something, but it's a much less sophisticated piece of kit than the high spec laptop that belonged to Hazel Partner.'

Greg paused for thought, looking at his notes and the summary on the whiteboard.

'Priorities for the interview with Lily Lai,' he said. 'One, details of her actions with regard to the planning and execution of the bomb attack on NASA. Two, the murders by poison of Nigel Atkinson and Hazel Partner. Three, whatever we can find out about the organisation above her level. Was she acting alone, or was there a bigger conspiracy? For example, can we nail the suppliers of the Semtex as well?'

# 30

## Lily Lai

Greg took a few moments to observe his interviewee from the adjacent viewing suite before going in. She was already seated on the far side of the small square table. In the harsh light of the interview room, she looked pale but composed. Evidently her brief, or someone, had brought her some fresh clothes, as she was neatly dressed in black trousers and white shirt. She'd hung a black cardigan over the back of her chair. Alongside her was a man Greg didn't know, presumably Mr Leavenham. He seemed young for his role, probably still in his thirties, nattily dressed in chinos and blazer, white shirt and striped tie. He had a bulging briefcase beside him on the floor and a laptop open on the edge of the table. Greg turned as someone came into the room behind him.

'Doesn't seem very bothered, does she?' remarked Chris.

Jim was behind her, also scrutinising their subject.

'Chris, I'd like you to observe from here. Jim, you come in

with me,' said Greg. 'We might swap over after an hour or two, particularly if I think that'll throw her a curve ball, but either way, I'd like comments, Chris. Right. Let's get started.'

Chris sat down in front of the two-way mirror as the men left the room. As she saw the door open, she switched on the intercom and got out her notebook.

Greg entered briskly, nodding a thank you at the uniformed officer standing in the corner.

'Good morning,' he said generally and sat down. Jim, on his left, was switching on the tape and checking all was working.

'I'm DCI Geldard and this is DI Henning, both of Norfolk police. Would you please introduce yourselves for the tape.'

'Professor Lai,' she said clearly.

'I'm Peter Leavenham of Parkes and Leavenham. And can I start by saying that my client has come here of her own free will after a very disturbing accident, and therefore I hope that this can be concluded rapidly.'

'The sooner we start, the sooner we can finish,' replied Greg. 'First of all, Professor Lily Lai, I must caution you that you do not have to say anything. But it may harm your defence if you do not mention when questioned something which you later rely on in court. Anything you do say may be given in evidence.

'As you've attended this morning voluntarily, you're free to leave at any moment. However, as we have some serious questions to ask about recent tragic events at the NASA and about your accident near Acle Bridge, I hope you'll feel able to assist us.'

There was a pause, and then Professor Lai asked, 'Are you arresting me?'

'Not at this point, no,' replied Greg. 'But there are some issues that give us grounds for suspicion that you may have committed an offence. I'm hopeful that a few questions and answers will clarify things.' Another pause, and then Greg added, 'Shall we proceed then? Let's start with the most recent events. What were you doing in North Walsham?'

'Shopping in Waitrose,' replied Lai succinctly.

'And where were you staying?'

'In a B&B.'

'Can I have the address please?'

'Sorry, I don't have it. I stopped on a back street when I saw a sign saying rooms to let. It was a spur-of-the-moment thing.'

'Perhaps if we show you a map, you can indicate where, roughly, it was?'

'Perhaps. Why does it matter?'

Greg ignored the question. 'Turning to your drive towards Acle yesterday. Where were you going?'

'I was returning to Norwich. To my home.'

'And why did you suddenly accelerate to dangerous speeds, to such an extent that you lost control, left the road and ended up in the river near the Acle bridge?'

'Because I realised I was being followed.'

'Why was that a problem?'

'Because my lab had been blown up, Chief Inspector. Don't you think you might find that a little frightening? I was fleeing for my life. Incidentally,' she added, 'if you're waiting for me to thank you for pulling me out, forget it. There would've been no accident if you hadn't chased me.'

'And on that subject,' interjected Mr Leavenham, 'we will be considering a formal complaint.'

Behind the two-way mirror Chris snorted eloquently.

'On the subject of the laboratory,' Jim interrupted, 'where were you on the day of the explosion?'

'I was working at home.'

'Really? Not at the laboratory at all?'

'Not that day, no. I had some data to analyse, and I often do that at home.'

Jim looked at Greg, who gave him a tiny nod. 'Did you know Hazel Partner?'

'The girl in IT? Yes, of course.'

'And did you stay at her home after the explosion?'

'No. I told you, I stayed in a B&B.'

'Have you ever visited Hazel in her home?'

'No,' Lai caught a glance from her brief and added, 'comment.'

'Now, why does that question cause a problem?' asked Jim of the air. 'I wouldn't have thought it was difficult. Either you've visited your colleague Hazel, or you haven't.'

Silence. Greg and Jim regarded the other two for a moment, allowing the silence to stretch out. Peter Leavenham made a note on his laptop and cleared his throat. 'If you have no further questions,' he began.

'Oh, we have more questions,' said Greg. 'We're just wondering why your client has suddenly gone no comment. We thought she was here to help. Perhaps it would be a good idea to take a break and you can have a chat with her. For the benefit of the tape, DCI Geldard and DI Henning are leaving the room. Constable Dennis here will see you get some tea and coffee,' he added.

Out in the corridor, 'Not here,' said Greg to Jim. 'Let's join

Chris in the viewing suite and discuss next steps there.'

Chris turned as they went in. 'Caught her in some handy lies,' she said with some satisfaction. 'And you haven't even started on the subject of the car yet. I look forward to hear her explaining how she comes to be driving Hazel's car!'

'Chris is right,' said Greg. 'I think we'll leave the car till the end. Let's challenge her on her whereabouts on the day of the explosion first. Then move to North Walsham, figuratively speaking.'

'What do you think her strategy is,' asked Jim. 'By all accounts she's an intelligent woman. Very intelligent. So, how does she think she's going to get away with all the lies?'

'At present, she doesn't know what we know. My guess is that part of her reason for being here voluntarily is to find that out. Once she knows how much evidence we've got against her she'll go no comment, then discuss with her brief how much credit she can get for shopping others. But let's go see, shall we?'

Tape back on and their return noted, Jim asked, 'Going back to the day of the explosion, you say you were at home that day.'

'Yes.'

'That would be your home in,' Jim shuffled though his papers. 'Taverham? Nowhere near the Science Park then.'

'Correct.'

'So, perhaps you'd like to explain why we have a witness that saw you leave the NASA compound by the rear gate shortly before the explosion?'

'They must have been mistaken.'

'I don't think so. They had a clear line of sight to the gate and they know you well by sight. They've stated they saw you get into a silver Golf, the one in fact which you put into the river yesterday.'

'No comment.' She flashed a worried look at Mr Leavenham.

'I think my client has given you enough help,' he said, rising from his seat.

'Just a few more questions,' said Jim. 'Our witness has stated that you were driven away in the silver Golf with a man subsequently identified as a Mr Nigel Atkinson.'

'She must have been mistaken. There are a lot of silver cars around.'

'Mr Atkinson himself has also made a statement.'

Even from the viewing suite, Chris could see the change in Lily Lai's demeanour. She stiffened and said, 'That's impossible.' Then snapped her jaw closed.

'Really. Why would that be?' enquired Greg, taking over the questioning. 'Because you thought he was dead? Like Hazel Partner?'

'No comment,' she said sullenly and stood up. 'I'm leaving now.'

'Not before time,' remarked Mr Leavenham, also standing.

'But not just yet,' said Greg, also standing. 'Lily Lai, I'm arresting you on suspicion of the murders of Nigel Atkinson, Hazel Partner and Jan Littleboys, the murders of eight casualties of the laboratory bombing, and of conspiracy to cause an explosion. You do not have to say anything. But it may harm your defence if you do not mention when questioned something which you later rely on in court. Anything you do say may be given in evidence. Interview adjourned at,' he looked at his watch, '1400. We'll be back,' he said.

In the viewing room, Greg sat down with Jim and Chris. 'OK,' he said. 'Three areas of interest. Her whereabouts on the day of the explosion – I have little doubt Mrs P's evidence will hold up in court and it's backed up by Nigel Atkinson's statement. We have a clear denial on record. No need to waste too much time on that.

'Her actions at Hazel Partner's house. There we have Atkinson's statement again, this time backed up by some forensics. Ned is happy he's got her fingerprints at the house and some of the samples may yet come up with a positive on DNA.'

Jim shifted in his seat. 'I'm a bit uncomfortable about relying so heavily on the Atkinson statement,' he said. 'What if the judge rules it inadmissible?'

'Then we have a problem, so it's up to us to make sure we have other evidence to back up the story. Some of what's coming out of the IT team is helpful. The fact that Hazel was hacking Lai's account is useful. What we don't know yet is what she found.'

'Nor do we have much other than Atkinson's word that it was she who poisoned the two of them.'

'We have a partial fingerprint on the bottle of paraquat,' objected Chris, 'and we're waiting to hear whether it was stored or synthesized in her lab. We're waiting on Craig Bennington getting back to us on that. We're also waiting on the final report from Hazel's post-mortem. There may be something there too.'

'How long before we get those results?' asked Greg.

'I'll chase, but last time I asked they were due any moment.'

'Then, since we now have her under arrest, I suggest we leave her to stew until after lunch. Let's regroup then, and see what else we can hit her with.'

'We'll need to watch our timing,' warned Jim. 'Deadlines will be looming.'

'Sure. But thanks to only having arrested her a few minutes ago, we can spare an hour or two to get our ducks in a row. The other issue is the car. What did they find exactly when they hauled it out of the river.'

'Not much.' Chris flicked through her notebook. 'The lab laptop as we noted earlier, currently with IT. An overnight bag containing a few clothes and toiletries. Mobile phone. A soggy map book. That was about it.'

'Can that lad in IT repeat his magic by mining the car's database?' asked Greg. 'He turned up all sorts of useful stuff from James Metcalfe's car. Not just where he'd been and when, but even how many people had been in the car!'

'He's trying,' said Chris, 'but no promises because of the water damage. And Ned's got the case full of damp clothes.'

'Ok. Let's meet again at one, and restart the interview at two.

It was an excited Chris that rushed into Greg's office on the dot of one.

'Got her,' she said. 'Bennington confirmed that Lai had submitted a research project connected to the synthesis of paraquat to see, or so she said, whether variants were possible that were less toxic but still effective herbicides. And Ned says he's got Hazel Partner's DNA and paraquat on stained clothing in the overnight case from the sunken car.'

'Even though it'd been in the river?' asked Greg.

'It seems the case was water resistant albeit not waterproof. Enough anyway that the traces survived. Ned reckons Hazel was sick over Lai while she was dragging her out to the garage. Presumably she wouldn't have dared leave the dirty clothes behind for us to find, so she stuffed them in her case with her other things.'

'She'll claim the clothes were Hazel's,' objected Jim

'But at the moment she's saying she didn't visit Hazel, and anyway, why would she take her smelly clothes away with her? Plus,' said Chris triumphantly, 'they're very different in size and shape. If these are Lai's clothes, they wouldn't fit Hazel.'

Reconvened at two, it was evident the atmosphere had changed. Lai was resentful and uncooperative. Peter Leavenham alternated between leaning back staring at the ceiling, and leaning forward with his hand up in attempt to intervene. He needn't have bothered. Lai ignored him and said nothing at all except, 'No comment'. Around six, Greg decided to adjourn for the day, with Lai remanded in custody overnight.

Back in his office he sat at his desk, stretched, and shuffled his papers together.

'So,' he said, 'she wasn't at the lab on the day of the explosions, evidence to the contrary. We have statements and forensic evidence that she murdered Partner and Atkinson. We have the security service evidence that she procured the Semtex and planned the explosion. I think we can satisfy CPS on every count. Well done the team. I think this warrants a small celebration this evening and she'll be in the magistrates' court tomorrow. No one needs to be there for that, they'll just send the case to the Crown Court, so I suggest we use the time constructively to pull all our material together and make sure we've dotted all the i's and crossed all the t's.'

'And the Crown Court bail hearing?' asked Chris.

'We'll need to check precise timings but it'll have to be before the end of the week. Yes, it would be good to have someone there for that. Chris, can you go?'

As Greg had predicted, the magistrates did their formal duty and the case of Regina vs Haigh, Nichols and Lai was adjourned to the Crown Court the following day. Chris duly attended, just to make sure Frank Parker opposed bail with his usual vigour, as she put it. Late morning she rang Greg from her mobile, standing in the car park outside the Norwich combined courts. It took several tries before she could get through as he seemed to be engaged for quite a while. When she did, her opening words were, 'You're not going to believe this!'

'Yes, I am,' said Greg grimly. 'I've just had Frank on the phone.'

'So you know her plea?'

'I know. Not guilty by reason of insanity.'

# 31

## Insane or evil?

Frank Parker entered the room like a thunderstorm and banged his papers on the desk. When the rumbles of thunder had faded he sat down and glared round at the assembled company of Greg, Jim and Chris.

'What the hell does she think she's going to achieve?' he snarled through clenched teeth. 'Insanity forsooth! I can't remember when I last faced that one in court.'

'Frank,' said Greg, 'can you outline for us precisely what insanity means in this context. Then we can work out what evidence might be needed to refute it.'

Frank sighed and leaned back in his chair to the point of danger. The wood creaked warningly but he ignored it.

'Essentially,' he replied, 'it means insane as defined legally. It has little to do with any medical or psychiatric diagnosis, although obviously expert witnesses will be called who will no doubt give evidence as to both. So, what she has got to demonstrate,' he could hardly bring himself to use her name, 'is that she is not competent, or was not competent at the time, to understand what she was doing, or was unable to understand that what she was doing was wrong. The textbook will tell you that every defendant is presumed sane unless the contrary is proved and that to successfully plead insanity, it must be clearly proved that at the time of committing the act the defendant was labouring under such a defect of reason, from disease of the mind, as not to know the nature and quality of the act they were doing. In this country, it's a very rare defence, although getting less rare, and it's also not usually very successful. But in this instance I can't rid myself of the thought that this is a very intelligent woman with a very experienced barrister in her corner.'

'So she doesn't necessarily have to prove clinical illness.'

'No. In fact medical experts are specifically required not to pronounce on whether she is or was insane in legal terms. It's a matter for the jury.'

'So where is she going with this?'

'I don't know.' Frank leaned forward so suddenly his chair banged down hard enough to rattle everyone's teeth. 'And I won't know for sure until I see more of the defence's case. But one thing I do know, and that's I'm going to need a damn good forensic psychiatrist. Bill,' he shouted loudly, and a young lawyer stuck his head round the door. 'Best forensic psychiatrist you can find. And I want them yesterday.'

Greg had been thinking hard and making notes.

'One question,' he said. 'Does she have to demonstrate that she had no idea what she was doing, or just that she couldn't know what the impact would be of what she was doing?' Frank eyed him sharply from under bushy brows.

'Are you reading my mind?' he asked.

'Not a stupid question then?'

'Far from it. If she could demonstrate that she planned and executed the actions for which we have evidence, but had no understanding of the probable impact, then she might have a faint chance of succeeding in her defence. If I was seeking to use insanity in her defence that's the way I'd go. Her actual actions were so well planned and thought through over a long period, it's hard to see how anyone could argue all of that was done with defective reason. Especially when at the same time she was a fully functioning senior scientist in a government laboratory with no apparent defects of reason. But if she could show there was a break in the logic between action and outcome, well then,' he shrugged.

'What about the siting of the car bomb. It's clear that was intended to cause maximum casualties,' said Greg.

'Clear to you and me perhaps, but if they argue she was so blinded by hate as to be oblivious to everything but her plans to blow up the lab, then…' And he shrugged again.

Leaving the CPS suite, Greg paused in the corridor.

'Jim, I'm going to go and have another chat with that counsellor, Neil,' he said. 'In the meantime, we need to revisit everything we've got that might give some clues as to her motive. If she had a logical motive for her actions, she'll have that much more difficulty demonstrating "defect of reason". Ask Sarah to have another chat with Newton and see what else we can get from them. And get IT to crawl over every document and message on those laptops. There has to be something.'

'Or she is mad, and there was no good reason.'

'In which case, we need evidence of just how dangerous she is. In one way, it doesn't much matter whether she's secured in prison or in hospital, provided she can't do it again.'

Neil was willing to be helpful, but cautious.

'I've said before, Greg, I can't give advice on someone I've never met, and CPS will need a forensic expert in the field, not someone like me.'

'Yes, I realise that,' replied Greg. 'They're looking around for the right person as we speak. This's to help me understand, if that's OK.'

'OK. I can spare a few minutes. But at most I may be able to suggest a few questions. Don't look to me for answers.'

'You talked before about hate having as its goal the elimination of its target. One of the things that's not clear in this whole case is why this target? Why enlist in the ranks of animal rights activists? There's nothing in her history that suggests she had any interest in animal welfare whatsoever.'

'Have you tried asking her?'

'Of course I have,' said Greg, frustrated. 'But she's gone no comment on me.'

'What about the ex-fiancé you mentioned?'

'He said she got very angry about a whole succession of slights and insults that she felt were aimed at her because of her gender and race. Most of the ones he mentioned were stupid, nasty insults of the sort sadly commonplace in some environments. He did mention one incident in particular,' he added thoughtfully. 'One where Lai felt she had been passed over for a new job or a promotion. He mentioned it specifically because he thought it was one instance where her assumptions about motive were wrong. But it was also an instance of when she was particularly angry.'

'Perhaps you need to find out what the examples he gives had in common. And particularly if there were more, later in her career.'

A further chat with Tom Bentley threw up little that was new.

'That new job she was after,' he said. 'I've done as you asked and checked back through my old diaries. It was a job at one of the big chemical companies. They had a big research programme looking for new active ingredients for pesticides, and an even bigger testing programme checking out the possibles. She was gutted when she didn't get the job.'

'The testing programme,' said Greg, following the germ of an idea. 'Would it have involved animals?'

'Oh, definitely. The safety and efficacy tests for pesticides are quite prescriptive. Most of the animals would be insects, of course, especially on the efficacy testing.'

'And the safety tests?'

'They commonly involve rats and mice. Sometimes rabbits and fish.'

Back in his car and returning to Norfolk, he had recourse to a quick phone call to Sarah, followed by another to Chris.

'Sarah,' he said, 'can you do some checking with Newton and any other contacts you have amongst the funny buggers. I want to know the date of the earliest link they have between Lily Lai and animal rights extremists, and what were the targets.'

'Chris, can you check the records for any demos, site

invasions or other problems connected with GMI Chemistry Ltd, particularly around and after the date Lily Lai was turned down for a job there.'

And then, 'Jim, can you have another chat with Craig Bennington? It's a very specific question. I want to know whether Lily Lai had applied for a new job or a promotion in the recent past.'

It was five o clock by the time some at least of the questions had been answered, and Greg grouped the team round the whiteboard in the ops room. Newly wiped down, it shone in the strip lighting, its emptiness somehow full of promise.

'OK,' said Greg, 'let's collect up your data, and I think you'll see where I'm going on this.' He drew a line down the centre of the board and labelled the top '1990'. 'OK, this is our time line. The left-hand column he labelled 'career path'; and right-hand column, 'animal rights events'.

'Jim, what happened in 1990?'

'Lily Lai was turned down for a job at GMI Chemistry Ltd. And broke off her engagement with Tom Bentley.'

'Sarah, what data do we have on animal rights activity targeting GMI?'

Early 1991, lab invaded and test animals stolen. Also, lab supplying them with test animals was broken into four months later and animals released. Lily Lai is suspected of having a hand in the planning, but no concrete proof. The information they have is not contemporaneous. It's a case of putting evidence together after the event. Quite some years after the event.'

'OK. We know that from 1990 to 2000 Lai continued to work in London, first at Imperial, and then in a more senior role at Queen Mary. Let's move to 2002 when she starts a new role at Porton Down. How did things go there, Chris?'

'I managed to get some detail from her HR file,' she replied, 'although they're pretty cagey about what she was working on. She started as a senior scientific officer. After three years she applied for promotion to principal scientific officer but didn't get it. According to her file, her science was very highly regarded but there were concerns about her people management skills, and that was the reason she was unsuccessful. The same thing happened again a couple of years later. Soon after that she left Porton Down and took up a role at NASA.'

'And over in this column?' Greg moved to the right of the board.

'Well there you could list two demos outside the Porton Down gate, one of which was suspected of being a distraction for a break-in on the site,' replied Sarah.

'Did they get away with anything?'

'No. The security was too good,' answered Chris; and Sarah added, 'That was when the security unit of the time started to take an interest in the animal rights crowd. Lai was on their lists as "of interest". It might be worth noting, too, that although their paths didn't cross, both Lai and Jack Haigh have links with Queen Mary.'

'So, to 2008 and her first role at NASA. This was the much-sought-after principal role, is that right?' Greg scribbled on the board again.

'Yes. And she stayed at that level through the move from Guildford to Norwich in 2010 and then for another four years until she was promoted to head of analytical chemistry in 2014.'

'OK,' said Greg slowly. 'I'm sure you're all seeing the pattern here. So, what happened recently that might have triggered more retaliation? Jim, you've spoken to Craig Bennington. Anything relevant?'

Jim looked up from his notes. 'Absolutely fits,' he said. 'According to Craig Bennington, Lily Lai applied for the role of deputy CEO at the end of 2016. She didn't get it. He did. Obviously as the other candidate he didn't take part in the interview of Lai, but reading between the lines afterwards, he concluded that the main point of difference between them, the thing that got him the job, was again people management skills. He said Lily was cool but polite with him afterwards. Not particularly helpful at agency board meetings, but not positively obstructive.'

Greg scribbled on the board again, then stood back.

'So what we have here,' he said, is a clear pattern of a slight, or something Lai interpreted as a slight, followed by revenge in the shape of an animal rights attack.'

'And the attacks seem to have escalated in severity,' added Jim.

Greg nodded. 'I think we need another word with Agent A.'

# 32

## Under cover

The conversation this time was a little different. Same safe house, but different atmosphere. Greg had specifically asked if they could have an off-the-record discussion, followed by, if needed, a carefully curated interview under caution. Agent A and her minders had agreed, subject to the Norfolk team leaving all recording devices, including phones, at the door. They'd stopped short of a strip search for wires but not much short, and Greg suspected they had been unobtrusively screened electronically.

With Jim involved in preparations for the forensic psychologist and Sarah up to her elbows in data files, this time Greg was accompanied by Chris, who was at least allowed to keep her notebook.

'Thank you for seeing us,' said Greg. 'Just to stress, we understand your constraints, and the last, absolutely the last thing we want to do is put you at risk, particularly if you're still in the field.'

Agent A gave a noncommittal smile and sipped her coffee. At least the funny buggers had good coffee, noted Greg as he followed suit.

'What we'd like to do is explore in more detail how you got to know Lily Lai, and what you know about her involvement in various animal rights events.'

'I've already told you,' interrupted Agent A, and Greg interrupted in his turn, 'Bear with me a moment. Let me explain what we're looking for, and then I'll leave it to you to decide what you can tell us.' He paused a moment to marshal his thoughts. 'You'll know that Lai is pleading not guilty by reason of insanity. We need to demonstrate that, far from being unaware of the consequences of her actions, the car bomb in Norwich was the culmination of a sequence of steadily escalating episodes of violence. So, what can you tell us about your involvement in the "Movement" and in particular Lai's use of it?'

There was a long pause. Then Agent A said, 'Some of this I can swear to in court. Some of it stays between us. I'll be clear which is which, and the history of my early involvement is part of the latter. My bosses here know this, but no one else does.' She hesitated again, then said, 'My first involvement with the animal rights crowd was as a student, before I joined the police.'

Greg was speechless for a moment. 'Yet they allowed you to go under cover in the same area?' he asked.

'It was my idea. I was aware from briefings that the intelligence community was getting worried about the potential for violence, that the demonstrations were escalating. I pointed out I had contacts in the field under my maiden name. So that's what I used. Also, like a lot of folk, I sort of reinvented myself when I went to uni and everyone knew me by a version of my middle name. In the Force, I used the first name my parents gave me. Both those factors helped create some distance between the two roles, and I was, of course, given a cover story.

'I took part in some fairly low level activity, then got involved with the "Management".' She drew quotation marks in the air. 'My cover was as a junior personnel officer in the civil service, so for them, my background was helpful when they were trying to place moles in specific places. From our point of view, naturally it meant we knew where the moles had been placed, which was very handy indeed.'

'And Lai?'

'My first contact with her was when the decision had been made to infiltrate GMI. I got the impression the decision was hers. It was definitely hers when we tried, and failed, to infiltrate Porton Down. Their procedures were too stringent. We couldn't get anyone in without telling them I was an undercover cop, and the decision made here was that wasn't a good idea.'

'And NASA?'

'Again, Lai's prints were all over it. The instruction to target NASA came from an IP address I recognised. It was either Lai, or someone using her ID.'

Greg paused to think and went over to the window. The top was open just a crack, and the smell of cut grass drifted in on the breeze. He turned back to Agent A.

'So, excluding your prior knowledge of the animal rights movement, you can make a statement linking Lily Lai to the infiltration of several activist targets, and you have evidence to back it up.'

'That's right.' She looked across at Chris. 'I'm happy to sit down with your sergeant and make a statement. And there's some evidence we can share from our files. Mainly messaging intercepted by GCHQ.'

'What about the Semtex?' he went on. 'What have you got that ties Lily to the acquisition of the explosives?'

'Ah, now that does get interesting. This was a departure for this group, so naturally we were very worried about what was going on. The decision was taken at a high level to prioritise scrutiny of Lai and a number of her known contacts. None of the usual team seemed to be involved and we don't know how the initial contact was made, but GCHQ picked up mobile phone traffic that linked Lai to the arrangements for the delivery and the payments. Subsequently we've also got banking data that looks as though Lai was involved, at least as a sort of post box, but we're still checking on that.'

'Why hasn't this been handed over to us?' demanded Greg. 'Surely this is key evidence for our investigation. I take it the Irish were involved somewhere along the line?'

'Well, no, that's the interesting bit. I know the Semtex was IDed as having passed through IRA hands, but we didn't find any recent links. The phone traffic and the bank details all point in the opposite direction. East rather than West and Lithuania in particular. Some of the conversations on the phones were in Lithuanian and the bank we traced the money to is in Vilnius.

Once Chris had the statement in the bag, and all the phone and banking evidence saved to an encrypted data stick, or at least all the evidence they were allowed, they got back into Greg's car. The first part of the journey was silent. The traffic was, unusually, flowing fairly freely and so were Greg's thoughts.

They had passed Barton Mills roundabout before he ventured a comment.

'Lithuanian,' he said. 'Coincidence or…' He didn't finish his sentence.

'We never did find the Lithuanians behind the modern slavery case,' said Chris thoughtfully. 'We nailed that bastard Metcalfe at Stalham Poultry and his fixer, Bakalov, but we never got whoever was pulling the strings from Vilnius.'

'My thoughts precisely,' replied Greg. 'Could be a complete coincidence, of course, but is it? How many Lithuanian gangsters have we got operating in Norfolk? And if there is more than one, how likely is it they are completely unconnected?' He drove on in silence for a while, tapping his fingers on his steering wheel.

'Not strictly necessary for a successful trial of Lily Lai,' remarked Chris.

'What isn't necessary?' Greg had been lost in his thoughts.

'Tracing the Lithuanian angle. But I can see we're going to do it. You do realise the funny buggers won't be pleased,' she added.

'Who said anything about we?' asked Greg, glancing sideways.

'Me. If we're going after Mr Big of Vilnius, we're doing it together. I'll see what my banking contacts can tell us. There're a few loose ends in this evidence,' she tapped her bag, 'that I think they might be able to help us tie up.'

'And I'll have a chat with Lukas Jankauskas,' said Greg. 'See what hints he might have for us. He was the best of all the Lithuanian workers we met at Stalham and he got pretty friendly with Ben. Chris,' he added, 'I'm not sure I'm comfortable with you being involved. These are dangerous people.'

'Precisely why you need me,' she replied. 'Someone has to watch your back and better me than anyone else. Moreover, Greg, what we have will never work if you start treating me differently. You can't kid glove me.'

'Fat chance,' he said with a grin. 'But you must understand, it's not easy for me to watch you walk into danger.'

'Not easy for me either,' she replied firmly, 'so much better we do it together. Deal?'

'Deal,' he said, hiding his misgivings.

Two quick phone calls, and Greg had his evening sorted.

'Just me this time,' he said to Chris quietly by his car. 'I've got hold of Ben too, so we're having an all blokes' evening with Lukas in the bar at the King's Arms. If there is anything he can tell me, I think he'll open up better if it's just the three of us.'

'I see,' said Chris, pretending to pout. 'What do I do? Wash my hair?'

'You could teach your parrot some words suitable for polite company,' suggested Greg, stealing a quick kiss as he got into his car. 'That'll take all evening.' He wound the window down and stuck his head out. 'I could call by later and see what progress you've made? If you're not too busy with all that hair?'

'Ring me when you leave the pub,' she said. 'I'll have Tallulah on standby. Bring a toothbrush.'

He was still grinning when he squeezed his car into the last space at the King's Arms. Rooks were circling the church tower nearby, and he saw them mob an optimistic seagull with harsh cries.

Ben and Lukas were already comfortably settled in the window seat and Greg pulled out the chair opposite.

'Thanks for this, Lukas,' he said. 'I really appreciate your time. How's Esther by the way?'

'Very well,' said Lukas. 'In fact, better than well. We're expecting our first child in a few months.'

Amid the cries of congratulations the drinks arrived and it was a few minutes later before Greg could pursue the reason for their meeting.

'When we had all that trouble at Stalham Poultry last year,' he started, 'it was clear there was involvement from organised crime in Lithuania. It came out in James Metcalfe's statements, and the Gangmaster and Labour Abuse Authority had some intelligence too, but that part of the investigation came to nothing.'

'Where's Metcalfe now?' asked Lukas.

'Residing at Her Majesty's pleasure. He started off in Norwich, but last time I asked they'd moved him to Bure.'

'And Bakalov?'

'He's still in Norwich. Word was that they had to move Metcalfe to get him away from Bakalov, and they upgraded our Romanian friend to category B at the same time. He's in the more secure part of Norwich.'

'Good. I do hope it is secure.' Lukas took a swig of his lager and put the glass down. 'I think,' he said, 'that he's still getting orders from his old bosses. You might see if you can find them that way. Find how the orders reach him.'

'Then track back,' said Greg, interested. 'That would make sense. I doubt it'd get us anywhere talking to Bakalov himself. He's as tight as a duck's arse.' As Lukas looked at him questioningly, he smiled and said, 'Ask Ben later. He'll explain.

It's a good thought though. Thanks, Lukas. I'll follow that up. What about other workers at the poultry plant? Are any still around that might be worth me talking to?'

'I'm not there now,' replied Lukas, and Greg noticed again how much his English had improved over the last year. The work, no doubt, of his interpreter wife.

'I got a new job. Teaching.'

'Wow, congratulations,' said Greg. 'Back to doing what you trained for!'

'Yes. Esther worked on my English. When I passed the tests they also approved my qualifications. It's a tough school I'm in, but no tougher than the turkey sheds, and some of my lads, they're getting the idea. I can see progress.' Lukas was flushed both with pride and with the reflected pleasure of Ben and Greg. 'We're making a home here now,' he said. 'And it's thanks to you and Ben. Now,' he said, 'to change the subject, Ben tells me you've met up with Mrs P again. How is she? She was the best of all people at Stalham.'

It was getting late when Greg, awash with low alcohol lager, got to Chris's little cottage. Once he'd said hello to Tallulah, had his ear nibbled and showered off the stresses of the day, he was glad to get into bed and settle down with Chris in his arms.

'So,' he said sleepily, just before nodding off, 'next stop we pop over to Norwich prison and make some enquiries about Bakalov's visitors.'

'Don't you need to check with the chief super first, to make sure she's happy with you getting involved?' asked Chris. But a soft snore told her she was talking to herself.

# 33

## In court

From Greg's perspective, the first, combative element of the trial began well before the trial itself. It was Monday when Frank Parker brought him up to date on trial preparations and confirmed that they might not be able to use the Atkinson statement.

'I've notified Defence and the Court that we want to enter hearsay evidence,' was his opening comment. Greg sat up sharply in the battered leather chair before the desk, where he had been lounging relatively comfortably.

'Hearsay? When it's in a properly recorded statement taken under caution,' he asked. 'I thought that was allowed.'

'And I still hope it will be,' replied Parker, sitting back down behind the desk and shuffling papers. 'But I have to get permission all the same. I have three arguments. One,' and he held up a finger, 'the hearsay is contained in a statement specifically and appropriately prepared for criminal proceedings.

Two,' the second finger went up, 'the witness is unavailable by virtue of being dead. Three,' third finger, 'as the unavailability of the witness is, according to that witness, due to the actions of the defendant, then justice is served by hearing the evidence. It should be irrefutable,' He paused on the last word with irony. 'However, courts and judges have their own inner logic. We can only wait and see.'

Three days later, some of his panic assuaged, Greg was in Courtroom Two in Norwich, seated behind Frank Parker and his leading QC, listening to the mellifluous tones of one of the country's more expensive advocates setting out the case for the prosecution.

'At first glance this case may have appeared to you straightforward,' he began, surveying the jury over his black-rimmed glasses. 'But you will now have seen on the top of the indictment sheet the usher kindly passed to you a moment ago, the range of offences with which these defendants are charged. My task today is to explain why they differ between the different individuals currently in the dock, and how the evidence we will be placing before you justifies these indictments.

'To take the most serious first, in the order listed on the sheet in front of you, Professor Lai Liling, also known as Lily Lai, is charged with causing an explosion likely to endanger life or cause serious injury to property. She is also charged with the murders of Jan Littleboys, Nigel Atkinson and Hazel Partner. Why are the deaths of these three victims picked out and treated as murder? Because in the case of Jan Littleboys, evidence will be placed before you that she was deliberately trapped in a locked room by Lily Lai so that she would die in the fires caused by the explosion, and in so doing provide a simulacrum of Lai herself and thus obscure the fact that she had survived the disaster engulfing the laboratory. By contrast, Atkinson and Partner were killed by the administration of a toxic substance, to be precise a form of the commercial weed killer paraquat, and we have both a witness statement and forensic evidence that this poison was administered by Lai herself.

'By contrast, the other two defendants, Jack Haigh and Pat Nichols are charged with conspiracy to cause an explosion likely to endanger life and property. These charges carry a maximum sentence of life imprisonment. Life imprisonment,' he repeated in a tone that boomed across the courtroom, stilling the shuffling from the reporters' seats and echoed by the subdued sniffles of Jack Haigh's mother in the public gallery. 'A serious penalty for a serious offence and therefore one that requires, demands, that you are as certain as you can be that these two men and one woman are indeed guilty as charged.

'You have also heard that all three defendants plead not guilty to these offences, but you will not yet be aware that the basis for their plea differs greatly from one to another. Pat Nichols denies any wrongdoing, regardless of the evidence that places him firmly at the heart of the conspiracy as bomb maker. Jack Haigh, on the other hand, pleads not guilty to conspiracy to endanger life because he maintains that he had understood a warning would be given and the laboratory evacuated. Whether this belief was reasonable or reckless is for you to determine. What is not disputed is that he has admitted having a hand in the preparations for the explosion.

'Finally, Lily Lai has entered a plea of not guilty on grounds of insanity.'

A susurration disturbed the quiet calm of the courtroom and the jurors looked at each other, as Sir Frederick took a carefully timed sip of water.

'Do not mistake me,' he went on. 'No one is arguing that Lily Lai is insane now and is therefore unfit to plead and to be tried in this court. No less than three psychiatric experts have examined her and are agreed on that point. No one, not even the learned defence is disputing those findings. This is insanity as defined in law, and as it is very important to the case I will take the time to explain the essence now. I have no doubt His Lordship will return to the matter in greater and learned detail in his summing up.

'Ms Lai's plea is based on her assertion that, at the time she undertook these acts, she was labouring under such a defect of reason, from disease of the mind, as not to know the nature and quality of the act she was doing. Or in other words, that while she was sufficiently aware as to be able to organise the explosion, she was,' and he repeated the key words, 'labouring under such a defect of reason, from disease of the mind, as to be unaware of the likely outcome of the blast. It is for the defence to demonstrate to you that this defect of reason existed, and for me to show that, in all the circumstances of this case, it cannot be assumed to be so.'

By the time Sir Frederick resumed his seat, the jury were in no doubt that they were about to face a demanding and complicated week. Some were already looking a little pale.

As Greg stood down from his lengthy spell in the witness box, he was satisfied that the key points of the cases against Lai, Nichols and Haigh were clear in the jury's mind. Witness statements, forensic evidence, CCTV – all combined in a powerful story of linked facts, and more than adequately traced the actions from planning the explosion, through preparation of the car bomb, the placing of it in the NASA car park, the tidying into oblivion by Lily Lai of the three potential witnesses, the aftermath at the farm near Blickling and the subsequent events in the River Bure. The immaculately turned-out Mrs P was a particularly effective witness, even more so than Greg had expected, and he noted with a grin that she, of all the lay witnesses, had listened to and taken on board the advice given by the Witness Service volunteer in the briefing prior to her appearance on the stand. With every question from whatever source, she turned and directed her answer to the jury. She answered each question precisely and then stopped. On the rare occasion she didn't know an answer she said so, and when Defence lost himself in a rambling question her response was terse. 'I'm sorry,' she said, 'if there was a question, I didn't understand it. Could you repeat it, please.'

Even the judge had hidden a smile. She was also completely unshakable and wholly convincing. By the time she finished, the jury were in no doubt that she had seen Lily Lai leave the laboratory by the rear entrance, get into Hazel Partner's car and leave with the man identified via CCTV as the driver of the car bomb.

Nigel Atkinson's evidence was, to Greg's huge relief and Defence's depression, read into the court record. The words of the dying man visibly left echoes in the minds of the jury. The ashen faces of Hazel Partner's mother and father, now sitting next to Jack Haigh's mum in the public gallery, also played their part. To Greg, observing the twelve assorted men and women closely, their attitudes to Lily Lai were clearly hardening. In fact, he was just beginning to relax into his uncomfortable seat behind the prosecution team when, as Frank Parker put it later, the excrement hit the air conditioning.

It was the first witness after the adjournment for lunch. During the short break the ushers had taken the opportunity to obscure the witness box and the entrance to it with screens, and once His Lordship had taken his seat, Sir Frederick called Agent A. There was a rustle as, Greg assumed, she took her seat. The screens were so arranged that she was visible to the jury and judge, but not the defendants nor the public gallery. She took the oath in a muffled voice, and in the introduction to his first question, Sir Frederick reminded her to speak up. Her answer to his first question therefore rang out loud and clear, and Jack Haigh, slumped in the dock, jumped as though electrocuted. Greg heard the bang as he leapt to his feet behind him, but turned to look only when he shouted,

'That's Meg. That's Meg. I'd know her voice anywhere. It's Meg I tell you. I want to speak to my brief,' he added. 'Now! I need to speak to you,' he pointed as he shouted, and a spray of spittle hit the screen before him. The dock officer tried to reach him to calm him down, Greg turned to see if he needed help and the defence solicitor took a step towards him. The scene was fast approaching chaos, when the judge took a quick decision.

'Clear the court,' he commanded, and one usher escorted the jury hurriedly from their seats while a second cleared the public gallery. The dock officer, reinforced by colleagues, started to return the defendants to the cells, with Jack clinging to a gap in the glass as he tried to address his solicitor. In moments the court was empty of all except lawyers and, still behind the screens, Agent A.

Once the jury, defendants and public had vacated the court, His Lordship leaned forward with a weary look on his face.

'I think you have some work to do,' he remarked to the assembled company. 'Mr Gadd, I suggest an urgent word with your client. He seems to have something on his mind. At the least it's clear he knows the identity, or at least an identity,' he amended, 'of Agent A.

'Sir Frederick, a word with your witness would also seem advisable. I will see you both in my chambers in an hour.' And he swept from the court as everyone else scrambled to their feet.

'Come on,' muttered Frank to Greg, 'I think we'd all better have a word with Ms A.'

Agent A was discreetly ushered to a side room near the public entrance to the court, while Greg and Frank followed obediently in the wake of the magnificent Sir Frederick, sweeping along in his wig and robes. Once in the side room he was quick to doff the former, dropping it with a sigh on the table before him.

'Right, tell me what I need to know,' he snapped. 'Clearly the witness knows you. Equally clearly, it's not as a police officer, so the logical conclusion is that he knows you in your undercover role. I don't think it's unreasonable to assume that comes to an end, here and now. So, what do I need to know about your contacts with Jack Haigh?'

For the first time since he met her, Greg noted that Agent A looked uncomfortable. She shifted in her seat, her expression was troubled, and she took her time replying, lifting her hair back from her brow before she spoke.

'In my undercover role, I was involved in the arrangements that resulted in Jack Haigh working at NASA,' she said carefully.

Greg thought back through the many conversations he'd had with Haigh, and the statements he'd made.

'You *are* Meg,' he said flatly. 'And your involvement with Jack Haigh goes back before your undercover work. You knew him back at Queen Mary and you were his introduction to animal rights. You were the contact who told him to go for the NASA job.'

Frank Parker spoke up from his place by the door. 'And Jack Haigh will be explaining this to his defence team, who will shortly be in front of His Lordship arguing that Jack Haigh was not only deceived as to the nature of the intended consequences of the bomb attack, but was led into it via a honey trap set up by the police! Jesus wept!'

Sir Frederick leaned back in his chair, now balanced dangerously on two legs. 'Any similar involvement with the other two?' he demanded.

'No. I met them only in later years and had no direct involvement with either. I know them only via electronic comms and telephone.'

Sir Frederick crashed forward and the chair wobbled as he leaned on the table, pointing at Agent A now aka Meg. 'Then we cut our losses,' he said. 'We accept the plea of guilty to conspiracy to cause an explosion, with the recognition that Jack Haigh pleaded guilty promptly, was misled as to the nature of the explosion planned and was encouraged to take part by someone he trusted. A sentence at the minimal end of the spectrum is the most we can reasonably hope for or expect. In fact,' he added, 'I find myself feeling sorry for the poor sod. Between you and Lily

Lai he was well and truly stitched up.' He glared across the table and the flushed undercover officer glared back.

'Right, let's go and see His Lordship and hope we can get this sorted.'

The two lawyers bustled out, leaving Greg with Agent A. 'I find I'm agreeing with them,' Greg said. 'I've been feeling a bit sorry for Jack Haigh for a while. But if this messes up my case against Lily Lai, I'll have your head on a platter, and that's a promise.' He left the room and the door banged behind him.

By the time negotiations with the defence team had been completed and the judge was satisfied with proceedings, the day was so far advanced he adjourned the case to the next day. Jack was remanded back into custody to await sentencing, both his plea of guilty to the modified indictment and the mitigation advanced by his defence team accepted. Tuesday began, therefore, with only two defendants in the dock: an increasingly worried-looking Pat Nichols, sitting as far as he could get from an imperturbable Lily Lai, as though to dissociate himself from her as much as possible.

Greg, resuming his uncomfortable seat behind the prosecution team, thought he could smell his fear all the way across the courtroom and through the safety glass round the dock. He also thought it was justified. It was clear he was making a poor impression on the jury, who had little difficulty in following the clear line of evidence linking Nichols with the manufacture of the bomb. 'In the bag,' thought Greg and turned his attention to Lily Lai.

In truth, as the long and complicated saga of her involvement with the movement was exposed, and her actions on the day of the bombing and subsequently were outlined, he found his attention wandering to thoughts of the Lithuanian connection and the source of the Semtex. He surreptitiously flicked through his notebook to where he had listed the contacts for Bakalov that the prison had given him, then closed it guiltily as George, the forensic anthropologist, took the stand.

In that role, George was surprisingly impressive. The finicky mannerisms left behind, he gave his evidence clearly and with precision. He explained how and why he knew the remains in the locked storeroom were those of a European female, and how, despite the degraded and fire-damaged nature of the bones, they had been successful in extracting mitochondrial DNA, which had helped in the true identification. Ned took the stand and explained how and why they'd concluded the door to the storeroom had been both locked and jammed with a chair. The jury was shown photos of the scene immediately after the fire, and several turned green. The judge, noting the reaction, ordered a short recess, and everyone left the court.

Downstairs in the coffee bar, Greg met up with Ned. 'Went well I thought,' he remarked. 'In fact, I think we've done a good job on presenting the facts as a narrative the jury can follow.'

Ned nodded over his extra-large cup of tea. 'The bits I've seen, I agree,' he said. 'How well did the evidence about the Semtex go down?'

'OK, I think,' said Greg. 'Defence tried to suggest there was something funny about the undercover evidence, but the stuff from GCHQ was convincing and I think the jury got the key points. The major question now is how they handle the evidence about sanity. That's the issue for this afternoon.'

'I don't get that,' replied Ned. 'Why plead insanity anyway?

She won't be any better off in a secure hospital than in prison. She may end up serving a longer term. And neither Broadmoor nor Rampton are a rest cure.'

'I know,' said Greg thoughtfully, sipping his coffee. 'And that worries me. She's a very smart woman. I can't help feeling she's got something up her sleeve. Some cunning plan that gets her out of hospital after a short spell. A much shorter spell than a prison sentence anyway. I can't see how she'd do it, but I've just got this gut feeling that's what she's planning. And if she succeeded, she'd be out on the say-so of doctors rather than the criminal justice system. That's why I think we need to make damn sure she goes down for this. And to prison, not a hospital.'

Throughout the next day and a half, those were the thoughts running round in Greg's head as psychiatrist after psychologist gave evidence that Lily Lai was so badly affected by repeated onslaughts of hate crimes that she was rendered incapable of logical thought. Repeatedly changing position on his hard seat, Greg imagined he could see the jury, concentrating hard on the complex evidence, first wobble then waver. His heart was sinking by the time Sir Frederick stood up to cross examine Lily Lai.

Lai, on the stand in her smart black suit and white shirt with pie-frill collar, did not look a likely candidate for the funny farm. On the other hand, nor did she look like a cold-blooded killer.

'Good morning, Professor Lai,' he began formally. 'Let me take you back to some of the evidence we've already heard during this trial. Evidence dating as far back as 1990. Where were you working in 1990?'

Lai replied, 'Either Imperial College or the then Queen Mary College, depending on whether you are referring to the beginning or the end of the year.'

'Quite right,' said Sir Frederick. 'And did you apply for a job elsewhere during that year?'

'I think I applied for several,' she replied.

'The one I'm thinking about is the job at GMI about which you and we have already heard evidence. What happened to your application?'

'I was turned down,' she said coolly.

'Why?'

'Because I am a woman and Chinese,' she replied.

'And we have already heard from a police source that you were involved in planning an invasion of the GMI laboratories immediately after your failure to obtain the job.'

Lai said nothing.

'Do you have no comment?' asked Sir Frederick.

'I didn't hear a question,' she replied, and Sir Frederick added, 'No problem, we'll move on. Where did you work next?'

'Porton Down,' she replied.

'And at what grade?'

'Senior scientific officer.'

'Were you successful in obtaining promotion to the next level?' asked Sir Frederick.

'No.'

'Why not?'

'They said I wasn't a good manager, but it was prejudice again,' she replied. This time, Greg thought he could detect a slight flush building in her cheeks.

Over the next hours, Sir Frederick took Lily Lai through her entire career, up to and including NASA, skilfully drawing out her thoughts about how she had been treated, creating a narrative of repeated decisions by a series of senior managements that were each concerned about her people management skills, about her ability to work in a team. And linking each repeated disappointment to one of a series of steadily escalating animal rights attacks on premises and people.

By the end, Lily Lai was visibly angry. Reliving the many disappointments seemed to have reawakened the bitterness that rankled in her heart and the hate that had eventually consumed her. At the end she burst out, without reference to a question and ignoring instructions from the judge, 'I don't know why you're forcing me to go through all this. You're just proving what I've said all along. I've been ignored, mistreated, picked on all my life. Is it so surprising I wanted to hit back? So surprising that I lashed out without knowing what I was doing?'

Sir Frederick let a silence fall before he responded. 'Ignoring for the moment,' he said weightily, 'that you can't have been simultaneously picked on *and* ignored, you have made my point for me.

'Your counsel has sought to argue that your repeated experiences of prejudice and mistreatment caused such a defect of reason that you could not know the nature and quality of what you did. I, on the other hand, have sought to show that for each perceived slight or disappointment there was an appropriately timed act of revenge. Do you deny that?'

Lily maintained a mutinous silence, despite instruction from the judge that she must answer the question. Sir Frederick ran again through the sequence, asking each time whether the event that followed the disappointment happened with her connivance or inspiration, but each time she refused to answer.

In the end His Lordship intervened. 'I think it is clear

that the witness is not going to respond,' he remarked. 'Time to move on, Sir Frederick.'

Greg watched as Mr Gadd attempted to redress the balance but, watching the jury, felt that Sir Frederick had edged it. From their faces, he felt that the hard facts presented by the prosecution had countermanded the complex arguments from the defence. He felt a renewed confidence in their assessment of Lily Lai. He was therefore both disappointed and disconcerted when, having been dismissed by His Lordship to consider their verdicts, time dragged on and on with no sign of a decision. In the end they were dismissed to a hotel for the night, and Greg went home to Chris.

'Nothing,' he said. 'No decision.' And he brooded all evening on what he could have done or said differently.

The following morning Chris came with him to the court and stayed for the long wait for a verdict. At lunchtime they were at last called back into Court Number Two and the jury filed in. Greg watched them closely, but couldn't decide from their demeanour what decisions had been reached. He noticed Chris, from the public gallery, subjecting them to the same level of scrutiny.

The clerk to the court put the question to the foreman of the jury, a middle-aged lady in jeans topped by twinset and pearls.

'With regard Lily Lai and the charge of causing an explosion likely to endanger life or cause serious injury to property, do you find the defendant guilty or not guilty?'

The lady in twinset looked up and, 'Guilty,' she said in a clear voice.

The clerk took her through the remaining three charges of murder and 'guilty' said the foreman each time. The jury beside her looked steadily more and more relieved as their verdicts were given.

Pat Nichols went the same way. Only when it came to the end did the foreman break with custom.

'I have been asked to say, My Lord,' she added, 'that we would respectfully like to urge clemency with regard to the other defendant who pleaded guilty to a lesser charge. We feel he was led astray and deceived. My fellow jurors have asked me to raise this with you.'

The judge regarded her over his spectacles and smiled. 'Thank you for your care and attention during a long trial,' he said. 'I note what you say. Perhaps you would be seated, and I will pass sentence.

'Lily Lai, you have been found guilty,' and he listed the indictments, the list seeming longer with each repetition. 'I sentence you to imprisonment for life, with a recommendation that you serve at least forty years.

'Pat Nichols, you have been found guilty of conspiracy to cause an explosion likely to endanger life and property. In light of your previous good character and the evidence that you were deceived as to the precise intentions of the attack on the National Agricultural Science Agency, I sentence you to imprisonment for a term of six years.'

As Pat collapsed with his head in his hands, the judge went on to address the remaining, white-faced figure in the dock. 'Jack Haigh, you have pleaded guilty to conspiracy to cause an explosion. In recognition of your guilty plea and your evident remorse as to the loss of life which ensued, which I am persuaded was unexpected by you, I sentence you to three years in prison.

'Take them down.'

# 34

## And after

Back at Wymondham, full of relief and the sense of let-down following a successful trial, Greg had just sat down to his desk when the phone rang.

'I've heard the result,' said Jim's voice.

'Yes, I tried to ring you from my car. Great isn't it?'

'It is,' replied Jim, 'but that wasn't really why I rang. One of my contacts, one of the ones I asked about the Lithuanians visiting Bakalov. He's been in touch. He said two things. First, they're really bad news. Finger in every bad pie in Norfolk and beyond, and with a very nasty violent streak. Second, he said, don't.'

'Don't what?'

'Just don't. I think he meant there would be repercussions if we went after them.'

'Repercussions are what I'm after,' said Greg firmly. 'I want these people put away. Or we'll have no peace in Norfolk.'

'There is an alternative argument,' said Jim. 'Along the lines of, better the devil you know. If we know who they are we can limit their worst excesses. And…'

'And what?'

'I think he's scared and he doesn't scare easily. And that really scares me to be honest.'

Greg thought a moment. 'Let's talk about it tomorrow,' he suggested. 'I hear what you say, Jim, but I'm not happy just to let it drop. Not now we have a name.'

Greg put the phone down thoughtfully. He had too much respect for Jim to ignore his advice but, after all, what was the worst they could do? He, and even Chris, could look after themselves. They weren't stupid. They could take precautions. He remembered Chris's advice and went off whistling. 'I must have a word with Margaret,' he thought.

It was the early hours of a chilly morning when Greg was woken by an unmusical cacophony from his iPad. Barely awake, he lifted the cover and clicked yes to a FaceTime call before he realised what he'd done. Behind him, Chris rolled over in bed with a sleepy complaint. He realised with shock that the figure on the screen was Isabelle, a baby clutched to her shoulder.

'Greg! Greg, we need your help,' she said. Tears streaked her face and sobs distorted her voice. 'I've had a phone call. We've been threatened. They said they'd do terrible things. To me and my baby. Please help,' she said. 'I'm here all alone and he's all I have now. Oh God, I wish he was yours. You have to help me Greg!'

Lightning Source UK Ltd.
Milton Keynes UK
UKHW010755110522
402816UK00003B/462

9 781800 421950